Rewriting Love

Lana Pickering

Contents

ACKNOWLEDGMENTS

First, let me start by sending out a huge thank you to everyone who has made this book possible. It takes a village to raise a child, but it takes a smart and savvy crew to publish a book.

Let me move on to the sappy, tear-jerking thank you. I dedicated this book to my mother, because she and I always shared a love of romance novels. She really is the one who started me on this path so long ago. I miss you Mom, every day and I hope this makes you proud. To my dad, who has always put me on a pedestal higher than I deserve, who has always believed I could do whatever I put my mind to, no matter what.

To my husband, Darren, thank you for knowing how to make me laugh and for keeping the romance alive, no matter how many years we've been together. Love you babe. A special thanks to my son, Kevin, who without his knowledge gave me the perfect teenage personality for my book.

Thank you to the rest of my family for all your love and support, which has given me the encouragement to take this journey. A very special thank you to my sister, Cheryl Taylor, and my niece, Robin Taylor, for being there and talking me off the ledge and being the best cheerleaders ever!

Now, let me thank those who gave their time and hard work to make this book possible. To my beta-readers, Tara Ashley, Christine Cairns and Lindsay Smith, I appreciate all of your feedback and telling me what I needed to know to make my book better, and for being just as excited about this book as I am. Thank you to Sarah Stokes for copyediting my book and helping me through the editing phase. I learned so much. To Nadia Morel for taking my random thoughts about my cover and putting together an amazingly romantic cover, you're the best!

A heartfelt thank you to my many friends and colleagues who have listened to me prattle on for hours about my book and never told me it was too much. You guys rock!

Through this whole process, the highs and lows, I have been blessed to have such wonderful people in my life. Thanks for everything.

Lana

Prologue

The street lights glared off the wet road like rays of the sun, blinding him as he drove. Anthony hated coming to this part of the city. The filthy alleyways and beggars on every corner made his skin crawl. However, this was the level he had to lower himself to in order to keep his secrets hidden. He needed to make sure the contract was complete. It would mean one less worry on his mind, but it had nearly killed him to make this choice. Martin had been his friend most of his life and loved him like a brother. But the guy had started getting sloppy and that was something that couldn't be tolerated, in Anthony's line of work, not even for someone he loved.

Turning into the dark alley beside the old abandoned plastics plant, his headlights illuminated the car straight ahead. He could see Gino waiting patiently, probably listening to the sports channel on the radio getting the scores for the Cubs game. He was a good, stand-up guy and had pulled Anthony's ass out the fire many times. It was essential to have someone you could count on in this business and Gino was his man. Technically, Gino could have been a capo by now, but that's why he kept him close. The saying, 'keep your friends close and your enemies closer' was his mantra.

As he pulled up, Gino jumped out of his car and headed towards him. He was a young guy, in his early thirties with traditional Italian looks of black hair and dark eyes. He must have come straight from his family dinner, as he was all spiffed up in his Sunday best. Getting into the passenger seat, all Gino said was, "Hey, Anthony."

"What's the news?" Anthony fidgeted with the rearview mirror to keep the road in sight.

Gino turned to face him. "It's done. I was listening to the scanners and there was no one alive at the scene."

Anthony smiled a bittersweet smile. "Good job, Gino. You always come through for me. I'll make sure to let Mr. C know what a great job you did."

"Thanks Anthony, that means a lot. I know this wasn't an easy decision for you."

"Well you can't get careless in this business and he was gettin' careless." Anthony rubbed his eyes as he struggled to justify ending his friend's life.

"So, what's our next move?"

"Now we wait to see if anything surfaces. Julia will start going through Martin's things and I'm going to be there to make sure any evidence is taken care of. I need to find out where he kept the key for the safety deposit box at the bank. If anything, he would have hidden the notebook there to keep it from Julia. I can't stand the thought of having to do anything to Martin's wife or son, but I'm not going down because he was a jamook."

Anthony thought the world of Julia and Ian. Christ, he had been there when Ian was born. He just needed to get in and check out the house to see where Martin might have stashed the key. Once he had a chance to see what was in the house he would know where else to look. All he needed was to get a hold of the black notebook and he could burn it to ash. Damn Martin for keeping information! Everyone in the business knew you never wrote things down because they'd only come back to bite you in the ass.

"Don't beat yourself up Anthony, he cost you two hundred large. Martin was an idiot, and he was going to eventually take us all down with him."

Anthony shook his head as he glanced down at his hands, sighing heavily. "If we don't find that book, he still could."

Chapter 1

(Two-and-a-half years later)

The faint sound of rain on the windshield pulled Julia out of her thoughts. At least it wasn't raining too hard at this point, as driving on unknown roads in the rain was not her idea of a good time. Actually, driving anywhere when it rained was not her idea of fun at all. The music on the radio changed to something upbeat. She turned it up, just slightly, to keep her mind off the weather. Julia glanced over to the passenger seat where her son lay reclined with his headphones on. *Well at least if he's sleeping we aren't arguing,* she thought.

Second guessing herself for the past week, she wondered if her decision to move was to rash. If only Ian hadn't gotten in with the wrong crowd of people in Chicago. But those kids were having a bad influence on him. The last straw was having the police show up at her door with Ian in the back seat of their cruiser. He and his 'peeps' were caught vandalizing a warehouse. There were no charges laid and only a warning given, but there was no way Julia was going to allow him to go down that road.

Between that offence, the underage drinking at a party, smoking cigarettes out behind the school and the joint she'd found in his dresser, which he'd said didn't belong to him, it was more than enough. After the police left that night, she pulled up the house listings online for the farthest possible location from Chicago, while still remaining in the state. That was why they were currently heading to Heritage Falls, Illinois. The school year hadn't started yet, so Ian would be able to start fresh come September.

Telling Ian they were moving erupted in arguments and threats that he would run away. She, in turn, yelled and screamed and told him she wished he was old enough to leave. Then she broke down into tears and so did he. They held each other and cried, because nothing had been the same since Martin had died.

It had been almost two and a half years since his death, taken so suddenly in that car accident. Now every time she drove in the rain she cringed. Martin's car had skidded out of control on a rainy night because of the wet roads. Their lives had been shattered in mere seconds. They say time heals, but it was a painfully slow process.

Focusing on Ian again, she smiled. Even though she was second guessing herself, this move did feel right. She had been scared to death of leaving Chicago, but now they were finally moving forward and it felt good. This was their opportunity to start over; to start a new life. She wanted this for Ian. He deserved to have a fresh start, with new friends and a new school. This was a great time for him to find himself. All she had to do was hope he met some good kids with good morals. Fingers crossed, she said to herself.

They'd been lucky to be able to sell their home privately in Chicago. Living in a highly regarded neighborhood, the house was snapped up without even having to put a sign on the lawn. Since it had sold so quickly, and the closing had been short, it allowed them to move even sooner than Julia had hoped. She purchased the new house from Mr. and Mrs. Bulger, who'd decided they wanted to move closer to their grandchildren in Florida. Julia didn't even have to deal with the details, as her friend Paige dealt with everything.

Now she was left to deal with more practical things. Julia had a very good mind for tasks and she had plenty facing her once they arrived. She arranged for Ian's school to forward his documents, so she would need to get him registered as soon as possible. Next, she would have to find a new doctor and dentist, as those were essential when you had a child. She also needed to find a pharmacy, a grocery store and a garage. Finding a bank was also a priority as she needed to be able to transfer her accounts and get a safety deposit box. She had taken everything out of the box at her old bank just yesterday, after taking the key out of the old ballerina figurine Martin had given her for her birthday.

There were some bank certificates and a folder with some fancy coins, which Martin had been saving for Ian. Some other papers and a couple of notebooks were also in there, but Julia didn't want to deal with any of it. It was hard enough knowing she would be leaving behind their life together in Chicago, so she didn't want to think too deeply about it. She just wanted to put it all in a box and leave it for another day.

After Martin's death she'd been left to go through so much of his stuff. Their wills and other insurance papers were at the house in the wall safe. Since neither Martin nor she had a lot of family she struggled through most of the paperwork herself. Lucky for her, Paige and Martin's childhood friend, Anthony, had been so supportive. Anthony was a godsend when it came to Ian too. He took him out to a ball game, the batting cages and just hung out with him. She was so grateful her son had someone to connect with when it all first happened.

But Anthony stopped coming around. He still called often – Julia knew he was a busy guy and he had things to do. Then about a year ago, the calls stopped and it was as if Anthony just vanished. Julia was hurt to think he would forget all about them, but without Martin to bring him here he must have just moved on. She wasn't even able to get a hold of him to let him know they were moving.

Slowing down to be sure she could read the house numbers on the side of the road, she could see the mailboxes with last names on them. She would have to add that item to the list of things to do. She was about to drive by when she realized the driveway was on her left. She had only seen pictures of the house, so she was totally going on a wish and a prayer as to where it was. She pulled in and instantly she felt at home.

The driveway was lined with big maple trees on both sides. Over to the right, there was a small pond and some beautiful gardens. She had already been thinking about hiring a handyman, so perhaps she would find someone who had a green thumb too. Further down the drive she could see a large red barn on the left. She had been told the house had a barn, but to be honest, she hadn't really thought about it. Pulling up to the side of the house, she could see the fenced in backyard that held the pool, and the forest in behind it.

The house itself was a two story, brown brick home with a large porch on the main floor and an upper-level balcony on the front of the house. There were wide stone steps up to the front door, and on either side of those were gorgeous flowerbeds. She would definitely have to get a gardener. Julia never had much of a green thumb. Her house in the city had been beautiful, but they had a lawn care service that would come and handle all of the maintenance. Julia and Martin had been far too busy with their careers to deal with any yard work.

Mr. and Mrs. Bulger had left the name of a handyman with their relator. Maybe she would just use their recommendation if he was any good at gardening. She had agreed to continue with the Bulger's agreement to lease a portion of the property to the neighbors, Mr. and Mrs. Vincent. The area was just field and she didn't want to have to deal with that much land. Mr. Vincent grew various crops like soybean, corn and wheat. She would rather see it put to good use then sit unproductive. She had been told the forest actually separated the house from the field so any noise during planting and harvest would be minimal.

Stepping out of the SUV, Julia stretched out her legs and back. It had been a long drive and she was glad to be out of the confines of the truck. Taking one more look around, she leaned into the truck. "Yo, sleepy head, we're here."

Ian slowly lengthened out his legs and arms as best he could inside the truck. Sitting up, he took in his surroundings. Looking over at his mother, he said with a serious tone, "Please tell me there's Internet service."

Julia laughed. "How did I know that would be the first question you asked me? Oh, right, because teenagers can't possibly go five minutes without being connected, unless they're asleep."

Ian stared at her with concern on his face. "Mom, please don't joke. This is serious."

Rolling her eyes, she headed to the back of the SUV to start unloading. "Yes, my child, the Internet guys will be here tomorrow morning to install. Sorry I couldn't get them here today, but I wasn't exactly sure what time we were going to arrive. Tomorrow was the best I could do. You'll just have to deal with it for now. Besides, you're going to be too busy today to be playing on the Internet."

Ian walked to the back of the truck and asked, "Doing what?"

Julia pulled out a sleeping bag and gave it a little shove into Ian's stomach. "Unpacking."

Mumbling, Ian grabbed the sleeping bag and headed towards the house. He stopped and spun around to stare at her, panic on his face. "Do you think they deliver out here?"

"Deliver what?" Julia wasn't sure what he was talking about.

"Food, Mom. We're going to starve!"

"We're not going to starve. That's why there are grocery stores. We stock up and make meals. Besides, I'm sure we can order stuff and go pick it up."

Ian huffed out a breath. "Bet there's no good pizza places here anyways. You can't get as good a pizza as you can get at Sal's." He turned and walked to the front porch.

Julia called out to Ian, who slowly glanced back at her. "Please give this a chance, babe. This will be an adjustment for the both of us, but we agreed."

Ian stared at her for a minute then said in a slightly sarcastic tone, "Well, you decided and I was forced to agree, but if that's your story…"

She felt her anger rise as she tilted her head to one side, saying, "OK, how about we agree that your actions have led us down the path to our current location."

She watched as Ian's shoulders slumped. "Mom, it wasn't that big a deal."

"Really? Not that big a deal? Hmm, police officers, to me, are a big deal." She sighed and peered up at the sky for a moment then back at her son. "You know what? I'm not arguing about this anymore. We're here and we will be starting Life 2.0 right now. Comprende?"

Sighing, Ian looked at her, "Comprende."

Anthony's knuckles whitened as he gripped the phone. He sat listening to the ringing on the other end, while his leg bounced, showing his nerves. He was just about to hang up when the line connected.

"Hello?" Gino's voice came over the line.

Anthony cleared his throat, as he had been waiting for his turn to use the phone for well over an hour. "Gino, give me the scoop. I only get the phone for eight minutes."

"We might have a problem here, Anthony. Julia moved." Anthony's mind spun from the implications this could have. Steadying himself, he spoke in a clipped tone. "What the fuck do you mean she moved? Haven't you been watching her place?"

Anthony could tell Gino was anxious from the tone of his voice. "Shorty and I drove by her place yesterday and it's empty. All the curtains and everything are gone."

"Son of a bitch. Did you see a for sale sign?" His hand trembled as he thought about the magnitude of the situation. He was already locked up; he couldn't risk being put in here for any longer than the two-year term he was already serving. Damn Carlo for getting him mixed up in a stupid computer scheme.

Gino must have moved away from the house as his voice was slightly louder now. "No, but I heard on the police scanner her kid had gotten into trouble with the cops. They dropped him off at home with a warning about three weeks ago."

Rubbing his hands over his face, he said, "Damn it! Were you watching her like I told you too?"

"Yes Anthony, I would go by once a week to scope it out. No more than that, you said it might raise suspicions. I was even borrowing other cars."

Anthony sighed loudly, "Do you think she went to the bank?"

Gino huffed out an impatient breath. "If I didn't know she left, how the hell would I know if she went to the bank? I'm just as worried about this as you are. "

Standing up to pace as far as the cord would allow he said, "Shit. OK, well start asking questions. Maybe poke around and ask some of the neighbors. Dino's got a cousin working in a real estate office. Ask him to see if he can get some info on the sale of the house. If I wasn't stuck in this shit hole I would have known what was happening with her."

"Yeah, damn cops. I still can't believe they pinched you on some stupid computer hacking bullshit. Carlo always was an ass."

Anthony could see the next inmate waiting through the glass door. Just then the signal that the call was coming to an end sounded and he hurried to finish his call. "My lawyer is working on it, but he better hurry the hell up".

There was movement on the other end and he heard Gino say, "I'll ask around and see what I can find out."

"Thanks, G. And give my love to your ma." Then the line went dead. Hanging up the receiver, he left the enclosed space to go back to his cell. Any chance of getting sleep for the next while had just evaporated into thin air.

Chapter 2

"No goddamn way am I giving you a cent, Francine." Jake ran his hand through his light brown hair, as the other hand held on to the phone receiver with a vice grip. Every passing day he hated her just a little bit more. His ex-wife was the most conniving woman on the planet. If she thought for even a second he was going to give her money, then she'd definitely been smoking something that had fried her brain.

With a huff on the other end to the line she started again, "But Jake, you can't expect me to entertain the girls if I don't have any money. It takes money to raise kids ya know."

Oh, there was no way she was trying to tell him about raising kids. What the hell would she know about raising their kids? She had made a beeline out of their home faster than a bolt of lightning nine years ago. "Oh really, and you know so much about raising the girls?"

"I take care of them too, Jake. Don't come off like you're the only one who has a hand in bring them up." He could practically hear the sneer on her face as she spoke.

It took all his willpower not to smash the phone to smithereens. "Really? You take care of them? You are supposed to have them for one weekend every month, Fran, and do you know how many times you've actually followed through? Do you? Six times, Fran. Six times in two and a half years! So do not preach to me about taking care of our girls, because you haven't been there for them in well over nine years."

His whole body shook as he continued, "I'm going to say this once. If you do not pick them up and take them on your weekend, which is coming up, I will be on the phone with my lawyer and you can kiss all access to the girls goodbye. I can't allow you to keep disappointing them. This is the final straw Francine. And don't ever ask me for money again. I don't owe you a single dime." Jake finally slammed the phone down in the cradle and wanted to punch something.

He stared at the phone again, then around his small office in the back of the garage and took a deep breath. Wow, this had been a really shitty day so far. First, it started with Danielle, his oldest daughter, having some kind of hair-induced meltdown, which was apparently his fault. He had bought the wrong brand of flat iron cream. He vaguely remembered asking the lady in the beauty aisle to pick one out. She thankfully did because he had no idea where to find it, but apparently, this was not the one she'd wanted, so the whole morning started off with drama.

Then his youngest daughter, Hailey, had a grand idea to help out. Unfortunately it sent Danielle into hysterics because she doused too much of another product on her hair and had almost fried it off. Hailey had started crying and apologizing, saying that she was just trying to help, Danielle wouldn't apologize for yelling at Hailey, and both girls had tears streaming down their faces. So before they wigged out anymore, Jake had started yelling. He sent Danielle to go wash all the stuff out of her hair and told her to just leave the flatiron for a morning when she had more time. He then told her to write down the name of the actual product she wanted and he would try and find it. Turning to Hailey, who was the sweetest girl on earth, he calmed her down and told her sometimes it was safer to just let Danielle figure things out on her own.

Just when he thought things had calmed down, his cellphone rang. It was Randy from the parts dealer in Harrisburg. He told Jake the Prothane ball joint boots that Jake needed for the Ford Mustang he currently had on one of the hoists in the garage weren't going to be available for another four days. Damn it, he needed those parts today. Now he was going to have to go and source another auto parts store to find them.

Jake finally got the girls to his sister's house, but then some moron cut him off while he had his coffee mug in his hand. This caused him to slam on his brakes and wear half of his streaming-hot coffee all over his work shirt and pants. Great, he had to walk into the garage looking like he pissed his pants and had practically boiled his balls off. Fan-freaking-tastic. The only bright moment was that he kept extra clothes at work.

And now to top off the work day, as he had been having such a great day so far, he had to deal with his ex who thought the whole world owed her everything and that Jake was her own personal ATM. Some days he cursed the day he'd ever met her. Then he would remember his sweet daughters and think it was all worth it. But dealing with Francine just made his blood pressure spike.

It hadn't always been like that for them. He had loved her once, a very long time ago. She had been so kind and pretty when he had met her. Long blond hair, curvy body – yep, the ultimate teenage boy's fantasy. They had started going out in the eleventh grade, and had been together up until eight years ago. He had kicked her out when Hailey was only two.

Actually, if he was being honest, they had started drifting long before that, when he realized she was cheating on him. They had stopped having sex as soon as she got pregnant with Hailey. He hadn't had a serious relationship with anyone else since. He guessed the sight of finding your beloved wife banging your high school buddy on your kitchen table made a guy a bit jaded on the whole love and relationship thing. She had never been adventurous with their sex life. If it had been any more vanilla, she would have kept her clothes on for shit sake. Apparently, she had been saving all her moves for someone else, or many someone else's, who were not her husband.

He knew he needed to get back out in the dating scene again, but the thought scared the shit out of him. He had been out on a few dates when he and Francine separated. He had even had a few one night stands, but they were not much to write home about. However, he would be the first to admit that the possibility of having sex again did excite him, a bit. Oh, who was he kidding? He would give his left arm some days to have sex. But it had to be with the right person. He wouldn't put his heart on the line for just anyone. He had been out with a few people but it hadn't felt right. Using someone just to scratch an itch felt wrong. Maybe he'd get lucky one day and the perfect woman would just walk into his garage. Yeah right, like that would ever happen. He already knew all the single women in this town, and there was no way he would be caught dead with any of them. He wouldn't meet anyone unless he got out, and the opportunity to do so was slim. Until then he had lots to keep him busy and cold showers weren't so bad right? Yeah, let's not even think about it.

Julia and Ian headed into town with many errands to do. She wanted to get Ian registered for high school as soon as possible. The day was turning out to be beautiful. The sun was shining and the breeze was warm as it blew through the open truck windows. She looked over to see Ian with his headphones on, playing some game on his phone, oblivious to the beauty all around him.

Just as they took the second curve into town the falls came into view. Seeing a scenic stop area up ahead, she pulled off. She quickly shut off the truck and hopped out, wanting to take a closer look. The sound of the falls was incredible. It roared like it was alive, barely harnessed as it rushed past with a power only capable of being created by Mother Nature. There was a fine mist hanging in the air from the churning water and Julia could feel her face and hair dampen. The birds swooped and called to one another as the wind forced them higher. The whole scene was straight out of a painting.

She faintly heard the car door shut and knew that Ian had finally realized she had left the vehicle. He walked up beside her and stared at the falls. Just then a butterfly fluttered by, its yellow wings were highlighted by the sun. The air smelled like damp earth and pine from the forest surrounding the area on either side of the river.

Ian eventually said, "This place reminds me of that time that Dad took us camping. Do you remember?"

Julia laughed. "I do. He was so excited about that trip. Then it poured rain half the time and we ended up sleeping in the car. But it was great once the sun came out and we cooked hotdogs and marshmallows over the fire."

Glancing over at her, Ian laughed too. "Yeah and we went fishing and I caught a bass." Ian turned away and was quiet for a few minutes. "I think that was the last time I really saw him laugh."

She stared out across the water, feeling the weight of the moment. "Me too."

They both leaned on the railing in front of them. Just when she was thinking they should get going, Ian said, "Mom. I'm sorry about, well...everything."

Nodding her head and smiling, she looked over at Ian. "I know, baby."

"Sometimes I just miss him so much. When I would be off goofing around with my friends it made it easier to forget, ya know. But I never meant to get into trouble. I guess I just got caught up in it."

Wrapping her arm around his shoulder, she said, "I'm glad you realize those mistakes. I think this is a chance for us to start fresh. I want a new life for us, Ian. Living in Chicago just kept us surrounded by all the old memories. Here we can do things differently. So how about from this point on we keep the good memories, but keep facing forward and make some new ones." She gave his shoulder a squeeze.

Ian looked a little uncomfortable. "OK Mom. That's enough of the love fest."

Julia quickly let him go, saying, "Sorry, I forgot you're a man now, so hugging is off limits."

"Well I'm working on it. No chest hair yet, but I'm hopeful." Ian grinned at her.

Laughing, Julia headed for the truck. "OK, let's go. After we get you registered for school we can stop for lunch and then pick up some groceries. Oh, I think if we can locate a garage we should see if they can take a look at that the truck. I think that knocking noise might be getting worse. I don't want to take any chances."

She heard a big sigh come from Ian. "Fine, if we must. You know how much I love doing errands."

Julia shrugged her shoulders, saying, "I know, but these are important. Besides, maybe we'll find a comic book store or video game place or something equally as exciting." She could tell Ian was considering this as a bonus.

"OK, now you've peaked my interest." Ian shut off his phone and left his ear buds out.

She smiled. "I knew it would." Lifting up her fist, Ian gave her a fist bump and she turned up the radio and sang along, as Ian rolled his eyes.

$$\infty \quad \infty \quad \infty$$

As they pulled up in front of the high school, Julia took in the large two-story building. It was an average school, complete with large windows and a running track. She could see on the other side a large dome-shaped building that looked like it might house a pool. Maybe Ian could join the swim team again. He had stopped swimming right after Martin had passed and she knew a part of him must miss it.

They walked in through the main doors and could see all the wood and glass cabinets filled with trophies. The floors must have been recently polished as they were gleaming and the halls held a distinct smell of lemon cleaner. They located the office down one of the halls, which was eerily quiet and lonely. Soon enough though, they would be buzzing with the sound of kids talking and running shoes squeaking on those very shiny floors.

Opening the doors to the office, they could hear country music coming from an old radio on the counter. Stacks of files were plied all around so high they couldn't even see if there was anyone on the other side.

Puzzled, Julia she called out, "Hello?"

A muffled sound came from the other side of the counter. Then a high pitched voice answered, "Hello?"

"Hi there, I called this morning about the registration for my son, Ian Witmore?" Julia strained up on her tip toes to see if she could make out a person. The muffled sound came again, but this time the voice was clearer. "Oh my, just hold on."

Julia and Ian heard several things tumble and some loud thumps erupted. Suddenly, a portly lady appeared around the edge of the counter. She was wearing her hair in a large bun on the top of her head, almost making her seem like she had two heads. Two large, blue eyes stared at them through thick black frames. She had full rosy cheeks and bright red lipstick to top off the look. Julia was about to move forward when she realized the lady was almost in a frozen state, just staring at her. Ian leaned in and said, under his breath, "Mom, I think she's a fan."

Still staring at the lady, Julia moved forward and extended her hand. "Well Hello, I'm–" Before Julia could say another word the lady clamped onto her hand and started pumping it up and down like a jack hammer. "I know exactly who you are. I have read everything you've ever published. I am a huge fan." Julia heard Ian behind her, say, "Told you."

Holding on to Julia's hand, the lady never let go. "I can't believe you're really here! I was so excited when I found out your son was coming to our school. I told everyone I know, which is a lot of people since I know most everyone who lives in Heritage Falls."

Julia continued to smile at the lady, until it started to get a little uncomfortable. Turning slightly, she said, "Thank you so much, it's always nice to meet my fans. This is my son, Ian. And your name is…?"

The lady suddenly let go of Julia's hand as if coming out of her awestruck state and said, "Oh, of course! I'm Mrs. Kramer, Carol to you, the school secretary. Let me get the paperwork and we can get this done and you can be on your way." Looking around at the piles of files she said, mostly to herself, "Now where did I put that file?" Luckily, Mrs. Kramer was actually quite competent and left the paperwork in a safe place and not on the stacks on the counter. She had also brought in a copy of Julia's most recently published novel and asked Julia to sign it. The secretary was overcome with a case of the giggles she was so thrilled.

Once they finished up with Mrs. Kramer and said their goodbyes, they headed down the hall. There was a poster by the glass cabinets that they passed on the way in. Julia stopped and said to Ian, "Hey, this looks promising."

Ian stopped and read the poster advertising for tryouts for the swim team. "Yeah, maybe." He shrugged his shoulders and glanced at his mother.

Julia smiled at him. "New beginnings, remember."

Ian smiled, but sadness filled his eyes. "It reminds me of Dad. He used to love watching me swim. It just makes me miss him."

"But you love to swim. Do you think he would want you to give up something you love because it makes you sad? No way. He would want you to do the things you love. And babe, I don't want you to hold back on life because things remind you of him. He loved you so much. So how about you be the best you can be and live. OK?"

Ian looked away for a moment and Julia knew tears were brimming in those beautiful hazel eyes. He blinked a few times fast then said, "Yeah, OK, new beginnings."

She wrapped her arm briefly around his shoulders giving him a squeeze as she said, "That's my boy. Come on let's get something to eat."

They found a restaurant on the main street called Rosie's Diner. The place looked like a real old-fashion diner. The black-and-white checkered floors were offset by the stools with bright red seat covers lining the main counter area. The wide pass-through window to the kitchen had brass light fixtures which added to the authenticity. The booths were all made with the same red covering as the stools and had high-back seats for extra privacy. There was a jukebox in the corner and old movie and band posters lined every wall. Even the waitresses were decked out in traditional diner uniforms.

They ordered their lunch and marveled at the old posters. Ian even went over to check out the jukebox. Julia watched as he pulled out a quarter and selected a song. It was a rap song she had never heard before, but Ian liked it, so she just listened. Their meal came and they both agreed it is delicious. Ian had the cheeseburger and fries, and the plate was filled beyond overflowing. Julia had the BLT sandwich and a salad which she would never be able to eat all of, even if she had three meal times to finish it. Her son, of course, polished off all of his meal and one section of her sandwich. She had no idea where he put it all.

Heading out of the diner, Julia saw a garage just down the street. She quickly drove over and pulled into the garage, plainly named Jake's Garage. At the same time Ian spotted a video game place, Gamers Kingdom and Comics, straight across from the garage. They made a plan that Ian would go over and check out the store and Julia would go and deal with the truck issue. As she walked into the garage she could see there was only one bay with a car on the hoist. Well this looks promising, she thought to herself. Hopefully they could fit her in right now. There were voices drifting from the back, so she made her way down a hallway hoping to speak to the aforementioned Jake. She stepped up closer to the open door, when she overheard the conversation more clearly.

"...and then I told her, 'Hang on tight, baby, you're in for the ride of your life.'"

She quickly cleared her throat, not wanting to hear anything further about the conversation. "Hello?"

A deep voice called out from behind the door. "Hello."

"Yes, I was hoping to talk to someone about taking a look at my truck."

Julia could hear footsteps coming towards the door, and then, standing before her was a man. An extremely handsome man, with wide shoulders, a muscular build and the most intoxicating green eyes she has ever seen. His light brown hair was messy, like he either styled it that way or had been gripping it in his hands. He had to be at least six foot two inches, because at only five foot six herself, she needed to look way up. Then he smiled at her and she was blown away. Holy moly, he was easy on the eyes! She could have stared at him all day.

Chapter 3

Oh holy hell, where had she come from? This woman was gorgeous, no, scratch that, she was stunning! She had a classic beauty about her. Smooth skin, full lips and beautiful hazel eyes that had flecks of green in them. Her hair was auburn in color and was left loose around her shoulders. It was the kind of hair you wanted to push yours fingers into as you pulled her close. He wondered if someone had just answered his prayers.

Suddenly, he realized he had been just standing there staring at her like an idiot. Great, way to make an impression Jake. He cleared his throat and put his hand out, walking towards her. "Hey there, I'm Jake. Jake Vincent." Great, now he was sounding like James Bond. He was such a loser. The woman before him laughed and he felt his heart stutter. Her laugh actually sounded musical and he couldn't wait to hear her do it again.

"Hi, I'm Julia Witmore. I was hoping someone could take a look at my SUV today, if possible. If not, I'd like to schedule an appointment." She smiled and his heart skipped a beat. She was absolutely the most beautiful woman he had ever seen.

Still holding her soft, warm hand in his he said, "Well, I believe I can do that for you right now."

From behind the office door, Dean, his employee, chimed in, "Oh, I can do that boss."

Reluctantly, Jake released her hand and said over his shoulder, "No, that's OK, Dean. You'd better go back out and finish Mr. Tanner's Mustang. He'll be back around three o'clock." Luckily, he'd been able to get the parts he needed from another dealer.

Glancing back at Julia, he waved his hand for her to head back the way she'd come. He watched as she walked ahead and was privy to the best view ever. She had curves, lots of curves, and damn if it didn't add to the whole gorgeous package. She had a great walk, with just enough sway in her hips that you knew she wasn't doing it for his benefit. She had a natural grace about her, like she might have been a dancer. Hmm, he could watch her all day long. But just as he was fantasizing about her curves and how he would love to rub his hands over them, they were suddenly standing outside in front of her SUV. It was a red Chevy Tahoe and from the looks of it, not that old.

She took her keys out of her purse and handed them over to Jake. "We haven't had the truck for very long. We just moved out here from the city and I wanted to have a better vehicle for winter driving. I used to have a little Toyota, but it wasn't big enough to put our stuff in to travel out here."

Raising his eyebrow, he would admit he was intrigued. "So where was home before this?"

She turned to him and smiled. "Chicago. It's a long story. I'd rather not get into it."

So that was a definite shut down. Maybe he would just see what was wrong and then he could probe a little. Then he remembered something. "Hey, you're the lady who bought the old Bulger place, right?"

Her head ticked back a notch, as if slightly shocked. "Wow, I knew this place was small, but I didn't know everyone would know my business already." She tilted her head to one side, "Yes, I did buy their place. How did you know?"

Jake laughed at her serious tone and held his hands up in surrender. "No worries Julia, I'm not some weird stalker or something. My parents are the ones you leased your land to. They live in the house right beside you."

She seemed relieved and her sweet smile came back. "Oh yes, sorry. I didn't put your last name together. We just arrived yesterday and we haven't even really unpacked or anything." She glanced over at the SUV and said, "It started making this weird knocking noise about a half hour before we got here yesterday and I didn't want to leave it too long."

Jake looked at the truck and then back at her. "Good call. Knocking could mean a few different things, but let me get it on the hoist and see what the problem might be. You're welcome to wait in the lobby. I'll take a look, then we can discuss if it's something big or small. Sound all right?"

Julia nodded. "I'm just relieved you can do it right away. I'll go and wait for you." She then headed into the waiting area. It had a huge window which looked right into the garage bays. He watched as she took a seat and pulled out an e-reader from her purse. Good, if she was distracted he could sneak a couple of peeks her way and she wouldn't notice. Well, unless she was going to sneak some peeks, too. And wouldn't that just be the best thing ever.

He hopped into her truck and pulled it into the bay. Before he raised the car he took a quick look under the hood and inspected all the usual problem areas. When he checked the spark plugs he noticed a couple had dirty insulating tips, so he cleaned them all and replaced one. During this whole process he checked out Julia as she sat reading. She seemed to be lost in her story, oblivious to him or anyone else. He was just finishing up when he saw her staring at him. Had she been checking him out? Hot damn, if that didn't make him feel good? At least this attraction wasn't one sided, because that would just be sad.

He started up the truck and it purred just like it should. Jake went to clean off his hands and as he was walking back towards Julia, he noticed a teenage boy walking into the waiting area with a bag from the gaming store across the street. The boy glanced at him and instantly he could see the resemblance to Julia. He watched as the boy talked excitedly to his mother and she was absolutely absorbed in her son, like everything he said was the most important thing in the world.

She was a true mother. Francine had never looked at their girls that way. Usually she stared at them with boredom or loathing. But since she had hardly made an effort in the last two-and-a-half years he had hardly seen her at all. If she screwed up again he would make sure his lawyer took even that privilege away from her, because she didn't deserve it. His girls were the most precious things in his life and they deserved only the best. They deserved to have someone look at them the way Julia was focusing on her son right now.

He pulled himself out of his thoughts and headed in to see them. He could hear the boy's excited voice. "And Kyle actually goes to my school. Well, he's a junior, but he said he'll make sure he says, 'hi' and shows me around. He also told me Fallout 4 is coming out in November. It's going to be so cool. He said he watched some previews and it looks epic."

Jake smiled at the boy as he remembered when he was a kid. He had loved video games, still did. As he walked towards them he cleared his throat. "Sorry to interrupt, but I thought I should let you know I'm done with your truck."

Julia looked at him and gave him another heart-stopping smile. Standing up, she said, "Ian, this is Jake Vincent. His parents own the house next to ours. They're the one leasing the field beside our house."

Jake watched as Ian turned to him and put his hand out to shake his. "It's nice to meet you, sir."

Sir? Wow, great manners. He liked this kid already. "It's nice to meet you too, Ian."

He then watched as Ian finally looked around the waiting areas and his eyes widened. Jake had pictures of all the cars he and his family had fixed up and sold over the years. His father had always had a love of cars and he had passed it along to his sons.

"Mom, check this out! It's a 1966 Ford Mustang. What a beauty."

Jake's heart gave a double beat. He liked this kid even more. His girls had never really taken an interest in the whole cars and motors thing, so he was alone in his love of all things automotive.

"You like cars?" Jake watched as the boy walked over and stared at each of the photos. Pictures of all different classic muscle cars were hung on the wall. They ranged from Corvettes, Barracudas, El Caminos, Camaros and many others. Jake remembered each one with love. Then Ian surprised him and touched the picture of the very first car he, his dad, and his brother ever rebuilt. It was a Pontiac Firebird. Jake had decided to become a mechanic because of that car. It was also the reason that they had just purchased another Firebird. They had just started on the rebuild and he was enjoying every minute of it.

"Yeah, I like cars. Do you own all these?" Ian looked at him and Jake could see the interest staring back at him.

Jake smiled and said, "Well, I can't claim to own them all. My dad, brother and I like to tinker so we buy old broken-down junkers and rebuild them. As you can tell by the photos, we've been doing it for a long time."

Ian went to the next picture and said, "Wow, is that a Corvette? It's amazing."

Jake moved closer to the picture and smiled. "It's a favorite of mine, too." He turned to Ian. "You ever work on cars, Ian?"

Ian averted his eyes and pretended to look at some other pictures. "No, we lived in the city. My dad used to talk about an old truck he had, but…"

Jake listened as Ian's voice drifted off. He remembered something his mother had said about how the new neighbor having lost her husband in a car accident. It broke his heart as he watched to boy struggle not to break down.

"Hey, tell you what. If you want, we usually work in my dad's shop which, as luck would have it, just so happens to be right next to your house. So feel free anytime to come over and check it out."

Ian looked at Jake and smiled, excitement in his eyes. "Really? That would be great. What are you working on?"

Jake could feel himself get excited just talking about the new car. "It's a 1980 Pontiac Firebird Trans Am. She was pretty beat up when we got her, but she's gonna be a beauty." Jake stopped then and looked at Ian. "I actually have a nephew about your age. You're what, fourteen or fifteen, right?"

Ian nodded. "Fourteen."

"Yeah, Wyatt's fourteen too. Maybe I can introduce you before school starts so you'll at least know someone. It's hard enough being a freshman, but even harder when you're starting a new school and don't know anyone."

"Are you sure he'd be OK with that?" Ian suddenly seemed skeptical.

Jake rushed to reassure him. "Absolutely. Wyatt is a great kid, really easy going. Why don't you have your mom bring you over tonight? We can just hang out, check out the car and you can meet Wyatt. He's there all the time. I'm not forcing anything, you guys can just hang out with all of us and we'll see how it goes. Sound good?"

For the first time during this whole exchange, Jake glanced at Julia. She was watching Ian to see his reaction. Jake's heart melted just watching her.

She spoke then, encouraging Ian to see how he felt about it. "If you want to I have no problem with it. I wanted to go over and introduce myself anyway."

Ian looked from her to Jake and back again. Then, in an excited tone, he said, "Sure, that sounds great!"

Jake smiled at the two of them. "Good, it's settled then. I'd better get back to work, but I'll see you both tonight around seven."

Ian waved and headed out to the car. Julia watched him leave and then faced Jake with an appreciative smile on her face. "Thank you for doing this. I was worried about him meeting people since we live out in the country."

"He seems like a great kid, so it was no problem at all." Jake smiled at her and watched as she bit her bottom lip. Why was that the sexiest thing he had ever seen? Had he ever found that sexy before? He didn't think so.

Pulling back from the direction of his thoughts, he said, "I better let my mom know you're coming. You better come prepared to have your ears talked off. She can carry on a conversation like no other."

Julia laughed her musical laugh and Jake felt like that alone could lift a man's soul. "I will brace myself."

Then they both stood there staring at one another. Her smile dulled a little until she finally said, "So, how much do I owe you for fixing my car?"

God, he must look like an idiot just standing there thinking she was just enjoying his company. "Oh yeah, sorry, it wasn't really anything, so this one's on the house."

Julia shook her head. "Oh no, I need to pay you something for the work you did."

Jake decided to come up with a plan to ensure he would get to see her. "Do you bake?"

She nodded, a strange look coming over her face. Jake smiled wide and said, "Perfect. Make me something and we'll call it even."

"I don't really think…, no, I need to pay you for this, not just make you something." Julia looked slightly panicked.

Oh yeah, Jake was enjoying watching her get riled up. "Julia, you live in the country now and neighbors do things for each other. I fixed your car and you bake me something and we then we call it even."

She seemed totally unsure and extremely adorable. She bit her lip again and Jake thought his heart would explode. "If you're sure. Any special requests?"

Jake wanted to tell her all he wanted was her in a bikini with a can of whipped cream, but that was highly inappropriate, so he went with his second choice. "Anything cherry would be great."

Julia nodded and started to back towards the door. "Cherry. Got it. I'd better go. See you later."

Jake gave her a slight wink and a small wave. "See you then."

He watched as she got in her truck and drove away, sighing as he thought about seeing her tonight.

Suddenly, Dean was beside him with a goofy grin on his face. "Boss, I think you might just have a case of the hots for that lady. And don't say you don't, because I have never, ever, in the whole eight years I've worked here, ever seen you look at anyone that way." Jake stared out the window where Julia's tail lighted had just been as Dean said, "She is one classy lady."

Jake's eyes never left the window as he said, "She sure is."

Chapter 4

Julia and Ian stopped at the grocery store to pick up something for dinner. Ian wasn't thrilled to be there, but he pushed the cart and didn't grumble too much, especially when a few young girls stopped to stare at him, then quickly walked away, giggling and glancing back again.

Julia caught him smiling back at them. She cleared her throat and said, "Hey. Looks like you've got some fans of your own already."

Ian glared at her like he was really put out. "Mom. Let's just finish this up. I want to go home and try out my new video game." She watched as he again glanced back down the aisle to where the girls were watching him.

Julia just shook her head and started to move on saying, "Come on hot stuff. Let's get this done."

Behind her all she heard was, "Mom" said in a harsh whisper. Sometimes it was fun being the mother of a teenage boy; they were so easy to tease.

She finished getting all the groceries they would need, including the stuff she needed to make two cherry cobblers. She needed to make two because there was no way Ian was not going to want one.

They checked out and she caught Ian once again looking at the girls who had strategically placed themselves at the magazine rack so they could watch him. Julia smiled to herself. He was a handsome boy, the perfect mix of herself and her husband. She just hoped he got in with the right crowd here. Jake seemed like a really great guy and having him be a good influence on Ian eased her mind.

They started to head back home when she saw the bank. She needed to get this done today so she could mark that off her list, too. She pulled over and told Ian that she wouldn't be long. She grabbed the box from the back seat and headed inside. Walking in, she asked about moving her accounts and getting a safety deposit box. The clerk behind the counter, Joanne was very kind and efficient. She pulled the appropriate paperwork and they got started. In between the paperwork and getting set up for the deposit box, Julia peered in the box on her lap. She could still see the coin folios and certificates, but she wondered what the other stuff was. Just as she was about to pull out the other notebooks she could see Ian in the truck. The girls from the grocery store had actually stopped to talk to him. He was laughing and talking, and as she watched, one girl was flipping her hair, a sure sign she was flirting. He seemed really at ease, which surprised her, because her husband had been so awkward the first time he'd spoken to her.

Just then, Ian pointed her way and the three girls turned in tandem towards her and waved. She smiled and waved back. Joanne walked in and told her to follow her back to the deposit box area. She settled her box inside drawer number 235 and locked it up. She would deal with the other stuff later – there was nothing in there that needed to be dealt with now. Having this chore done was enough. She finished off the final paperwork and Joanne gave her a business card and told her to call if she needed anything further.

As she walked over to the truck she could see Ian still talking to the girls. Julia made her way over to them and they all smiled. She shook each of their hands. Their names were Carrie, Rachel and Danielle, and they all looked about Ian's age. They said their goodbyes and headed for home. Julia glanced over as Ian twisted in his seat to watch the girls as they walked away. Then he sat back with a goofy smile on his face.

Julia couldn't resist. "So which one is it?"

Ian looked at her, puzzled by her question. "Which one what?"

She smiled and rolled her eyes. As if he didn't know what she was asking. "Which one do you like? You have this love-struck grin on your face."

Ian let out a huff, and then said, "I'm not in love, Mom."

"OK, so you're not in love, but that's not what I asked. I asked which one you like. I bet I can guess." She said this last part in a sing-song voice.

Her son slid further down in the seat and wouldn't look her way. Maybe she should stop while she was ahead. It was obvious he wasn't about to discuss his likes or dislikes about girls. These were moments when a father was needed and she felt a pain in her heart knowing she could only tell him her side of things.

Just as she was about to give up on the whole teasing thing, she heard Ian say in a quiet voice, "Rachel."

Julia laughed. She knew it would be her. Did she know her son or what? "Oh yeah? She is really pretty. They all are, but I know you're partial to girls with dark hair."

Ian laughed and shook his head. "How can you possibly know I like girls with dark hair?"

Julia stared over at him with a matter-of-fact look. "All the movie stars that you like have dark hair. I know you have posters of some of your favorite female singers and they have dark hair. And once, when you were younger, you told me you liked girls with dark hair because it always made their eyes look darker and you like dark eyes too. And weren't Rachel's eyes dark blue? They were really beautiful."

Bringing his hand up to his face, Julia knew he was a bit embarrassed that she knew this about him. "Baby, don't be embarrassed. Moms just pick up on these things. We can't help it. But more importantly, now you've met a few more people that go to your school. And with the way they were checking you out, your name will be all over school before it even starts. New kids in small towns always cause a buzz. You're going to be Mister Popular before you step foot in school on the first day."

Ian was quiet for a while, then glancing over at her and said, "You really think so?"

"Absolutely. And who wouldn't want to be your friend? You're smart, funny, handsome and an all-around great guy. Plus if you decide to go out for the swim team you can show off your pecs and abs. It's a win-win for you and the girls!"

Ian started to bust a gut then. "Mom, you had me up until the pecs and abs thing. You think you're really funny, don't you?"

"You bet I do, babe. I should have been a comedian. Maybe there's still time. We could move to L.A. and I can put together a routine all about my son and his journey through puberty. Sound like a good idea?"

Ian looked serious then. "No, Mom, that sounds like a horrible idea. Let's just stay here." He was quiet then said, "But I will admit at times you are funny, but not funny enough to make a career out of it. You better stick to your books."

Julia gave him a contemplative look. "So, no stand-up routine for me? Well, maybe you're right. Books do put a roof over our heads and food in our bellies. Besides, I wouldn't nearly get enough time with my favorite guy if I'm on the road all the time."

Watching Ian he seemed to be considering this. "On second thought, this is starting to sound better all the time." He laughed again as she mock punched him in the arm.

"Very funny, lover boy." They laughed all the way home.

∞ ∞ ∞

Hours later, after baking two cherry cobblers, they piled back into the truck and headed over to the neighbors. Ian was staring out the window and she could tell he was a bit nervous.

As they pulled up to the Vincent residence she turned to him and said, "We'll stay as long as you want. If you want to leave after twenty minutes, then we'll leave. No pressure, OK?"

Ian nodded. "Yeah, sure. Let's go."

The house was similar to Julia's with the exception of the extra balcony on the second floor. It had the same wide, double doorway and stone steps. The gardens were beautiful and Julia could tell Jake's parents must be avid gardeners. Looking to the back of the property, she could see the large shop and people milling about inside.

Just as they were getting out of the truck, they heard the screen door creak open. A petite woman with short grey hair stepped out. "Hello there, neighbors."

Julia waved and said, "Oh, hello, I'm…"

She didn't get a chance to finish as Jake's mother said, "I know who you are Julia. Audrey, my daughter, and I were planning a welcome for you this weekend, but it seems Jake beat us to it." Then she walked down the steps and shook Julia's hand.

"I'm Lillian, and can I just say how wonderful it is to meet you in person. The girls and I are big fans."

Julia smiled at her. "Thank you so much."

Lillian gushed a little, still holding her hand. "We've read everything you've ever written."

Julia continued to smile saying, "It's so nice to meet my fans." She had never been good at the 'meet-the-adoring-fans' piece of her job, but Lillian seemed really nice, so she just kept shaking her hand.

As Julia watched, Lillian's smile grew even bigger. "You are even more beautiful in person than the back cover of your books!"

Feeling the blush creep up her face, Julia tried not to look uncomfortable. "Um, thank you?"

Lillian laughed. "Oh dear, there I go already making you blush. I will apologize in advance as sometimes my mental filter doesn't always work right and I have a tendency to blurt."

From behind Julia the sound of a gruff voice said, "Sometimes? Woman, it's all the time with you."

They all turned to the man approaching them. He looked just like Jake. Same green eyes, same mischievous glint in them, same great smile. He walked over to where Julia and Ian were standing and extended his hand.

"Hey, I'm Alfred. You can call me Al though, as no one calls me Alfred except my mother, and Lillian when she's mad at me." He smiled at his wife. "I'm very happy to meet you. I wanted to say thank you for carrying on the lease agreement we had with the Bulgers."

"Oh, it was no problem. The other part of the property is more than enough room for Ian and I."

She watched as Al's eyes shifted to Ian and his smile got wider. "Hello there young man." Al shook Ian's hand. "I hear you might have an interest in classic cars?"

"Yes sir. I haven't had an opportunity to work on one before, but I would definitely like to check it out." Ian glanced at his mother and Julia nodded.

Pulling Ian with him as he headed towards the shop, Julia could hear Al say, "That's the spirit. How about we head back to the shop and take a gander? We'll let the ladies chat."

Julia watched them walk into the shop and hoped, not for the first time, that Ian was going to make some good friends.

Jake watched from the shop as Julia walked into the house with his mother. It took a lot of effort not to run over to say hello, but he knew better. If his mother caught even the slightest inkling he might be interested in her, she would be all over Julia, trying to sell him off like a prized horse. It had happened before when Jake hadn't even been interested in the woman. Geez, it had been crazy awkward.

He looked over at the door when his dad and Ian walked in. Ian seemed a little nervous, but he chatted well enough with his father. Jake had been thinking about the kid since he had been at the garage earlier that day. It must be tough being that age and having no father. He hoped he could be a good friend to Ian, and his mom too.

Grant, Jake's brother, and Wyatt already had their heads in under the hood. They stopped once Al and Ian came in. Ian's eyes scoped out the shop until his eyes landed on Jake.

"Hey Jake, thanks again for inviting me over. The car looks really cool." Ian eyed the car lying in parts. "Well, I mean, the parts I can make out, anyway." Everyone laughed and the ice was officially broken.

Jake introduced Ian to Wyatt and they did this weird handshake, fist bump tap thing. It was like they were already part of some secret club only teenage boys were privileged to be in. Ian shook Grant's hand and the work began. They showed Ian everything they had done so far, and then explained the next steps. He listened intently, asking questions when he didn't understand. Jake was thrilled to have a new apprentice in the shop, and so was his dad. Wyatt was old hat at lots of things now, so having a newbie was kind of nice. Before they knew it, almost two hours had gone by.

Jake stretched and said, "I think we should call it a night, gentlemen. Some people in here need to get up for work in the morning. Not all of us can be on summer break." Wyatt looked at Ian and they fist bumped over being able to sleep in at least a little bit longer.

Wyatt turned to Ian and asked, "Hey, you want to hang tomorrow? I'm going to the skate park with a couple of friends. Do you board?"

Jake watched as Ian's face lit up. "Sick! I'd love to hang out, and yes, I totally board. I used to go all the time before I got in…" Ian stopped and then continued like it was a confession. "I got into some trouble with the police. Some of my friends and I got caught breaking windows in an old warehouse. I didn't even throw anything, but I was still there. That's one of the main reasons why my mom and I moved. She didn't want me to get into any more trouble. I haven't been to a skate park in a while. I would love to get back on my board. I'm sure my mom would be fine with it."

So there was another riddle solved for Jake. Just knowing Julia would move her son away from the city to keep him from making bad choices lifted her perfect mom status up a few more notches in his eyes.

They headed into the house to get something to eat. For Jake, it was a chance to scope out the hot new neighbor. As they trooped in and made their introductions to Julia, he could see his mother at the kitchen counter preparing food for the hungry masses that had just descended upon her kitchen. She was always whipping up something for them. Then his eyes tracked until they landed on Julia and the sight before him took his breath away. Not just because she was breathtakingly beautiful, but because as he watched, she was sitting with his two daughters laughing and having a great time. It warmed his heart to see it.

Just as he was going to make his way over to talk to her, Ian excitedly ran over to her saying, "Mom, you've got to see this car! It is going to be so amazing." Ian's eyes came to rest on Jake and he smiled.

Jake looked over to his daughters, just as Ian said, "Hey, didn't I meet you today? Danielle, right?" Instantly, Jake's boy-dar went up and now he wasn't sure if having this cute, totally cool boy near his teenage daughter was such a good idea. Hovering close, he waited for a response, watching to see if there was interest on Dani's face.

Dani nodded, "Hi Ian. It's nice to see you again. I didn't know you knew my grandparents." Jake waited, but no giggling happened. She had also spoken two full sentences, which was a sure sign she wasn't interested. If she was she wouldn't be able to speak at all and would have been blushing up a storm by now.

Ian just smiled, with no look of interest either. "Yeah, my Mom and I just met them today, we're their new neighbors. Are you going to the skate park tomorrow? Or is your friend Rachel? Wyatt and I are going. Maybe we'll see you there." Then, as smooth as any guy he had ever seen, Ian nodded and walked away, making a beeline for the food. Ian had just dropped a total bomb on the teenager in Jake's life and hadn't even flinched.

So it was Rachel he had a thing for. Staring at Danielle now, he watched as she whipped out her phone and started texting furiously. Danielle had always been the matchmaker among her friends. Jake bet she was texting something like, 'OMG, Rach, that cute Ian guy we met today, just, like, totally asked about you! AAAhhHH, can you believe it. He wants us to go to the skate park to hang out tomorrow. He asked for you specifically. OMG!!! Call me later and I will totally tell you everything.'

He wouldn't see her for the rest of the night once they got home, because she would have the phone attached to her head and the conversation would go on for hours. Sometimes he would give anything for a son. No drama, no giggling, no meltdowns. Just someone he could understand. But honestly, he loved his girls and wouldn't give them up for the world.

His focus moved to Julia. She was talking to Hailey now, who liked the fact that she had Julia's full attention. She was talking a mile a minute, her hands moving as she spoke, and Julia just sat there taking it all in as if Hailey was the most important person on the planet. It was exactly like he had seen her do with Ian earlier today. It was a skill to be able to completely focus on something or someone. He watched as Julia smiled and laughed with his daughter, and in that moment the world shifted, just a bit. She was totally throwing him off balance, like having her in the room filled the space with so much oxygen that it was almost making him dizzy.

He pulled his eyes away from Julia, only to land squarely on his sister. Audrey stared at him with an inquisitive look, like she knew what was going on, even if he didn't. He stared back at her and mouthed the words, "Don't say a damn word."

She got this mischievous glint in her eye as she raised an eyebrow. He could see she really wanted to say something to embarrass him. He continued to stare and shook his head slowly. Just when he thought he had been victorious at the stare down, his mother turned to him and said, "What's going on between you two? You better not be fighting. You're not too old to be sent to your rooms you know."

Audrey was the first to speak. "No, Mom, we're just having a discussion is all."

His mother eyed them both. "Funny discussion. I didn't even hear any conversation."

Jake just smiled at his mother, knowing he was almost always able to win her over. She walked away with suspicion clearly written on her face. Whew, that was close. He glared over at his sister, who was still looking like she wanted to create some serious embarrassment for him.

He headed over to Julia now and said, "Well Julia, I think your son has a talent as a mechanic. Ian, you can come over anytime."

Ian smiled at him with his mouth full. That kid could eat as much as Wyatt. The crazy teen metabolism, he remembered from when he was young.

Julia stood up. "This has been great. Thank you for having us over. I hope we can do this again sometime."

She smiled at Jake and before she could say another word, Lillian asked, "Well how about you come over for Sunday dinner? We'd love to have you."

Julia seemed stunned for a moment. Jake watched as she looked at his mother, then at him and finally at Ian. He was nodding and she didn't know what to say. "Oh, I don't want to impose…"

"It's not an imposition if you're invited." Jake smiled at her and for a moment she looked like he caught her off guard with his smile. So he continued, "Besides, Mom makes the best pot roast in the state." Then he winked at her and he actually saw her jaw drop. Then he remembered he had an audience.

Lillian laughed. "Is that a hint that you want pot roast?"

Jake shrugged. "Well if you're offering." And everyone laughed. It was common knowledge that Jake was a pot roast junkie.

Julia turned to Jake and said, "Come on out to the truck and I'll give you your payment for fixing my truck today." She had said it innocently enough, but everyone stopped in their tracks like she had propositioned him for sex or something. She glanced around and said in a matter of fact manner, "I made Jake a cherry cobbler in exchange for fixing my truck since he wouldn't take my money. Come out and get it before I leave." She waved to everyone as she headed for the door.

Ian called out, "Be right there, Mom!" He stood where he was and finished up his conversation with Wyatt about their outing the next day.

Jake followed Julia to her truck and watched as she leaned over into the back seat. It might have made him a total pervert, but he couldn't have looked away from her if he tried. As she stood back up, she produced a clear plastic covered casserole dish with the most delicious-looking cherry cobbler he had ever seen. She handed it to him and said in a whisper, "Thanks again for everything today. It was great. I hope you like the cobbler."

Standing with her under the big light in his parent's yard made him feel like he was a teenager again. Julia was beautiful with the light shining down on her. Her skin looked so soft that Jake's hand itched just to touch her. She smiled the sweetest smile and Jake couldn't wait to see her again.

"I'm glad you're coming to dinner on Sunday, it should be a great time." He took a step towards her, drawn to her as the light shined off the green flecks in her eyes. Just as he was contemplating doing the unthinkable and kiss her, he heard Ian come out the door. Stepping back, Jake took a deep breath and smiled at Ian as he came over to the truck. He said his goodbyes and waved them off, watching the taillights turn onto the road.

Heading back into the house after putting the cobbler in his truck, he was smiling to himself as he walked into the kitchen. Then he came to a full stop. Everyone, except for the kids who had already left the room, was staring at him. Realization hit him and his shoulders sagged. Before anyone could say a word he said, "I don't want to hear it. This is no one else's business but mine. If I like her, or she likes me, I don't want to talk about it. So just go do what you were doing." Hoping against hope, but he knew his family were notorious meddlers.

Everyone was quiet until his dad spoke up. "Son, you'd have to be dead not to be attracted to that woman. She's funny, crazy smart, talented and let's not forget she's beautiful. Hell, if I was thirty years younger and wasn't already married to the most wonderful woman in the world, I'd give you a run for your money." Jake glanced at his brother to see him nodding.

His mother watched him. "Jake, what are you afraid of?"

He so didn't want to get into this with them. "Mom, I'm not afraid. But… I need to take this at my own pace. She's had a couple of rough years and I don't want to push her away. Promise me you won't pester her. And no crossing your fingers behind your back. Just keep your word."

Walking over to the doorway of the living room he told the girls it was time to go. He needed to get away from his family before they had anything more to say about Julia. Coming over to his mother he kissed her on the cheek, gave his dad a quick hug and waved to his siblings, knowing he and Julia would be the topic of discussion as soon as he left.

His daughters piled into the truck and talked about the trip to the skate park tomorrow. Danielle had promised Hailey she could come. He loved listening to his girls when they were getting along. Just as they were turning down the road they lived on, Danielle turned to him and said, "So, Dad, Julia seems really nice. You should maybe ask her out sometime." Oh no, not her too. Why was his dating situation a hot topic tonight? Was it so obvious to everyone he needed to get out more? He guessed the girls saw it all the time so yeah, they would like him to date.

Jake glanced at her and said, "Let me think about it." That was all he was going to say about it. But as the night wore on his thoughts drifted back to Julia and how much he really would like to get to know her.

Chapter 5

The next few days were filled with unpacking and setting up the house. Ian helped out with the furniture, but Julia had wanted him to have an opportunity to get out and make some friends, so she had done a lot by herself. She didn't mind as she knew how she wanted things to be done.

She called Al one day to see if he knew of this Joe Green fella that Mr. and Mrs. Bulger had recommended. Al was quick to assure her Joe was a great handyman, complete with a green thumb. She called Joe right then, and he came over that afternoon. He was a tall, thin man, in his late fifties with only a thin ridge of hair around his head. He didn't talk a whole lot, but that suited Julia just fine.

She liked the fact he'd already done work on the property and knew the place quite well. They walked around the yard and the house to get a sense of what kinds of things Julia would like him to do. He'd taken care of the pool since the Bulgers had left, so Julia discussed what needed to be done for the end of the season. He said she had a few more weeks and then it would be time to close it up. She also wanted the gutters cleaned and the yard to be prepped for the winter. After an hour Joe left. He had given her a quote for the regular maintenance and they agreed on an hourly rate for anything over and above. Julia couldn't believe how reasonable his rates were. In the city, she would have paid three times as much.

There was a beautiful study in the house that used to be Mr. Bulger's. The walls were all dark cherry wood, with two walls being floor to ceiling bookshelves, which Julia was thrilled about. She was a lover of books, of course, and had tons of them. Picturing all of them at home on these shelves was very exciting. She set up her computer and monitor and all her other gadgets.

Julia had been a full-time author for about fifteen years now. She'd always loved to write and with Martin having such a good job as an attorney, she had been able to fulfill her dream. She had about twelve published novels under her belt already. She was actually working on a new genre and was anxious to move forward with it. Her editor was very happy and she was lucky the publisher was taking a chance on her going in this new direction. She was hoping to get a deal with them for a trilogy, but she would have to wait and see.

She had done very well financially with her writing. She actually didn't have to worry about money even after Martin had died. He had made sure they had life insurance and when his accidental death benefit was paid out, it had been a substantial amount. It had been hard enough losing him, so knowing they could live comfortably was what Julia thought of as a final gift from Martin.

Due to her books being so profitable, she was able to put money away for Ian's college fund and still have some of the luxuries they had before they lost Martin. Even the private sale of the house had been more lucrative than she could have hoped. She had purchased the new home and property and was still able to put some in the bank after all was settled.

Putting the finishing touches on her study she took in her new space. Yes, she could definitely write in here. The windows were big to let in lots of natural light and air if she wished. The desk set up was perfect and she was excited to get started again and lose herself in the world she was creating for her readers.

By Sunday the house was coming together, and she and Ian were settling in nicely. Just hours before heading off to the Vincent's house for dinner, Julia made something special and had picked up two bottles of wine to take with them.

As they pulled in the driveway, Julia wondered if there was a party going on. There were seven cars already parked. She hadn't expected there to be so many people. Julia stared at Ian then at the two bottles of wine and the dessert she had made. "I don't think this will be enough."

Ian looked at her, puzzled. "Mom, Mrs. Vincent said you didn't need to bring anything." Julia has seen Lillian briefly the other day and had told Julia just to bring themselves.

"I know, but it just felt wrong not to bring something." Julia was raised by strict parents who would be rolling over in their graves if she were invited somewhere for dinner and had not brought something.

Ian shrugged his shoulders, saying, "Wyatt says there's usually enough food to feed an army." Ian and Wyatt had hung out every day since they met. Julia was so happy he had made such a good friend. Jake hadn't been wrong – Wyatt was a great kid.

She hoped that once things got settled, she would have a chance to make some new friends, too. She had to admit she missed her friends in the city. But she just needed to give it some time. This invite to dinner was a perfect opportunity to perhaps meet some other people.

They gathered their few things and started making their way to the house. Just as they were about halfway up the driveway, she saw Jake and he called out, "Hello there, pretty lady!"

She smiled at him as her heart rate picked up. Why was this always happening around him? "Well hello yourself."

Jake walked straight towards her and lifted the edge of the foil to peek into see what was in the dish she brought. Leaning in, he took a deep sniff, closed his eyes and he groaned. The sound was so completely male and sexy that for a few seconds she just stood there staring at him like an idiot. Still leaning forward with his head only a few inches away, Jake said, "Mmm, what do we have here? It smells absolutely sinful."

Was it just her or did he sound downright dirty and suggestive? Wow, she really needed to stop reading those romance novels. They were putting all kinds of things in her head.

Jake had been watching her the whole time and a mischievous grin appeared on his face. "Maybe I should sample one out here before the crowd realizes you brought food." He had a twinkle in his eye as if he was trying to come off all innocent.

Staring at him now, all she said was, "I don't think so."

Jake's bottom lip popped out ever so slightly and all Julia could think of was wanting to give it a taste. "Aww, really? I just want one." He seemed a little pathetic, what with the lip and the sad puppy dog eyes going on. But his green eyes were mesmerizing and she could feel herself being drawn in.

Suddenly, Ian was beside them and said, "You're wasting your time Jake. She is immune to the sad face." Well, she was immune to Ian's sad face because, he'd use it to his full advantage if not, but Jake, on the other hand – damn, this man was crazy hot!

She smiled shyly and said, "I guess one won't hurt."

"What? Really Mom, you're going to cave the first time he shows you the puppy dog eyes?" Ian huffed and marched off towards the door, thoroughly disgusted with her for giving in so easily.

Julia watched as Jake pulled out a brownie and took a bite. His eyes closed again and the moan that came from him was enough to have her breath catch and her knees go a little wobbly. Who knew watching a man eat brownies could be this much of a turn on?

Finishing the brownie with more groans and sounds of absolute bliss, Julia watched as he licked each of his fingers slowly. Now if that was not a deliberate flirt, she didn't know what was.

"That was, by far, the best brownie I've ever had." Then, wincing, he said, "But don't tell my mother I said that."

Julia laughed as she watched Jake glance over his shoulder, as if Lillian was going to come out after him. "A piece of information for blackmail later. Hmm, that could come in handy."

Jake grinned. "Sweetheart, if you need me you just need to ask. With eyes that beautiful, it would be hard for me to refuse." He continued to smile as he took the container of brownies from her and headed into the house. Holy Moses, this man could seriously melt her panties right off!

As Julia walked in the door she was shocked at the amount of people inside. There were a few younger ones pushing little scooters, squealing as they went. The kitchen was packed with people everywhere, talking and laughing and having a great time. Meal preparations were underway and the smell in the room was mouthwatering. She scanned the crowd and felt a little overwhelmed.

She spotted Ian already in the den, sitting with Wyatt and Jake's daughters. They were having a great time playing some video game, and he seemed to already fit into the group. Unlike herself, who was currently feeling like the outsider that she was. If she had known so many people were going to be here, she might have said no to the invitation. She could get overwhelmed in crowds, and this was definitely a crowd.

Just then she heard Jake's voice beside her ear. "You're looking a bit lost, sweetheart."

His breath on her cheek sent a shiver straight down to her toes. How could one person have the ability to make her feel absolute out of control with just the sound of his voice?

"Sorry, it's just more people than I expected." Glancing over her shoulder at him, he smiled and her heart fluttered.

Feeling his hand rub along her lower back he said, "You don't have anything to apologize for. We're quite a crew to take in. Plus we have a few extras here today. Come on, let me introduce you." His hand felt warm and comforting as he moved her forward.

They started in the living room first, where she met Jake's niece, Jessica. Then, they headed into the living room to meet his Uncle Mel and Luke, his brother-in-law. They both smiled and shook her hand politely and just as quickly, let their eyes drift back to the football game on TV.

Heading into the chaos of the kitchen next, she was introduced to his Aunt Margo, and his cousins Kristen and Colby. His sister-in-law, Jennifer, stared awestruck as she shook her hand. Julia could tell she was a big fan. Lillian and Audrey called out their hellos, as they were busy getting food ready. She also met Jake's cousin Ted, who some might call nerdy, but who was quite thrilled to meet her. Then Al came in from outside. He came straight over and gave her a hug and kiss on the cheek, saying how happy he was that she had come. Jake gave him a weird look, but they moved into the fray and before Julia even knew what was happening, she had volunteered herself to help with dinner.

Lillian smiled at her and said, "You know you didn't need to bring anything, but thank you so much for the wine and brownies. They smell delicious."

Jake popped his head in between them and said with a huge smile, "They are."

Lillian laughed. "I see the hustler has already hit you up, has he?"

Hit up, hit on, that about covered it. Julia cleared her throat. "That he did."

Lillian looked at her with a gleam in her eye. "You know if you keep feeding him, he'll keep coming around right. He's like a stray dog."

A huff sounded from behind Julia and Jake sounded indignant as he said, "Mother, did you just call me a stray dog?"

Lillian laughed and shrugged her shoulders. "Only in the most affectionate way possible, dear." Julia watched as Jake shook his head at her then got pulled into another conversation.

Once the food was ready, everyone headed to the dining room. The table was long enough to fit everyone except the kids, who ate at the table in the kitchen. Lillian had done a lovely job setting the table and each spot had a place card to show who was sitting in what seat. Julia was not surprised when she found her name and she was seated between Jake and his brother Grant.

Jake leaned over and whispered, "My mother is playing a bit of matchmaker here. She's thrilled we have an equal number of boys and girls at the table."

Julia laughed. "I'm glad I could help out with the numbers for seating." She was impressed when Jake pulled her chair out and helped her slide into place.

Once he was seated in his own spot, he said, "No, thank you. Otherwise, I was going to be stuck sitting beside Ted." They both glanced down to see the aforementioned cousin. Not the most attractive individual and socially awkward wouldn't even start to describe him. Ted's voice was also very loud, so the thought of poor Jake sitting beside him made her cringe.

He leaned in closer, his eyes still on Ted. "I really owe you one."

Julia threw him an inquisitive look. "My, my, blackmail info and an IOU. I'm really racking up the favors." She watched as Jake laughed and gave her a wink.

Dinner was absolutely fantastic. The pot roast was melt-in-your-mouth good, just like Jake had said. The meal conversation was equally as good. She had been seated between Jake and Grant, and this meant she had been privy to all the smack talk, little digs and inside jokes they shared. Grant was a great little brother, making sure to try and embarrass Jake as much as possible, unless they were talking about Audrey – then they were on the same team. The stories were great and Julia especially liked the one about the time when Audrey had dressed both her brothers in dresses for a tea party. Lillian had taken photos and they were shared with any and all people who wished to see them. Julia made sure to mention that she would love to see the photos the next time she came over for tea. Lillian nodded and said she would show her all the embarrassing pictures of the boys she could find.

Jake was a good sport through it all. When the desserts came out everyone raved about the brownies and somehow Jake had been able to snag two more. As everyone continued to talk and have their tea and coffee, she could feel Jake's arm come around the back of her chair. She smiled to herself and continued to chat with Jake's Aunt Margo. Julia did however catch a look between Audrey and Lillian as they too noticed the arm around the back of the chair. Yes, they were definitely not missing a thing when it came to her and Jake.

Once the cleanup started all the men headed for the living room to continue watching the football game. Jake sat so he could still see her, and she was a bit embarrassed by his attention. The ladies were all talking and laughing and dishes were being moved around in different stages of the cleaning process. As Julia was drying another dish, the topic of conversation switched to Jake's ex, Francine. Thankfully, Dani and Hailey were in the den playing video games with the boys.

Lillian checked over her shoulder before she started. "If I get my hands on that little witch, I'll strangle her myself." Anger flashed in her eyes.

Audrey leaned in and said, "You might have to get in line, Mom."

Julia could see it wasn't just Lillian and Audrey that were mad, but Jennifer was livid too. Whoa, something big must have gone down. Julia whispered, "What happened?"

Lillian shook her head. "Just Franny using her kids to get what she wants again. She had the nerve to tell Jake she couldn't take the girls on her scheduled weekend because she didn't have any money. Jake told her he wouldn't give her a dime and if she didn't take the girls on her weekend he was calling his lawyer.

"So, Franny did come and get the girls on Saturday morning. First thing this morning she's dropping them off at 6:30, saying she has an appointment, and then she peeled out of the driveway. She didn't even kiss the girls goodbye or get out of the car. Then, Jake finds out from Dani that the girls did nothing at all on the weekend. They sat at Franny's new boyfriend's house and watched TV. There was hardly any food in the house and the place looked like it had been trashed before they even got there. Luckily, Jake always gives Dani money to take with them in case of emergencies, so she was at least able to get a pizza for her and Hailey."

Huffing out a breath, Lillian continued. "Dani confessed she gave her mom some of the money, because Franny told her she needed to pick up some medicine and she hadn't gotten her cheque yet."

Julia was shocked to hear this. "How much did she give her?"

Lillian shook her head again. "Well, Jake had given her a hundred and twenty dollars in case the girls needed it. They bought pizza and Dani gave the rest to her mom, so I'm guessing at least a hundred dollars. Hailey told Jake that Franny wasn't even home most of Saturday and hadn't even come home until this morning. That meant the girls were home with the boyfriend all night. Dani said she basically barricaded her and Hailey in one room when the boyfriend ended up having friends over. Dani has only met this guy one other time and her mother left them alone with him!

"Needless to say, Jake was livid. He will be on the phone tomorrow with his lawyer. He was in quite the foul mood when he got here today. He and Dani got into it after he told her she should have called him and he would have come over and picked them up. Dani said it wasn't fair to him to have to take care of them all the time and her mother needed to take some of the responsibility. They were both angry when they walked in and haven't spoken since."

Audrey sighed, "I will never understand what he ever saw in that girl."

Lillian looked out towards the den and smiled. "She did give me some beautiful grandbabies. All my grandchildren are beautiful. Being a grandma is the best job in the world."

Julia thought about that for a minute. Ian had sadly not had an opportunity to get to know any of his grandparents, as they were all gone when he was too young to know them. Martin had an Aunt Wanda that Julia stayed in touch with, but it wasn't the same. She and Martin had both been only children, so Ian was missing out on the full family experience.

The ladies continued to chat about different things. Julia talked about being an author and her new opportunity she had been given to write in a different genre. She learned all about Jennifer's job at the bank, which just happened to be Julia's new bank, and Audrey's work at the hospital. It was nice just sharing stories and talking to women facing some of the same issues she was facing.

Audrey turned to her and said, "Hey, how about the next time the girls get together you come out with us? We go out about once a month just to have a drink and chat. It's so much fun. You should come. It will at least get you out of the house and it's a good way to meet people. What do you say?"

Julia was thrilled. She couldn't believe how easily she had been accepted into this family. They were kind people and she was so happy they were pulling her into their lives. "Actually, that would be great. When is the next one?"

Jennifer pulled out her phone and said, "It's on the eighteenth of this month. We usually just go to Gilly's for a drink and appetizers. Sound good?"

"It's a date!" Julia said enthusiastically. Now she had something to look forward to.

Julia stood up a little while later, thanking Lillian for the wonderful dinner and saying goodbye to everyone. Ian seemed tired from all the food he'd consumed. He said his goodbyes and headed for the truck. She was just exiting the house when she saw Jake coming up from the shop.

Smiling, she said, "I wasn't sure if I was going to see you before I left. Having fun in the shop?"

Jake came closer as he said, "Yeah, my uncle and cousin wanted to see the car. You were looking for me?"

She laughed. "Just to say goodbye."

"No other reason?" She couldn't miss the twinkle in his eye.

"Nope, that was it."

Jake seemed disappointed for a moment. Stepping closer, he said, "Damn. I was hoping I had made more of an impression on you and maybe you were going to ask me out."

With a puzzled look, Julia said, "Ask you out? Well Mr. Vincent, I have to know someone a lot longer than a week before I ask them out."

"How long?" Jake watched her closely, as if trying to read her.

Julia thought hard and said, "At least a few weeks, maybe more."

Jake stared at her, as if measuring her answer. "We've known each other for a week now."

"Yes." Julia could practically hear the wheels turning in his head.

Jake nodded. "So, I have to wait two or three more weeks before you'll ask me out."

Julia thought about this for a second. "Wait, why do I have to do the asking? And before you ask, the same rules apply."

Jake looked at her with playfully sad eyes and said, "I don't like rejection, so I leave the asking to others."

"Aww, and how's that working out for you?" Julia stifled a giggle.

Jake glanced down at the ground for a minute then back at her as he answered, "Well to be honest, I haven't been out on a date in a long time."

She looked at him matter-of-factly. "Then maybe you should change your approach. Put yourself out there. You never know what could happen."

Jake's eyes heated as he stared at her. "In that case, I might have to make an exception for you then. Three weeks, right?"

Julia nodded as she watched him. The light from the shop illuminated him from the side and she could see him wanting to ask her more, but he didn't. Instead he leaned in closer and said, "OK, I'll wait. But perhaps I should give you something to consider in the meantime."

Before she could respond, his hands came up and cupped her face as he brushed his warm firm lips over hers. They were so soft that Julia just wanted to curl into him like a warm hug. He smelled like pine and soap and the combination made her head spin. He pressed in closer to her and she let out a soft moan. Suddenly, she felt his tongue run along the seam of her lips and she couldn't help but open for him. She wanted to taste him, too. As he gently dipped in for his first taste, all she could do was revel in the sensation of his kiss. She grabbed the front of his shirt to pull herself closer. Mmm, he tasted so good, like mint and something dark. It had been so long since she'd kissed someone she'd almost forgotten how incredible it was to share that intimacy. Just as she is about to try and deepen the kiss, Jake drew away slowly.

When she opened her eyes, the heat in his stare was plain to see. "I knew it would be good, but it was a million times better than I could have imagined." His eyes travelled back down to her lips again. Just as she was thinking she should lean back in for another taste, she heard Ian call to her from the truck. Reluctantly, Julia let go of his shirt.

"You'd better go. I know how impatient teenagers can be." He was still holding her face and he ran his thumb along her lower lip. He dropped his hands, and she stepped back.

Glancing towards the truck and taking another step away she said, "See you soon."

Jake smiled at her with the heat still simmering in his eyes. "I'm counting on it."

Julia got in the truck and Ian was staring at her. "What took you so long? Did you forget something?"

Julia smiled at him. Yeah, part of my heart. "Uh-huh, I left my purse, but I got it now."

Ian nodded and yawned. "Let's get going. I'm exhausted. I ate so much, I think I could easily go three days without eating and still be full."

Julia looked at him as if he just grew two more heads. "Doubtful. You're a teenager. Your whole life revolves around food. Well, food and video games. And girls."

Ian rolled his eyes. "Mom, I'm not talking about girls."

"All right, just food and video games then." She started the truck and they headed home.

Chapter 6

As Anthony made his way into the non-contact visitation area, he could see Gino waiting. Other inmates were exiting or entering to talk to their visitors. The room was too bright and it showed all the cracks in the linoleum floor and the dirty vinyl seats. The room smelt like body odor and pine cleaner. He made his way over and picked up the phone. Gino eyed the guards warily, but picked up the receiver on his side.

Gino smiled a sad smile and said, "Hey, Anthony. You doing OK?" For all of Gino's faults he was a pretty good guy, unless he had a contract on you – then, you were dead.

"I'm doing fine. Met with my lawyer last week and he says he's pretty close to being able to get me outta here."

Gino nodded. "That's good. I thought I'd come and see you to let you know what I found out. I didn't want to get cut off on the phone, that's why I came in person." Anthony knew Gino hated to even step foot in this place. He was doing him a huge favor by even coming here.

Anthony nodded. "Give me some good news."

Gino leaned forward, dropping his voice down to make sure he wasn't heard. "Dino's cousin was able to find out who sold the house. The real estate agent is some guy by the name of Robert

Axford. He apparently went and met with Julia at the house after one of her friends suggested him. Because the house was in such a fancy neighborhood, and houses there are in high demand, the sign never made it out on the lawn before the whole bidding war happened. She listed the house and it was sold within twelve hours. That's why we didn't see a sign."

Anthony nodded, thinking about why Julia had left so fast. It seemed strange that she would just up and move so quickly.

Gino continued in the same low tone. "Dino's cousin checked to find out where she had moved to, but it wasn't listed. That means, apparently, she didn't buy locally, she moved out of the city. She said she poked around to see if this Robert Axford guy remembered the name of the friend, but he said he couldn't remember. He sells a lot of houses, so the list of someone recommending him would be long."

Cursing quietly, Anthony stared at Gino with concern in his eyes. "Damn it, Gino! What if Julia knows? Were you able to check with the neighbors?"

Gino nodded. "Yeah, I actually sent Nina there as if they were long lost friends. She spoke to the one of the neighbors and asked where Julia had gone. Nina said it had been years and she was hoping to reconnect with Julia, or some shit. The neighbor was really friendly and she told Nina she couldn't remember anything specific other than Julia was moving to the country. Apparently Julia and Martin kept to themselves a lot, because they were always working. They offered to take Nina's number and stuff, but she said she would check on Facebook."

His brain started to churn then. Why hadn't he thought of this before? Maybe Julia could be found through one of her social media accounts. She was a published author, so she must have accounts for that sort of thing.

Glancing at Gino, he said, "Hey isn't Big Tony's son into computers and hacking and stuff? Do you think he could dig around see if her social media sites say anything? I mean it's worth a shot, right? Otherwise, we have no idea how far she's gone. Find out if he can do this for us. I'm willing to pay the kid." This might be a dead end, or it might be just the ticket.

Gino smiled his first genuine smile since he walked in the place. "Good thinking. I thought about talking to her publishing company, but they keep a tight lid on all that info."

Peering over to the guards, Anthony sighed. "Shit, I really wish I was out of here. Let's work those angles and I'll call you for updates. If we do get information, hopefully my lawyer can get me out of here sooner rather than later and we can go see what she's been up to."

They said their goodbyes and Anthony headed back to his cell. He could have gone and hung out, but associating with people on the inside just seemed to keep you on the inside. He had so few people to talk to or that came to visit him, it made him think, not for the first time, he should start seriously thinking about a family. But he liked to have lots women, not just one, so he didn't think settling down would suit his lifestyle. Nah, he just needed to worry about getting out of here. Then he could move on with his life once the threat of information getting out was eliminated.

Four days had gone by, and Jake hadn't heard anything from Julia. School was starting next week so he understood they were probably getting settled into the new house and getting ready for school. As it was, the impending start of school brought with it an increase of drama for Dani. Between outfit freak outs and manicure meltdowns, his household was in a constant state of chaos. It also seemed to be the meeting place for all of Dani's friends, so the pandemonium was brought to a whole new level.

Hailey was at least being easy this year. She didn't seem too concerned at all about going into fifth grade. She did, however, seem to be enjoying the constant dropping in of Dani's friends, and they all treated her well so he didn't mind it. Hailey had always been the easier of the two. When she grew tired of the girls upstairs, she would find him and they would hang out together. But now it was Thursday and he was trying to figure out when he was going to get an opportunity to see Julia again. He had thought about just dropping by the house, but that just seemed too pushy. He thought maybe he could get Ian's number and text to see if he wanted to come over to the shop, but then he thought Wyatt would think that was weird, so he dropped that idea, too.

Just as he was running out of ideas Hailey said, "Hey, Dad, do you think Julia and Ian were invited to go to Uncle Luke and Aunt

Audrey's party this weekend? I hope so, I really like her. She is so nice and pretty. She really listens when you talk to her. She said she might have some books for me once she finishes unpacking. I told her how much I like to read and she said she had some perfect books, just for someone my age."

As Jake watched, he could see the adoration for Julia in his youngest daughter's eyes. He couldn't blame her, Julia was great. She was beautiful, smart and funny. She was everything a guy could want, and apparently, everything a young girl who craved the attention of a mother figure could want, too.

"Hmm, you know what? I'm not sure, but let me call Aunt Audrey and find out." He smiled as Hailey headed off to see what disaster her sister was dealing with now.

Picking up his cell phone, he dialed the number and he moved about the kitchen getting stuff ready for dinner. It rang a few times and Audrey picked up. "Hey, little bro, what can I do for you?"

Jake rolled his eyes. He hated the 'little' title. "Hey sis, Hailey was just asking me if Julia and Ian will be at the party on Saturday. She really likes her and was hoping she had been invited."

He could practically hear his sister smile on the other end of the phone. "Oh Hailey wanted to know, did she? Well, you can tell her yes; Julia and Ian will be coming on Saturday. And, tell Hailey I told her to bring her swimsuit because maybe Hailey would be able to go swimming with her. And tell Hailey Julia asked me if she would be there along with her dad and sister."

His heart gave a little flutter knowing Julia asked if he was coming too. He rolled his eyes at Audrey and the dramatic way she answered his question.

"Who else is going to be there? I hope Terry isn't coming this year. He made a complete ass of himself last year."

She laughed. "No, he is definitely not invited this year. Just the usual people. Oh, and Luke saw Dylan Lincoln and got cornered into inviting him too."

Jake's vision instantly flashed red. "Why did he invite him?! He's a pompous ass. Always bragging and gloating over all his money. I can't stand him." Not to mention he was the one who was screwing his ex on their kitchen table. But he had only ever told Grant who he had caught Francine with and had sworn him to secrecy.

Sighing, Audrey said, "I know he's a bit of windbag, but we had invited a group to come and he hangs out with them. Why do you hate him so much?"

"I don't hate him, I just can't stand him." Actually, maybe he did hate him. "Just keep him away from any new guests that might be coming. I don't need to have him trying to get in good with Julia. He's a player and she doesn't need any part of that."

Audrey laughed. "Is this because of the kiss I just happened to witness the other night at Mom and Dad's? Because, little bro, that was some hot and steamy lip lock. Oh-la-la!"

Jake could feel his cheeks get a bit red. "Seriously, were you spying on us? That's so seventh grade, Audrey."

She giggled. "That might be, but you should know Dad and Grant were also watching."

"Christ, Audrey! You guys are worse than a bunch of old women. Stop spying on me!"

He could hear her tsking on the other end. "Now where is the fun in that, little brother?" And the line went dead.

Argh! He texted her back.

> *Hey I wasn't finished. Can u give me Julia's cell #?*
> *Wanted to ask about her truck.*

Jake waited a few seconds until his phone chimed.

> *Really? U want 2 ask about her truck? LAME! If u want*
> *to talk 2 her ask if she needs any help with the house?*
> *The truck thing - super cheesy!*

Shit, she was right. Grudgingly, he decided to go with her idea.

> *Fine, will do. Just give me the #.*

The phone chimed again.

> *Yes, I am full of fantastic ideas. Let me know if u need*
> *any guidance from your older and infinitely wiser sister.*

Oh brother. He thought for a second, then sent back a text.

> *Oh u mean much older and decrepit sister?*

He knew how sensitive she was about her age, so he was probably going to pay for that one.

> *Hey, u want that number or not, jerk!!*

Oh no! Time to lay it on thick.

> *Yes please, oh wise, beautiful and caring sister.* ☺

He hoped it made up for the decrepit comment.

See, that's the kind of respect I deserve. 555-7986.

Jake laughed to himself as he logged Julia's number into his phone under the name 'Incredibly Sexy Lady'. Then, he went and got dinner on the table and called the girls.

Julia dropped over to Lillian's for tea on Thursday afternoon, after receiving a phone invite. She had finished all the unpacking and getting each room set up and was just doing some editing when she had gotten the call. She was feeling in need of a break.

Pulling up in the driveway she saw Alfred in the shop and waved. He waved back with a big grin on his face. She headed inside and Lillian had the table set for tea.

Lillian was smiling at her when she came in. "Well, there she is. You settling in OK, hon?"

Julia nodded. "Yeah, Ian seems excited about school starting and that's a miracle in itself." She was quiet for a second. "I was so worried about him in Chicago. He was hanging out with some bad kids. I couldn't have him growing up there. That's the reason we moved. He seemed to be drifting, you know? I know it's only been a short time since we've been here, but he already seems different. Wyatt is having a good influence on him. All your guys are, really. And Ian talks about Jake like he's known him forever."

Lillian nodded. "Jake's always been like that. Always the cool guy, life of the party. Everyone wanted to be his friend. Even when he was going through hard times. And believe me, when he was with

Franny there were many hard times. Sometimes I wish he never had gotten involved with her. Then I think of Dani and Hailey and I wouldn't change it for the world. And neither would Jake – those girls are everything to him."

Julia could see the sad expression on Lillian's face and she said, "But at least he has you guys, right? It must have been great for him to have his family so close by. I wish I would've had that when Martin passed away. It was hard having no family around, but at least I had friends."

Leaning over and taking Julia's hand in her own, Lillian said, "Well you're here now and even though it hasn't been long, we're here for you anytime. And so is Jake."

Tears welled in her eyes and almost spilled over as Julia glanced at the hand holding hers. She had almost forgotten what it was like to have someone so mothering, making her feel safe. She squeezed Lillian's hand one last time, saying, "Thank you. You have no idea how much that means to me."

"Sweetheart, you deserve to have so much in your life. You're too young to be alone." Lillian grabbed the tea pot and topped off each of their cups. "And I told my son I wouldn't meddle, so I'm only going to say one thing about it. He's a good, strong man. I raised him right and he is not the type to do you wrong. He's loving and kind and has a big heart. So, if you are looking or thinking about looking, you couldn't do any better than my Jake. Now that's all I'm going to say. And don't tell him I mentioned it."

Julia laughed. Listening to Lillian talk up her son was so heartwarming. She knew Jake was a great guy, but she didn't want to move to fast. She needed to take it at her own pace, even if she did get heart palpitations thinking about the kiss they shared.

Her phone vibrated in her pocket and she took it out, thinking maybe Ian needed her. She peered at the screen, but didn't recognize the number. She was about to delete it when she saw the first line.

> *Hey Julia, it's me Jake. Audrey gave me ur number. Just wanted 2 check if u needed help with anything. Just let me know. Also wanted 2 say, just over two weeks!! Text me anytime. Talk 2 u later, pretty lady.*

She couldn't help but smile.

Chapter 7

Julia and Ian were in the car on their way to Luke and Audrey's place for their annual summer bash pool party. Ian had been texting back and forth with different people, finding out who was coming. She could tell his social circle was expanding and it made her happy.

Ian started laughing as he read his latest text. "Oh man, this party is going to be so epic! Apparently, they have a bonfire in the evening and even have fireworks." He started texting again, smiling to himself. Julia was excited for him. The kids he was hanging out with were really good kids. She wasn't delusional to think that they were perfect, but overall they were pretty great.

They pulled onto the street where the Parkers lived and the road was packed. Cars lined both sides and all the activity seemed to be right where they needed to go. Julia had only been by one time to pick up Wyatt, but she hadn't been inside. The exterior of the house was gorgeous. It was a two-story stone home with columns in the front. It was quite large and a little on the intimidating side. But Audrey and Luke were really nice people and so inviting. Julia could see them becoming good friends.

She was glad she accepted the invitation. Audrey had said it would be a great way for her to meet people and make some connections in the community. It felt good to be making changes after such an emotional summer. She felt that within the next couple of months, she and Ian would be settled into their new lives.

She found a place to park and just as they were getting out of the car, Ian gasped. "Oh my God. She's here." Julia watched as Ian's smile spread and even his eyes sparkled.

"Who's here?" she asked. Julia saw Ian glance over at her and she was sure he wasn't going to answer. Just as she was about to pull the handle to get out he said quietly, "Rachel. She was supposed to go away this weekend, but she convinced her parents to let her stay so she could come to the party." Ian was blushing all over.

"Is that a good thing?" Julia was curious about his response to this news.

Ian looked over at her. "Danielle told Wyatt that the reason she changed her plans was because I was coming to the party."

Ah, that explained the blush! Julia smiled at him. "Of course she changed her plans for you. You're hot, especially now with your new haircut."

Ian rolled his eyes at her. "Mom, stop." But she saw him check the mirror on the sun visor to make sure the styling job he had done was still in place. The new cut made him look older, more mature and she felt a little ache in her heart as she realized her little boy was slipping way.

To lighten the mood, she said, "Well come on, stud, let's get in there so you can show off the new lid."

They got all of their stuff out of the back of the truck and were just heading up to the house when Jake appeared in front of them.

"Fancy meeting you two here." His smile was breathtaking. He walked towards them wearing white board shorts and a light blue T-shirt which showed off his well-muscled arms and broad chest. Sweet Jesus, she could get used to that view.

Ian walked up to him, balancing everything in one arm so he could fist bump Jake. "Hey, how's it going?"

"It's going great now that you're here, bud." Jake smiled warmly at her son and a little part of her heart melted. Jake turned to her and took several items out of her arms, which was great as they were already starting to ache.

Julia let out a breath, saying, "Thanks. It was getting kind of heavy."

Jake smiled at her and she could feel the heat in his stare. "I thought I was witnessing a damsel in distress."

She laughed. "Distress seems like a bit of overkill, but I do appreciate it."

Ian had already moved farther down the street and called out, "Come on, Mom!"

Jake looked over his shoulder at him and said, "Why don't you head on in Ian, I can help your mom. Wyatt's out back."

Before Ian could get too far Julia called out, "But take those two bowls and put them in the fridge!"

Ian moved swiftly then yelling back over his shoulder, "Yeah, OK, Mom! See you in there!"

Jake turned back to her and she realized they were the only ones standing out on the street. She looked over just as Jake said, "You need me to take anything else?" His eyes sparkled as he watched her.

She glanced down at the remaining items in her hands and said, "No, I'm balanced now."

She watched as Jake stepped closer and said in a soft voice, "Good, because I wanted a chance to remind you of our agreement and to give you a proper hello." He leaned in and brushed his soft warm lips against hers. She could taste something sugary on his lips and she wanted to lean in deeper for more. She heard a small groan come from him and her insides turned to jelly. Ever so slowly he pulled away and stared into her eyes.

"I think we should be glad we're both holding stuff, because if not, I don't think that kiss would be ending anytime soon." Jake explored her face and his eyes landed back on her lips. Before she realized what she was doing, her tongue ran over her bottom lip and she could taste his sweetness again. Jake grew serious and she could see his eyes dilate watching the movement.

Julia's breathing was uneven as she reflected on the kiss, then she said, "Um...well that was...mmm. Wait, what agreement?"

Jake had a mischievous grin on his face as he said, "The agreement we made stating that I can ask you out in three weeks, which is actually only two weeks now."

With a puzzled look, she said. "That wasn't an agreement. It was just a conversation."

He looked at her, almost as if he was offended. "It most certainly was an agreement. And I've already been scoping out good date sites."

She tilted her head to one side, surprised he had already put so much thought into this. "You have?"

He nodded slowly. "Absolutely."

She grinned at him, wondering what he'd come up with for their date. "So what ideas do you have for this supposed agreed-upon date?"

Jake leaned against a random car along the road and said, "Well since I haven't actually dated in a long time, I was thinking the Ice Cream Hut, but then I remembered the place burned down a while ago. Then I thought maybe the drive-in, which would be my first choice, but might not be appropriate for a first date. I don't want you to think I'm just taking you there so we can make out. I wouldn't want you to think I'm easy, and you might try and take advantage of me."

Julia burst out laughing. "So you think we can't go to the drive in because I'll try and take advantage of you?"

"Well, I'm not sure. Maybe I don't want to give you the wrong impression about me." Jake tried acting innocent.

Julia started walking as she said, "Too late. I think I already have an impression of you, and trust me, the innocent look is not fooling me at all."

Glancing over her shoulder, she watched as he started trailing behind her with a wounded look on his face. "Aww Julia, that hurts my feelings. I guess I'm just going to have to prove you wrong." He lengthened his stride so they were walking side by side again.

Julia glanced over. "You can try, but it's going to take a lot." She winked at him and watched as he almost missed a step.

Just as she was about to walk up the front steps, Jake said, "Hey, wait. Before we go in, all kidding aside, watch out for some of the guys that will, no doubt, be hitting on you."

Julia's eyebrow went up at his statement. "What? No guys are going to hit on me."

Jake's eyes made a slow track up and down her body, making her whole body tingle. "Hell yes, they will. I could hardly keep my eyes off of you the first time we met, so I know they'll hit on you. But just remember if anyone starts bothering you, just look for me and I'll come over."

She looked at him with a jokingly adoring look, batting her eyes for the full effect. "Like my own personal knight in shining armor?"

Jake smirked. "Hey, I like that. Yes, I'm your knight in shining armor."

Before she could say anything further, he was already through the door. She followed and was amazed as she glanced around the inside of the house. It was beautiful inside, all modern furniture and vaulted ceilings. The kitchen was to die for, with its plentiful cupboards and huge island, all in browns, beiges and creams.

There were people everywhere, most of whom she didn't recognize, but they all knew Jake. Julia could tell by a few of the looks she was getting from the women Jake was a hot commodity.

They didn't want her treading on their territory. She wasn't stupid enough to think other women wouldn't be looking, but the way their claws were out she was feeling a bit out of her element. Let's hope she found others who were friendlier.

Platters and bowls of food were everywhere. Jake set her platter down and turned to her before she could process all the activity. He moved in close and whispered, "I'm going to go outside, but remember knight in shining armor, right here." He pointed at his chest, then winked as he walked away.

She smiled at him and then searched for a place on the counter to set down her other platter. Just as she found a spot she heard someone clear their throat behind her. As she glanced over, she could see the two ladies that had been giving her the evil eye as she walked in with Jake. Oh this should be fun, she thought.

The first lady was a tall blonde with legs up to her armpits – she was about as artificial as a mannequin. The enhanced double-E breasts, the Botoxed lips and the smooth face lifted skin were almost laughable in Julia's eyes. The fake-looking woman took a step forward and extended her hand saying, "Hello, I don't believe we've met. My name is Ramona, and you are?"

Julia stared at the extended hand and decided that good impressions go a long way, so she would keep an open mind about these two. "Pleasure to meet you. I'm Julia Witmore." She watched to see if the name triggered any recognition, but the blank stare she received meant these ladies were apparently not fans of her work.

The lady behind Ramona moved forward. She was just about as altered as her friend. The woman had black hair, pin straight and if her face was pulled back any further her eyes would be permanently shut. Her breast size was not quite as dramatic, but by the look of this woman she mustn't eat, like, ever.

Julia glanced at her and since no movement came, she extended her hand to the dark-haired woman. "It's nice to meet you, too. And you are…?"

The dark-haired woman looked at Julia's hand and finally took it, just as Julia was about to pull it away. "My name is Carla. So, how do you know Jake?" Carla's eyes roamed over Julia with a disdainful look and she could feel herself go on the defensive.

So they're just going to start with the claws first and forget about the niceties. Two can play this game. Julia looked at them with the sweetest smile and said, "You know how it is. He fixed my truck and one thing lead to another. I just moved to town and he has been such a gentleman, showing me around and introducing me to his family. The Vincent's are just wonderful people, don't you think? Well, I hope you ladies enjoy the rest of the party. I'm just going to find my friends. See ya'."

Julia bolted out of there like her butt was on fire. If Carla stared at her any longer with that just-bit-into-a-lemon look, she might have said something nasty. Who knew she was going to have to be on alert for just walking in the door with Jake?

She made her way out on to the patio when a feminine voice called out over the noise. "Julia! Over here!"

Focusing in the direction of the voice, she saw Audrey sitting with a large group of women. She recognized a few of them and she felt relief flow through her. Yes, allies! She made her way over and a chair was placed for her and introductions were made. This group of women were nothing like the ones inside and Julia was grateful.

As Julia was taking a seat, Audrey whispered, "I see it didn't take him long to locate you."

"Who?" Julia played innocent, knowing full well what Jake's sister was referring too.

Smiling ear to ear, Audrey said, "Jake. I just happened to be watching out the window a few minutes ago and that was some kiss hello."

Julia could feel the blush from her toes to the top of her head. "Oh, um…yeah."

Jennifer spoke a little louder, as she said, "Look at that girl blush! Must have been some kiss." Julia glanced at her and Jennifer winked.

Worried that everyone would get the wrong impression, she quickly said, "We're just friends."

Audrey laughed. "What? I can honestly say I've never kissed any of my friends like that."

"Unless it's a friend with benefits, that is." Jennifer added, wagging her eyebrows.

The ladies laughed and waited for Julia to answer. "No, definitely no benefits. We don't know each other very well."

Staring at Julia with the smile still plastered on her face Audrey leaned closer and said, "Oh, give it time, sunshine. I think my brother is quite smitten."

Julia smiled at her and laughed. "Did you just say smitten? What is this, the 1800s?"

Audrey shrugged her shoulders. "I'm just saying I think he's interested. Like, really interested."

Julia glanced over to where all the men were standing and sure enough, Jake was watching her. He held up his beer as if to say cheers. She smiled and looked back at the ladies. "Well, the one thing I will say is… he sure does know how to make a girl feel welcome."

The whole table laughed and a drink was placed in Julia's hand. Several of the ladies asked her about her next book and were genuinely kind and interested in what she did. These were the kind of people Julia was hoping to meet. All of them had good careers and children and she felt a connection to them.

Her chair faced out towards the crowd and she could see the pool and the rest of the grounds from there. There was a group of men standing around the barbeque, talking and drinking beer. Most of the kids were in the pool having a blast, including her own son. When he spotted her, he waved and smiled. She returned his wave and watched as he did a cannonball off the diving board. The girls in the pool cheered and Julia knew Ian was trying hard to impress them.

A few of the ladies went into the kitchen to start bring out the food, but they told Julia to just relax. So she spoke with a few of the other ladies at the table while her eyes roamed the crowd. Jake suddenly stepped into her line of vision and she smiled. He mouthed the words, 'You OK?' and she nodded. She was just about to look away when she heard Ian say, "Hey Jake, come on in, the water's great."

Audrey and Jennifer had just returned to their seats as Jake headed to the pool. As if in slow motion, he took his shirt off and tossed it on a nearby chair. Julia's mouth went dry and she couldn't have pealed her eyes away if she had wanted to. She knew he would be well-built under the shirt, but, wow, he was even better than she could have expected. All tanned, rippling abs and wide shoulders that flowed down into a perfect V at his waist. His board shorts rode low and she could see the defined indent of his oblique muscles. He was a fantastic specimen of a man.

"Earth to Julia. See something you like? Ladies, I think the sight of my brother shirtless has rendered her speechless!" Audrey was grinning from ear to ear.

They all laughed and it pulled Julia out of her daze. "What? No, I'm fine. Sorry, what were we talking about?" Her face had grown very warm and she was feeling a full body flush.

Turning to glance at Audrey, she could see they weren't going to let this go. "I hope you know he probably did that on purpose, just for you. He wouldn't have made such a production for anyone else.

There are many ladies here he wouldn't give the time of day to, but he must really like you."

Julia almost choked when Audrey made reference to the 'ladies'. She looked at her and said, "You mean the ladies I met inside when I first arrived – Ramona and Carla?"

Audrey started nodding right away. "Those are the ones. Or, as we secretly like to call them, the Barbie Twins. I'm always surprised Ramona can stay standing up right without falling on her face from the weight of those things. And watch out for Carla, she is one nasty bitch."

Glancing over at a table that was positioned closer to the BBQ, Julia could see the Barbie twins fawning all over the men. She could tell the married men of the group were giving them a wide berth. The others seemed to be enjoying the attention. Well, there was no way in hell she would even step near those women again.

The afternoon flew by fast and Julia was truly enjoying the company. Jake's whole family was here and she had met several people, including Donna Nickerson, the owner of the local bookstore. Once Donna found out who Julia was, she was thrilled. She was a very sweet lady in her mid-forties, with curly brown hair that seemed to have a life of its own, especially with the humidity. She had a funny giggle and Julia enjoyed talking to her about books and the publishing process.

A couple of the ladies decided they wanted to go for a dip in the pool, since most of the kids had gone to play Frisbee. After the heat of the afternoon, Julia thought this was a great idea. She had actually worn her suit under her yellow sundress. As she walked to the edge of the pool she became a bit self-conscious. She knew she had a nice body, but nowhere near super model status. As she quickly looked around, she realized no one was even paying attention to her, so she slipped her sundress over her head to reveal a pretty blue two-piece suit underneath. It fit her perfectly, and helped to enhance the amount of cleavage she had. Just as she headed to the shallow end, her eyes met up with Jake. He was standing over talking to a couple of guys and she could almost feel the heat of his stare on her exposed skin. Her breath hitched and she felt like they were the only two people in the yard. Looking away from him, she shook her head and stepped into the water.

Chapter 8

Shhiiittt, all of his blood just shifted to the lower half of his body. Julia looked incredible and if he didn't turn away soon he was going to totally embarrass himself in front of his two buddies. He took a long pull from his ice-cold beer and hoped a case of brain freeze might help him to forget about the smoking hot body he'd just seen. He stopped drinking, but Julia was still trying to get into the water in that form-fitting bikini. It would be etched forever in his mind. He was just about to look away when she dipped under, then broke the surface. Every fantasy he had ever had paled in comparison to watching Julia in the water, fully wet. As she dipped her head back so her hair would be out of her face, he could clearly see the outline of her hard nipples. Oh God, his knees almost buckled. Luckily his buddies were listening to Luke and weren't watching him.

She was a goddess, all curvy lines and rosy skin. He could stand there leaning against the patio railing and watch her for hours. She slipped back under the water and swam to the other side of the pool, just out of his sight. Jake desperately wanted to take a few steps so he could see her again, but then she swam back. Again, he watched her stand and the water ran in rivulets down her body. What he wouldn't give to use his tongue to follow each and every one of them as they fast tracked into her bikini top, then on to much darker and forbidden places.

"Wow, that's quite the view you've got there, bro." Jake heard his brother's low voice in his ear, but didn't break away from the sight of Julia. It was going to take a lot more than Grant to pull him away from the most gorgeous woman on the planet.

But Grant's next statement had Jake seeing red. "You're not the only one watching her, just so you know. Dylan's been keeping a close eye on her too."

Jake quickly scanned the crowd and for the first time he saw Dylan, who was now making his way over to Julia and the other ladies in the pool. No fucking way was he going to let that asshat anywhere near her! She was way too good for the likes of Dylan 'The Shit Head' Lincoln. He was one of the slimiest guys Jake knew.

Grant was well aware of Jake's hatred for Dylan. The two of them watched as Dylan sat in one of the patio chairs and started to chat Julia up like they were old friends. Grant grunted beside Jake. "What a douche that guy is. Did you hear his daddy just purchased another car dealership in Toledo? It will be just another thing for him to brag about."

Just as Jake started towards the pool, he heard his brother whisper, "Oh, shit, three o'clock, bro."

Before he could even take another step, Carla was right in his face, followed by a cloud of perfume so strong it made his eyes water. Intermingled with that was the strong smell of wine on her breath. He glanced down just in time to see her run her hands over his chest. Revulsion from the touch streaked up his spine. The Barbie Twins, as they were called, had tried and failed on many occasions to get involved with him. But the fake bodies and high-maintenance lifestyle turned him off completely. Jake quickly grabbed both of Carla's wrists and pushed them away from his body.

She peered up at him with overly puffy lips and pouted. "Oh, come on, Jake. You know I don't like to play hard to get, because I know how hard you can get." Carla licked her lips.

Jake glared at her with complete disgust and said low enough so he didn't totally embarrass her, "No, you don't know, as I would never allow you to lay a finger on that part of me. We've been down this road before and it will always end the same way."

He glanced over at Dylan and quickly had an idea form. He watched her rejected expression and said in a much kinder voice, "But you know who would be looking for some attention? Dylan Lincoln. He's right there over at the pool. Why don't you go on over and see if he'll sit with you during the fireworks."

Carla didn't look very pleased, but made her way over to where Dylan sat talking to Julia and a few of the other ladies in the pool. Jake followed behind Carla, making his way over. There was no way in hell Julia was going to be subject to this asshole's cheap moves, and Carla was just the distraction he needed.

Jake watched as Carla swung her hips over to Dylan, practically falling into his lap. Must have been all the wine in her system. Dylan caught her and managed to ease her down on his lap without bodily harm. Well that couldn't have turned out better. He watched as Dylan and Carla had a quick exchange and then she was up and leaving again. Crap! Jake quickly came over and sat on the edge of the pool, dipping his legs in, close enough to Julia so it was obvious he wanted to talk to her.

Dylan cleared his throat and said, "Hey, Jake, um – we were talking here."

Jake turned only slightly, saying, "I'm sorry, I thought you and Carla were having a moment. I wanted to come over and talk to all of these lovely ladies. Hey ladies, how y'all doing this afternoon?" He winked at Julia and watched as she blushed.

"Well, I wasn't having a moment with Carla, so if you don't mind, I was just about to ask Julia out for coffee tomorrow." Dylan was staring daggers at him.

Jake's hands balled into fists and all he wanted to do was punch Dylan right in his surgically altered nose. Turning a little more to face Dylan, he said, "As it so happens, Julia is already booked for coffee tomorrow."

Dylan drew his brows together and said, "Then, the next day."

Looking thoughtful, Jake glanced at Julia, then back at Dylan. "She's booked for the next several months for coffee, tea, dinners, lunches or anything else you wish to share with her."

Dylan smiled, but it didn't reach his eyes. "I'm sure she can fit me in at some point, since I'm such a nice guy."

"Yeah, that might have worked Dylan, if you were a nice guy, but we both know that doesn't apply to you." Jake stared hard at Dylan. The tension between them was so thick you could cut it.

Just as Jake was envisioning grinding Dylan's face into the concrete patio, he heard Julia beside him. "OK well, that's more testosterone than I can take. I think I'm going to get myself a drink. Audrey, let's go whip up another batch of margaritas." Most of the women cheered with the mention of margaritas.

Jake heard Julia splash through the water to the edge of the pool. He pulled his eyes away from Dylan and watched as Julia slowly walked up the pool stairs. Water ran down her legs and all Jake wanted to do was run his hands up and down those thighs and cup her ass in that blue bikini. She headed towards the house and several of the ladies followed, his sister being one of them.

Looking back to Dylan, Jake couldn't help the sneer that appeared on his face. "Man, just leave her alone. Julia's been thorough a lot and she is way too good for the likes of you."

Jake watched as Dylan's eyes followed Julia all the way back to her seat. He wanted to grab the dickhead right by the throat. Dylan slowly pulled his eyes off of her and back to Jake. "Aww, don't be jealous, Jake. You know how much I like to share. I mean we've shared a woman before, why not this one, too?"

His whole body shook with anger. It took every ounce of restraint he had not to jump up and pound Dylan's face into an unrecognizable pulp. Grant and Luke must have sensed the tension or overheard what was said, because before Jake knew it they were both standing in between the two very angry men.

Staring directly at Dylan, Luke said in a stern voice, "Dylan, I think perhaps it's best you leave."

Dylan's head whipped over to look at Luke. "Why do I have to leave? Jake here is the one being the asshole."

Luke shook his head. "No, actually I heard what you said and I think it's you who is being the asshole. My party, my rules – and Jake is family."

Dylan glared back at Jake, who had just stood up from his spot beside the pool. Anger flashed in Dylan's eyes. "This isn't over Jake. This competition has just started, and I never lose."

Jake took a step forward and Grant held him back from going any further. "Go near Julia and I swear Dylan, you'll be sorry. Julia deserves better than a slime ball like you. I believe my brother-in-law asked you to leave."

All the men waited to see how this was going to play out. Dylan backed up a step and headed for the back gate on the other side of the yard. Everyone watched until they saw Dylan exit before both Luke and Grant looked at Jake.

"You OK, man?" Grant was the first to speak. Jake knew what he meant. He wanted to know if the reminder about Francine was bothering him. He also realized Luke must know too.

He looked at both men and said in a low tone. "Yeah, I'm fine. I can't believe he brought that up. I need you guys to promise me you'll let me know if he tries to make a move on her. He's just a player. Julia needs someone better in her life than that ass wipe."

Both Grant and Luke nodded. They were all on the same page. Luke stepped forward and put his hand on Jake's arm. "I haven't mentioned the fact I knew about the Francine thing because, well, it's just shitty, and I figured that you didn't want to talk about it. But I have heard he's been with a lot of married women in this town. Believe me when I say there's a line forming to take that jackass down. I'll make sure to spread the word and have eyes and ears on him."

Jake glanced at Luke and smiled. Luke had been in their lives now for at least thirty years and he felt like just as much of a brother as Grant was. "Thanks LP; I know I can count on the both of you." He took a big breath then continued, "I don't know about you two, but I could definitely use a beer right now."

They all laughed and headed to the cooler to get another beer. Jake lagged behind and looked over to where Julia and the ladies were sitting. She was watching him with a serious look on her face. He knew he was going to have to tell her about why he'd done that, but not right now. He turned away from her, as she seemed to be searching and he was feeling a bit raw. He would tell her later. Now, he needed a beer and a chance to cool down.

Later that evening, the men got the fireworks set up and everyone placed blankets and chairs around the yard to watch the show. One of the guys was a firefighter, so he handled the safety aspects of the evening. Luke was in his element with pyrotechnics. When they were kids, Luke always wanted to light stuff on fire. Jake was always surprised the guy didn't get into more trouble but then again, Jake and Grant were probably the ones who kept him out of trouble with fire, but got him in trouble in other ways.

The show was just about to start when Jake glanced around to see if he could find Julia. As his eyes scanned the crowd, he saw her raise her arm to wave him over. His stomach did a little flip knowing she wanted to see him, even after the caveman move he'd made today.

He weaved through the crowd and saw she had laid out two blankets – her and Hailey on one with a spot for him. On the other one were Dani, Rachel, Wyatt and Ian just laughing and having a good time. Hailey was chatting Julia's ear off about school starting and the new teacher she was going to have. He felt the same strange pull in his heart, seeing Julia being so attentive to his little girl.

Jake took his spot and sat down, making sure to brush his leg against hers. Before he could say anything to her, Ian spoke up. "What can we expect to see in this show, Jake. What kind of fireworks did you guys get?"

Jake smiled at Ian. "I didn't do the actual purchasing; I just chipped in the money. But I did see a couple of Arctic Blasts, an Electric Storm, a Glitter King and some Red Devils. There are other things there, but I didn't look any further after I saw the Red Devils. It should be a great show."

The kids seemed satisfied, and they went back to laughing and talking amongst themselves. He glanced to Julia just in time to see her put a small blanket over Hailey's legs. He leaned forward to stare at his daughter. "You cold, Haileybug?"

Watching as Hailey leaned a little bit closer to Julia she said, "Just a little bit. But Julia has it covered."

Julia leaned towards Jake and whispered, "I think someone is just tired. It's been a busy day." She looked back at Hailey and brushed her hair back from her face in a gesture so sweet Jake was overcome with emotion. Hailey closed her eyes as if soaking up the kindness Julia was giving her. Guilt filled him – the exchange made him feel like maybe he wasn't doing a good job as a father. He tried to be Dani and Hailey's everything, but sometimes it was hard to get things done that had to be done. He did so much for them, but maybe he wasn't doing all that he should.

Julia glanced at him again and said, as if she had been reading his thoughts, "You've done a great job with your girls Jake. They are both kind, caring, loving girls. You should be so proud."

Wow, she had no idea how much he needed to hear that. "Thank you. Ian is a fantastic kid, too. He told me about what happened in Chicago, but I think he was just trying to find his way."

Julia bumped his shoulder and he moved a bit closer to her. He could smell the light floral scent on her skin and slowly he leaned in to her ear and said, "I know you want to ask me questions about what happened today, but let's just enjoy tonight, OK?"

He stayed close so when she turned her face towards him, their lips were only a few inches apart. The lights had been shut off in the house so the backyard was dark and Jake was tempted to move in and kiss her sweet lips. He could feel her breath across his cheek and just as he moved in the first firework went off, scaring them both. Julia laughed first and Jake did, too.

For the next hour they watched the show, keeping their lips to themselves. The fireworks were awesome and the kids were thrilled – well, most were thrilled. Jake glanced over to find Hailey curled up with her head on Julia's lap, sound asleep. The show ended and Jake said to Julia, "You called it. I didn't realize she was so tired."

Julia ran her hand along Hailey's head. "She played hard today. She must have been swimming for four hours. I was tired just watching her."

Jake stood up slowly and came around to Hailey's side. "I'm going to take her upstairs to bed. Audrey and Luke have a room here just for the girls."

Julia nodded her head. "You need any help?" She asked as she stood up, brushing off her pants.

Jake grunted a little. "Actually, yeah. You can help me get her in her PJs. Geez Louise, she is getting too heavy to be carried to bed."

Grabbing the blankets off the ground and placing them over her arm, she laughed. "Come on now, a big strong guy like you? I'm sure she's no problem."

Jake gaped at her. "Well thank you for the compliment, but she has really grown this year, and when she sleeps, she's like dead weight. Let's get her upstairs."

They made their way up through the crowd and into the house. They took the winding staircase to the room Audrey had done up so the girls had somewhere to stay when they slept over. Thank God for his siblings and parents, he never would have made it without them.

The room was done up in purples and greens and had a two twin beds. There was a dresser in the middle and Jake said over his shoulder to Julia, "Hailey's got some pajamas in the second drawer. Can you get one?"

Julia opened the drawer and pulled out a yellow nightgown with little daisies on it. She walked behind Jake while he set Hailey on the edge of the bed to sit her up. Julia came forward and pulled off Hailey's shirt. She had an undershirt on and Julia left that in place as she slipped the nightgown over her head and pulled Hailey's arms through. Then Julia pulled back the covers and Jake scooped Hailey under and tucked her in. She never even woke up.

They smiled at each other, making their way to the door. Jake flicked off the light. Just as Julia was about to walk out, he wrapped his arm around her waist, pulling her back. Sliding the door so it was almost closed while they are still inside the room, he spun her to face him.

"Thank you for helping me with Hailey. I think she likes you." Jake could only see the outline of Julia's face and a slight reflection of light in her eyes.

She ran her hands over his chest and Jake could feel his pulse speed up. "Both your girls are very special Jake. I feel privileged to have been able to get to know them."

A lump formed in Jake's throat. It seemed strange that anyone other than his family would think so highly of his daughters. Julia made him feel like a great dad when she said stuff like that.

"Thank you. I sometimes think I'm scrambling as a parent now that they're getting older. When they were young they made me feel like a superhero, able to scare all the monsters from their rooms and to reach stuff on high shelves without even jumping. Now they look at me sometimes like I have no concept of anything modern and I'm, well, old."

Julia buried her face in his chest and he could feel her quietly laugh. She grinned up at him and said, "When Ian was young I felt like I could conquer anything for him. The fixer of scrapes and booboos with a single kiss. I was a wizard in the kitchen, making the greatest of dinners. I can't forget the fact that my multitasking abilities were second-to-none and he always told me I was the best mom ever. Then, this past summer, I went from the one person left in the world he still had to love, to public enemy number one. I cried so much during that time. I had already lost so much and I felt his friends were trying to steal him away from me. But moving here and meeting you and your family has helped with our relationship. I feel like he's coming back to me. So believe me when I say, thank you for everything you've done."

Jake's hand came up and cupped her cheek. He could see the sheen of unshed tears. Leaning forward he kissed her sweetly. This kiss wasn't about passion or sex, this kiss was just a simple thank you to a wonderful woman who was helping to restore his heart.

Pulling away, he could feel the corners of her mouth curve up. "How about we go and sit at the bonfire for a while before I head home? Not sure if Ian's coming with me tonight or not, but I have stuff to do tomorrow so I need to get some sleep." She was still standing close and her breath gently flowed over his lips as she spoke.

He knew they needed to head downstairs before he took this in a whole different direction. "OK, come on. I bet they have hotdogs for cooking over the fire." He moved her out of the way as he opened the door and they headed downstairs after closing it.

"How can you possibly be hungry? You had three plates at dinner." Julia stared at him with a puzzled look.

Jake laid his hand on his stomach and rubbed it in a circular motion. "I'm not sure. I've always been a big eater. By the way, the pasta salad you brought was amazing. Maybe there is some of it left."

They reached the bottom of the steps and Julia laughed. "Tell you what, I'll go out and find us a place to sit while you rummage around in the fridge."

"Nah, I'm good. I'd rather just spend my time with you." Jake took her hand as they headed towards the back of the house.

Julia looked surprised. "Wow, choosing me over food? I must have made quite the impression."

Bringing her hand up to his lips to kiss, he said, "You have no idea."

Chapter 9

Julia woke in the morning to the sound of rain hitting the window. Well at least yesterday had been a beautiful day for the summer bash. Thinking about the great day they had yesterday brought thoughts of Jake to her mind. The rest of the evening at the bonfire had been really nice – she and Jake had found a perfect spot by the fire and he had been able to pack away three hotdogs. When she was ready to go, he had walked her out to her truck. Ian was slower to follow her out as Rachel was still there. Jake and Julia caught a quick glimpse of Ian giving Rachel a kiss goodbye. Julia felt a slight pain in her heart as she realized her little boy was taking a big step towards manhood. Ian had practically floated to the truck. He got in without even acknowledging either of them. Jake had told her to text when she got home and gave her a quick kiss before she drove away.

Now, it was a rainy Sunday and Julia knew it would be full of editing and proofreading. It was early but she couldn't sleep anymore. She headed for the bathroom, got washed up and brushed her teeth. Putting on her favorite white button-down cotton top and yoga pants, she headed to her office where she had her special coffee maker – there was no way she could even consider editing today without her caffeine fix.

Once her thermal mug was full and she had her comfy slippers on, she was all set to work. Ian would undoubtedly sleep for another few hours so the house would be nice and quiet. Starting her computer and pulling out the notes she'd made she began the arduous process.

Hours, and what seemed like four gallons of coffee later, Julia came out of her writing fog. Glancing over at the clock on the wall, she was shocked to see it was now twelve. She had been at this for five hours! Rubbing the back of her neck, she was just about to get up when she let out a small scream. There, standing in her doorway, was Jake.

He seemed alarmed and said, "I'm so sorry! Ian let me in a few minutes ago and when I came in here you were so focused I almost turned around and left." He stared at her with heat in his eyes and added, "And can I say the sexy librarian look that you're rocking right now has fulfilled every fantasy I've ever had."

Julia laughed as she slipped her glasses off and pulled the pencil out of the bun in her hair. Shaking it out, she heard a groan from Jake. "Wow, you really know how to bring a fantasy to life, Julia."

She stood up and walked towards him. "I'm sure the rest of the ensemble will kill the fantasy. There is nothing sexy about yoga pants and comfy slippers."

"Speak for yourself. Just witnessing the whole 'letting your hair down' thing has my head spinning." Jake grinned at her with laughter in his eyes.

She watched as he just stood, looking at her, and said, "To what do I owe the pleasure of your company today? It's not really a nice day for a country drive."

Jake smiled and shrugged his shoulders. "Audrey had all of your dishes cleaned before I left her house this morning so I told her I would drop them off. Also, I kind of wanted to talk to you about the incident yesterday. I feel I owe you an explanation."

Julia focused on Jake's face and could see sadness in his eyes. "Jake, you don't owe me anything. It's obvious you and Dylan have some history. I just happen to be in the crossfire."

Jake glanced down at the floor. If he wanted to talk she would let him ease into the conversation. To help she said, "Hey, you hungry? Because I'm starved. I was thinking about making a grilled ham and cheese. You want one?"

Jake nodded and looked grateful that he didn't have to explain anything just yet. They went into the kitchen and she started to pull things out of the cupboard and fridge. Jake took a seat at the breakfast bar, watching her as she worked her culinary magic.

She pulled out thick French bread slices, three different types of grated cheese and black forest ham. Setting the pan on the stove, she set to work and within fifteen minutes she had several sandwiches done. She handed Jake a couple and plated two more just as Ian walked into the kitchen. Julia knew he would be down once the smell from the kitchen had wafted up to his room. He took them, kissed her on the cheek saying 'thanks' and 'hello' to Jake, before he disappeared. She put the last one on her plate and sat beside Jake. She had pulled out milk before sitting down and poured each of them a glass.

Looking over at Jake, she watched as he took a huge bite and moaned. Swallowing, he smiled at her and said, "This is the best grilled cheese sandwich I've ever had." He dug in and devoured both sandwiches before Julia had even finished her first half. He downed his milk and looked like he might slip into a dairy-induced coma.

He turned to her as he wiped his mouth on his napkin. "Seriously, I would marry you on your grilled cheese skills alone."

Julia turned pink at the compliment. She finished her sandwich then shifted towards Jake. He was watching her and smiled at her shyly.

Clearing his throat, he finally told Julia about what had happened. "Francine and I had been fighting a lot. She was partying quite a bit and staying out 'till all hours. I was trying to keep the garage from going under and taking care of both kids. She was spending more money than we could spare. I had moved most of our money into new accounts so I could be sure the mortgage on the house and garage would get paid.

"She was home all day with the girls, but one day I came home to find Danielle crying with a huge bump on her head. She said she had fallen off the counter while trying to get something to eat because she was so hungry. I found Hailey in her crib, her diaper packed full.

She had a raging diaper rash all over her bottom and legs. Francine was sound asleep and the smell of pot filled our bedroom. I was furious. I got the girls cleaned up and fed and took them over to my Mom and Dad's place. I came back to find her still asleep. I took every bit of marijuana, liquor, pills, anything else I could find and flushed them all. Then, I woke her up. She tried to tell me she hadn't been sleeping too long. When she realized what time it was, she tried to justify leaving our kids hungry and dirty, saying she was too tired from taking care of them all the time.

"I told her if I ever found her in that state again with our kids in the house she would never see them again. She went into an absolute rage when she found out what I had done with all of her stashes. A week after the incident I came home to find she and Dylan, buck naked, screwing on our kitchen table. They were both stoned out of their minds and they barely acknowledged me until I grabbed Dylan by the hair, pulled him off her and slammed his face into the door frame and I shoved him outside.

"She started yelling at me, saying Dylan was more man then I would ever be. I was frantically looking for the girls when she told me she had dropped the girls off with my mother. It took everything I had not to grab her and toss her out the door with Dylan. She started threating to leave and I told her to go. Just go and take that piece of shit Dylan with her when she left."

Jake took a deep breath before continuing. "I wasn't even upset they were screwing. I knew she had been with other guys and I had been turned off for a long time. We hadn't had sex after she had

Hailey. I was actually relieved it was over. She is the least mothering person I know. If I had known back in high school what I know now, I don't know if I would have married her. The only thing good to ever come out of our relationship were the girls."

He looked at her with sadness in his eyes. "Dylan was one of my best friends before that happened. We had grown up together. I was hurt he would do that to me. He's always been a player, but I never thought he would ever screw around with my wife. We steer clear of each other now. But I went crazy when I saw him talking to you. I couldn't let that jerk try and impress you with all his money and charm. He's a user Julia, and you deserve so much better. I apologize for the way I acted, but given the choice, I'd do it again."

He reached out then and took her hand. Running his thumb over her palm, she felt the heat creep up her arm. She felt bad for the situation he'd been put in and wished she could take away some of the pain in his eyes.

Julia gripped his hand. "As I said, you don't need to apologize to me Jake. I kind of figured it was something like that. Most of the ladies I sat with yesterday told me to stay away from him. Apparently, he has hit on a lot of them and he isn't great at taking no for an answer. I appreciate you looking out for me and I will make sure to give him a wide berth."

She watched as Jake let out the breath he was holding. "That would be a great idea. He tends to use his wealth and power in this town to get what he wants. If he ever starts to pressure you, let me know, and I'll take care of it."

Smiling at him, she said, "To be honest, I've never been impressed by wealth, and I'm not interested in having a sugar daddy by any means. I've done very well with my novels, so I definitely don't need anyone to take care of us. And as for power, I can't be won over by someone who would be willing to manipulate people to get what they want."

Jake continued to rub his thumb over her palm, watching the motion. The silence between them grew, but it wasn't strained or uncomfortable. She wondered where he'd gone in his mind that gave him such a faraway look. Finally, he peered into her eyes and she couldn't read his expression. She was just about to ask when he moved in his chair and kissed her so tenderly it almost took her breath away. His soft, warm lips pressed against hers, not demanding, not pressuring her, just gentle and tender. She reached up and brushed her finger tips along his jaw, feeling his five o'clock shadow. Moving in slightly, she could feel Jake's hand push into her hair and pull her closer, deepening the kiss. It was such a possessive move and for a moment it caught her off guard. Laying her hand on his chest, she could feel his strength and she wasn't sure if she was ready to take it all on.

Pushing back gently, she looked into his eyes and could see heat simmering there – and something more. With his hand still buried in her hair, he held her and let his eyes roam her face. Somehow that was almost more intimate then the kiss, like he was searching for something she wasn't ready to expose yet.

He must have sensed her discomfort, because he slowly let her go and settled back into the chair. She ran her fingers over her lips and watched as his eyes tracked the movement. Before she was able to say anything, he pushed the chair back and said, "I think I'd better go. The girls are at Mom and Dad's and I have some things to get done." Taking her hand he kissed her knuckles. "Thank you very much for the amazing lunch. Don't hesitate to call if you need anything. I will call you about our date soon." Then he was gone.

She sat there so stunned she didn't know what to do with herself. She stared out the window until Ian came in and said, "Hey, where's Jake? Did he leave?"

Julia quickly turned to look at her son and said in an overly bright tone, "Yeah, he had some stuff to get done and needed to pick up the girls."

Ian frowned slightly as he stared at her. "Mom, you feeling all right? You look a little flushed. Are you coming down with something?"

She laughed, as it was always funny when your own words came from your child. "No, baby, I'm fine. I think I'm going to go and do a bit more work. Then how about we go and do something, maybe go to the show or watch Netflix or something?"

He nodded and smiled. "Sounds great. I'll just be playing video games until you're ready."

After cleaning up the mess from lunch and completing another chapter, she and Ian went to the movies and saw the action film that was playing, then they went back to Rosie's Diner for supper. It was a great night and one Julia could get used to.

The whole time they were out, there was no mention of missing Chicago or any of his old friends. And strangely only a few references to Martin. Later that evening as she was lying in bed, she felt guilty about how Martin had been mentioned less and less lately. It made her a bit sad to think they were moving on. But the therapist that she'd seen after Martin's death said this would be a sign of her getting on with life.

Thinking about Jake and the kiss they shared this afternoon made her realize she was moving forward, even if it seemed really scary. Just as she was about to drift off to sleep her phone buzzed. She lifted it up and saw Jake had sent her a text.

I just wanted 2 say good night. I enjoyed our time together this afternoon. U were on my mind. Night, pretty lady.

She smiled to herself and thought about the pain he had shared with her today. He was such a great person and he deserved someone who would value a relationship with him. Was that someone her? She wasn't sure yet, but only time would tell.

I enjoyed our time 2. Goodnight, my knight.

She rolled over and let her mind drift until she was dreaming of moonlit kisses and whispers.

Chapter 10

With the school year upon them and the start of many extracurricular activities for the girls, Jake felt like the next two weeks flew by. He'd been swamped at the garage. Two of his guys had come down with some flu bug, which meant he had to call in his one part-time mechanic, who spent more time talking then he did working.

Jake's lawyer had called to let him know the amendment to Francine's visitation had gone through. Due to the issues he'd brought forward, she was now only able to see the girls during supervised visits once a month. He hadn't heard from her yet, but he knew he would. He'd felt one small flicker of guilt until he remembered she'd left the girls alone at the boyfriend's house. They didn't even know him and Jake was not comfortable with having his girls alone in the house of some strange man.

The one nice thing about the last couple of weeks was Julia. They hadn't really seen each other, but they had texted every day. She said they were busy with the start of school and that she was trying to finalize the new book with her editor. In their most recent text, he mentioned that their date night was coming soon. She said that he had waited long enough and if he still wanted to go out she would be available on Saturday. He had asked her out for Friday, but she was already going to Gilly's Pub that night for ladies night.

He was slightly disappointed, but he understood it was important for Julia to make some friends. He agreed to Saturday night and told her he'd pick her up at her place at six thirty. He was extremely happy about the date and apparently it showed.

On Friday, Dean was finally back to work after being out for five days with the flu. Jake could tell Dean had been watching him throughout the morning when they sat down to have lunch and Dean said, "So, what gives, man? You've been smiling like a fool all morning."

Jake couldn't help the smile that was continually plastered on his face. He hadn't felt this excited in he didn't know how long. "Well, it just so happens that I have a date tomorrow night."

Dean leaned forward in his seat. "A real date? You? Please tell me it's the classy lady that was here a few weeks ago"

He just nodded and Dean smiled at him. "Oh man, she was gorgeous! Her name was Julia, right? Jake, you are one lucky man." Looking at Jake with a mischievous grin, he said, "Maybe you'll finally get some and stop being such a grouch all the time. I don't know how you've gone so long."

Jake frowned at him. "How do you know I haven't been getting any? As far as you know, I could be out with a different woman getting some every night."

Dean scoffed. "I totally call bullshit right now. You're too busy with the girls, work and your re-builds to ever have time for a woman, let alone a new one every night. And you my friend are not that kind of guy. I've known you since freshman year and you've only ever been serious with Francine. You've dated a couple of times sure, but you are the kind of guy who has to get to know someone before you put yourself out there, especially since everything went to shit with your ex. So, don't tell me you have woman every night. But, I hope for your sake Julia is someone who you like enough to get to know."

Jake glanced at the sandwich that he'd picked up at Rosie's Diner. "She is definitely someone I want to get to know. She's funny, smart, kind, not to mention beautiful. I'm going to tell you something, but I will kick the shit out of out of you if you repeat it. It has been a really long time since I've been with someone, and it's not because the invitations haven't been there. But I want something more than just a one night stand. I have the girls to think of and I don't want to be the kind of guy who's with a bunch of different woman all the time. What would I be teaching the girls? That it's OK to sleep around? That it's fine to just shuffle through life never having a committed relationship? No way! They see their mother do that enough. I need to set an example for them."

Running his hand over his face he looked at Dean. "That being said though, I really hope eventually something might happen between us, because damn, I am getting a serious case of blue balls, man." They both laughed and finished up their lunch.

Heading back out to work on a Chevy Impala, Jake focused on the job and finished up quickly. He texted Dani and found out that she was staying overnight at Rachel's house. He sent her a reply telling her to be careful and to let him know if she needed anything. Dani kept stuff at Rachel's house so he doubted she would, but it was important to him that she knew he was there for her.

The end of the day came and Dean said he would lock up once he was finished. He was just about out the door when Dean yelled, "Have fun on your date, Boss!" Jake waved to him and headed out.

He was picking Hailey up from his sister's place. He worked later than school got out, so Dani and Hailey went there after school to wait for him. He honestly didn't know how he ever would have worked things out if it wasn't for his family. Truly, he was blessed to have them in his life.

He pulled into Audrey's just in time to see his sister step outside. She was dressed in her 'girls night out' clothes. She had on a nice skirt and blouse and her high-heeled boots. He hopped out of the truck and whistled. "Wow, pretty fancy for Gilly's, don't you think? If I didn't know how much you love your husband, I might be thinking you were trying to pick up some guy."

She punched him in the arm. "As if! I can barely keep up with his needs. How could I possibly fit in another man?"

He winced, saying, "TMI Audrey. I don't need to know about your husband's needs. If you remember correctly, I punched him out for finding out about his needs when we were in high school."

He had literally punched Luke out when he heard Audrey and he had done the deed. Afterwards, Luke came to him and told him they were in love and wanted to get married. Jake forgave him and they went back to being best buds.

Audrey shook her head at him. "Yes, I remember. You gave him a fat lip and he couldn't kiss me properly for a week! You could be such a hot head sometimes."

Jake laughed. "Well, since I had done it to save your honor you should have been grateful. Instead, you practically beat the crap out of me. I had to lie to Mom and say I got beat up by Ryan Miller so she wouldn't question why we were fighting. So there, I saved your ass then, too. I am truly the best brother ever. Grant knows it; you just need to come around."

Audrey leaned into him and gave him a hug. He pulled her in and hugged her back. She headed to her car saying, "I know you're the best brother ever. I'm going to pick up Julia right now. I heard through the grapevine someone has a date tomorrow." She said the last part in a sing song voice.

He frowned at her. "How did you hear that?"

"Since she didn't want to leave Ian alone, he's staying here tomorrow night. Actually, he's here now – he and Wyatt are going out to the movies and Ian's sleeping over." Just as she was about to get in the car, she said, "Where are you taking her, lover boy?"

Jake rolled his eyes at his sister. "If you must know, I've made reservations at Paradou for dinner. I thought we could take a stroll along the water front to digest, and then Ted's band is playing at The Rapids, so I thought we would go and hear him play. Does this meet your approval?"

She stared at him with questioning eyes. "Did you seriously come up with this plan yourself or did you have help?"

Damn it, why couldn't she just say it sounded good? He huffed out a breath. "Well, nosey pants, the girls chose the restaurant and suggest the walk on the waterfront. But it was my idea to go and see Ted's band."

Audrey nodded, "Just wanted to make sure you were giving credit where credit was due. They told me all this anyway. Have a good night, Little Brother." He watched her pull away. So, his girls had ratted him out! He would have to start making pinky swears mandatory when it came to his dating plans.

Walking into his sister's house, he found everyone hanging out in the kitchen. They all said their hellos and Hailey waved from her seat. Coming up behind her, he bent over and kissed the top of her head. He watched as she flipped through some recipe books. "Whatcha doing, Haileybug?"

She moved her head so she could look up into his face. He couldn't help the surge of love as he stared into eyes that matched his. She was so special.

"Today at school they were talking about having to bring in a recipe that represented our heritage.

I know we're English and so I was looking for recipes for something English."

Luke smiled at her and said, "Oh yeah, like bangers and mash. My grandmothers were the best."

Hailey wrinkled her nose. "What is bangers and mash?"

"Oh, its sausage and mashed potatoes, it's so good." Luke rubbed his stomach at the memory.

Shaking her head she grimaced. "Gross! No, I need something I can take to school. I was hoping to make a dessert or something. Hey, Dad, can you take me out to Grandma's house? I bet she knows a great recipe."

He ran his hand over her head and said, "Sure, baby. Maybe she'll even take pity on us and feed us dinner while we're there."

Ian and Wyatt were snacking on pizza. Ian offered Jake a piece. "No I'm good, Bud, but thanks. Hey, what movie are you guys going to see?"

Wyatt rolled his eyes and said with utter boredom, "I don't know, some chick flick. Rachel and Danielle and some other girls wanted to go and asked us to come." Jake watched as Ian glanced away and smiled.

"Oh, so is this a date night then?" Jake smiled as Ian's eyes went wide.

Wyatt shook his head. "No, we're just hanging out, right, Ian?"

Jake continued to smile as the two boys looked at each other, then back at him. Ian was a really bad liar but that was good – for Julia. Jake stared hard at Ian until he saw the boy's shoulders deflate. "OK, it's kind of a date, for me and Rachel, but we're just hanging with our friends, too. Please don't tell my mom. She'll make a thing out of it and I don't need that."

Without skipping a beat, Hailey jumped in. "Hey Dad, maybe you and Julia could have a double date with Ian and Rachel! That would be fun, right?"

Looking at his little girl, he watched as she beamed her perfect smile. Glancing back at Ian, he waited to see what he thought of Jake dating his mom.

Ian was looking a little uncomfortable as he glanced over at Hailey. "Thanks for the idea Hailey, but I think maybe your dad and my mom would rather spend some time alone, just the two of them. You know, getting to know one another. Besides, I'm not sure I'd want to hang out with them on their date. No offence, Jake, but I wouldn't want to cramp your style." Ian smiled a genuine smile at him and it helped to release some of the tension in his chest.

Jake looked back at Hailey and said, "As nice as that would be, I wouldn't want to cramp Ian's style either. But you won't have to worry about dating for a long time, so don't you worry about it."

She seemed puzzled and said, "How long do I have to wait to date?"

"Until you're twenty five. Is that OK with you?" Jake waited to see if she would freak out. When she seemed to be considering this he laughed.

She nodded and said seriously, "Fine. But, I think you're going to have a hard time convincing Dani that she can't date until she's twenty five. She already likes someone."

Jakes brow creased and he said almost sternly, "Who does she like?"

He watched as both Ian and Wyatt leaned into hear this piece of information. Even Luke seemed interested. Hailey looked at the group of men watching her, hanging on her answer.

"Do you honestly think I'm going to drop that kind of information in this room? She'd kill me! Nice try Dad. Let's go to Grandma's house." Then she got up and went to grab her coat.

Damn, he would have to dig for more information on the ride over to his mother's. He looked at the boys and Luke and said in a whispered tone, "OK, if anyone finds out who she likes we agree to share. Agreed?" He held out his fist and Luke bumped his fist on top of his without a moment's hesitation. Ian and Wyatt looked at each other and shrugged, bumping the top of Jake's fist.

Hailey came around the corner with her coat on. She smiled and said, "Really, Dad? Good grief, she'll never tell anyone, so you're wasting your time."

Well, he would see about that.

∞ ∞ ∞

As Julia walked into Gilly's bar, she could see some of the ladies she'd met at Audrey's party. Jennifer was there along with Carol, Gail and Sue. There were also a couple of ladies she didn't know, but she was excited to meet more new people. They headed to their seats and a waitress came straight over to take their order.

However, before Julia could even get her jacket off she heard her name being called from the bar. Glancing over, she saw Dylan waving to her. Oh great, just what I don't need this evening. She nodded slightly and quickly sat down. All she kept chanting in her head was, please don't come over, please don't come over. But apparently that was not to be, because Dylan appeared by her side.

He looked around the table and said hello to everyone. They answered unenthusiastically, but this didn't seem to deter Dylan. He leaned down close to her ear and said, "Hey, Julia, why don't you leave the hen party and come over so we can get to know one another?" The smell of hard liquor poured off him.

Thankfully, Audrey must have seen the distress on her face because she said, "Hey, Dylan, why don't you head back to the bar? We're here for a girl's night and so that means no dicks allowed. So, off you go. Thanks, bye."

He glared at Audrey and a sneer spread across his face. To Julia he said, "I'll be right at the bar when you change your mind."

As he turned to go, Audrey said, "Yeah, don't hold your breath Dylan. She's not going to change her mind."

Dylan stopped but didn't turn around. Julia could see Audrey's statement bothered him. He then moved on to take his seat back at the bar. Luckily Julia faced way from the bar so she didn't need to see if Dylan was staring at her. Just knowing what she knew about him now made her skin crawl.

As the evening progressed, Julia stopped thinking about Dylan and was having a great time with the ladies. The two new ladies she met, Lynda and Anne, were really nice and fans of her work.

At one point, after a few drinks, Jennifer leaned over and said, "So, tell us Julia, are you looking forward to your date tomorrow night?"

Anne was an adorable lady with a heart-shaped face, and she asked, "Who's the lucky guy?"

Julia was about to say, when Audrey and Jennifer answered at the same time. "Jake."

The rest of the table gasped. Not the response I expected. They were staring at her like she just won the lottery.

Carol was the first to speak. "Let me just say, on behalf of all the women of this town, oh my God, you lucky woman! Jake has been like the elusive prize for many, myself included, but I'm married now. But some are still waiting, sad but true. And you walk into town and – bam! - he asks you out. But, if I'm being honest, and it's not just the margaritas talking, it's no wonder, because you are absolutely gorgeous. I can see why he chose you. You're a really classy lady, too. If I was a guy, I'd totally do you. OK, wait; maybe it is the margaritas talking."

The whole table erupted in laughter, including Julia. When they quieted she leaned forward, in a conspiratorial manor and said, "Thank you for the compliment, Carol. I'm not sure why he asked me out, but he was definitely persistent. I will share one thing with you though... his kisses... they taste like heaven and feel like total sin." She smiled as the ladies started to hoot and whistle. Yes, she was definitely having a blast.

A little while later she needed to go to the ladies room. She excused herself from the table and headed to the back of the bar. She was almost to the hallway leading to the bathrooms when someone grabbed her around the waist and pulled her back. She didn't have to see him to know it was Dylan. He reeked of alcohol and she gagged when he pulled her face around as if to kiss her. Pulling away, she tried to get free, but he held her tight against his chest. His one arm banded tight around her waist while the other groped her in some really inappropriate places. While he roamed her body he slurred into her ear. "Oh yeah, I knew you'd feel amazing. Here lemme get you going, then we can go out the back and I'll make you feel like a million bucks."

She said no several times, but could feel his hand heading south and fear slid down her back. Then she remembered the self-defense course she and Paige took. She slammed her elbow into his solar plexus with as much force as she could manage. Then she smashed her heel down on his instep. He let go and she swung around and punched her other elbow square into his face. He grabbed for his nose as blood squirting between his fingers. Finally, she slammed her knee into his groan so hard she was sure she had broken something. He dropped like a bag of rocks to the floor, holding his face and groin, cursing and swearing. The music stopped just as she yelled out, "I said no, asshole!!"

Everyone turned to stare at her and their eyes tracked to the heap of writhing body at her feet. She could feel herself coming apart, her face heating from embarrassment and the need to flee from what could have happened. She spun around and raced to the restroom. Once there, she locked herself into a stall and cried. Her whole body shook and she couldn't seem to get ahold of herself. She had never felt so violated. Audrey and Jennifer were asking her to open the door, but she couldn't make her muscles move. It was as if she was frozen. She could still feel Dylan's hands on her. There was no way she could go back out there. She couldn't face Dylan again.

Sitting on the toilet seat lid with her knees drawn up to her chest, she thought she heard a male voice whisper as it entered the ladies room. Just as she was starting to panic, the man said, "Hey Julia! Open up sweetheart, it's me – Jake."

Oh God, he was here! She didn't know whether to be relieved or embarrassed. Relief won out as she finally got her body to move off the seat and slide the lock open. Jake gently opened the door and let himself inside locking it again.

Staring up into his worried eyes, she fell apart again. He tentatively wrapped his arms around her, asking her the whole time if it was all right to do so. She nodded as tears streamed down her face and suddenly he was holding her to his chest, telling her everything was going to be OK. He told her Dylan had been dragged outside by the bouncers and the police had been called. Jake told her if she wished to press charges there were people who were willing to come forward as witnesses.

All she wanted to do in that moment was disappear. Julia didn't want to see anyone else, she just wanted Jake to keep holding her, to forget about this whole mess. He eventually pulled away, brushing her hair away from her face. She must look like hell – her face felt swollen and blotchy. He didn't even flinch as he peered into her eyes and said, "How about I take you home, OK? I think I've seen enough of the ladies room to last me a lifetime."

Julia couldn't help but laugh. He was the sweetest man. Jake wiped her remaining tears and kissed her on the forehead. He opened the stall door and they left the restroom. The first thing she noticed was that everyone was back to doing their own thing and they weren't looking at her at all. Some glanced her way, but they just let her walk to her table with Jake's arm wrapped protectively around her.

Audrey was the first one out of her seat as they approached and she pulled her in for hug. "I am so sorry Julia. We didn't see what was happening until we heard your voice. I can't believe he'd do that! Jake's going to take you home. I'll come and see you tomorrow. You go and get some rest."

Jake picked up her purse and jacket as they headed for the door. The ladies waved goodbye and she smiled sadly as they exited the bar. He had her in the truck headed home within a few minutes.

Focusing out the front window she couldn't seem to wrap her head around what had happened. She hoped Jake didn't think she had encouraged Dylan. It would break her heart if Jake thought she was that kind of person.

As the yellow lines slipped by along the center of the road, she said, "I wish I understood why he did it. I didn't encourage him at all – I barely spoke to him. I didn't want him to touch me, but I couldn't get away. He just kept talking and touching me. All I wanted to do was get away from him. It all happened so fast." Quietly, she said, "I'm sorry to have ruined your night, Jake."

The next thing she heard was gravel under the tires as they pulled off to the side of the road. Jake had his seat belt off within seconds as he jumped out of the truck, slamming the door. The next thing she saw were the headlights illuminating him as he yelled into the night and slammed his fist onto the hood of his truck. She watched as he picked up a stick and beat the ground with it a few times. Whipping it into the darkness once he was through, Jake stood still with his hands gripping his hair.

His shoulders slumped and he looked defeated. All Julia could think of in that moment was that it was her fault. Her heart broke and she couldn't stay away from him a moment longer. Opening the truck door she slipped down onto the gravel. She walked around to the front of the truck, and now she was highlighted by the beams. Stepping up behind him she wrapped her arms around his waist, pressing her face into his back. Slowly, he turned around and held her. She heard him take a deep breath and whisper in her ear, "You have nothing to be sorry about, Julia. I'm sorry I lost it. I don't do well with feeling helpless. I know it's irrational to feel bad that I wasn't there, but it doesn't seem to matter in my mind. I just hate the thought of Dylan being anywhere near you."

She breathed in deep and the wonderful scent of his aftershave and maleness soothed her. He felt so strong as she soaked up the feeling of comfort just having him near. "If it makes you feel better, I kneed him so hard in the groin that I don't think he's ever going to be able to procreate, like, ever." She felt his laugh before she heard it. It was good to feel the tension leave his body.

They got back into the truck and drove the rest of the way to Julia's house in silence. Pulling up to her house, Jake was out of the truck before she could even undo her seatbelt. As they approached the front door, hands linked, Julia said, "Thank you for the ride home, Jake. I really appreciate it. I'll let you get back to the girls now."

"What are you talking about? I'm not leaving. I'm staying with you tonight." He was serious. She wasn't sure how she felt about that. He held out his other hand and she realized he wanted her keys.

She glanced at his hand and said, with more calm then she felt, "It's OK Jake, you don't need to stay. I'll be f-fine." Crap, she would have sounded way more certain if she hadn't stuttered at the end.

His eyebrow went up and she knew he wasn't going to be leaving anytime soon. Reluctantly, she handed over her keys, watching as he unlocked her door and ushered her inside. He closed and locked the door behind them as she pushed her code into the alarm system she had installed. When she turned towards him he was watching her. All she wanted to do was have a shower and crawl into bed.

He must have understood because he walked over to her and said, "Why don't you go and get ready for bed? I'm just going to make a phone call to Mom."

She nodded and went upstairs to her room. Heading into her bathroom she quickly stripped out of her clothes and stepped into the hot shower. It felt good to have the water pelt her skin with the steaming spray. It was as if it was washing away the feel of Dylan's hands. She felt immensely better when she got out. Toweling off her body and putting on her loose-fitting pajamas, she brushed out her hair. She stepped into her bedroom to find Jake standing in the doorway. He had his arms crossed over his chest, leaning on the door frame as his eyes tracked her every move. He didn't approach, just stood there and waited for her.

He finally spoke, with a gentle, almost whispered voice, "I'm just going to sleep on the couch. I don't want to give you the wrong impression. I can be a gentleman, unlike others in this town."

Julia remained standing beside her bed and she wasn't sure what possessed her when she heard herself say, "Don't go. Can you just stay here for a little while? On top of the covers, of course. You can be a gentleman on top of the covers."

Jake let a slow smile cross his face and nodded. Making his way over to the bed he waited until she was under the covers then shut off the lights. As he lay beside her on the bed, she realized it had been a long time since she'd felt the bed dip beside her with the weight of a man. He lay close, but didn't touch her. She snuggled further into the covers and then she heard Jake say, "Go to sleep, Julia. I'm not going anywhere."

He moved just a little closer to her and she could feel his breath on the back of her neck. It was comforting to know he was there.

Eventually, she relaxed and her eyes grew heavy. She listened to Jake's breathing and realized he was close to sleep. She eased closer to him and could feel his body heat though the blankets. It felt so warm and safe that she quickly drifted off to sleep.

Chapter 11

Anthony waited impatiently for Gino to pick up the phone. Chewing on his fingernails seemed to be his favorite pastime nowadays. Suddenly, the line connected and he heard Gino's garbled voice. "Hello?" There was a series of coughs and hacks. Sounded like Gino was under the weather, which means he probably hadn't been out finding information.

"Hey, G, just checking in. Sounds like you got a bad cold."

More coughing and hacking, then a weak voice said, "Hey, Anthony. Yeah, stupid cold has been hanging on for over a week."

Glad that there were miles separating him for the guys germs, he said, "I won't keep you long, but wanted to let you know my lawyer was able to get me out early. I get released on October first. I need you to keep looking into the situation so I can get it handled when I get out."

Gino was wheezing into the phone as he spoke, "That's great news! I have all my contacts working on the situation. I even have someone searching school records, so hopefully that will help." Coughing ensued and Anthony didn't want to listen to that for much longer.

"OK Gino, you go and get better. If it's not better soon call Guido and have his mom whip up one of her old country cures." He had that once and if you could get past the smell and the taste, it would heal what ailed you.

Gino recovered from his hacking and said, "Talk to you soon."

Anthony made his way back to his cell and started thinking about all the things he needed to do when he got out. Julia and Ian were high on the list, but the work of a mobster trying to rise to the top was never done. He needed to keep his ears to the ground if he wanted to be boss come April.

The sound of birds chirping woke Jake and he snuggled further into the pillow. As he become more aware of his surroundings he realized that something was different. A floral, fruity scent hit his nose and he felt the urge to bury his face in it. But why would that smell be in his room? Reaching out his arm he tried to scoop the comforter to his chest when he realized there was a body under it.

That's when it all came flooding back. He was in Julia's bed, well, on top of the covers, but still closer to a woman then he'd been in years. Pulling her back against him, he buried his face in her hair and took a deep breath. Mmm, she smelled amazing, like flowers, peaches and berries. She felt so soft and warm under his hand. Unfortunately, the more he thought about the way she smelled and the way she felt, his body started to respond. After everything that had happened to her last night this was the last thing he wanted to show her.

Leaning back just a bit to keep his morning wood from stabbing her in the backside, he was conscious of the way she was leaning back towards him. She began to roll and soon she was facing him, with the covers pushed down around her waist. He glanced down her body and he could see that her pajamas had shifted and a very beautiful, dark rose colored nipple was now exposed for his viewing pleasure. Oh, God! He could feel himself lengthen, and try as he might, no amount of thinking about baseball, his Aunt Doris's hairy legs or math problems was going to fix his situation. He really was trying to be a gentleman here.

Just as he considered leaving so he wouldn't be tempted, Julia shoved the covers to the bottom of the bed, and slung her leg over top of both of his. Now not only did he have to deal with an exposed nipple, but due to the lack of covers he could see she had on tiny, pink panties which left her whole thigh on display. He struggled with himself, all he wanted to do was run his hand along all the exposed skin and see if it was as soft as it looked. If he was a true gentleman, he would push her back and cover her up. But she felt so good pressed against him that he couldn't bring himself to do it. Gently, he put his arm around her, careful not to touch any skin and pulled her closer. Her face was now pressed against his chest and if he was honest, it felt incredible.

As he lay still he could feel her slowly waking. The little twitches and movements, the stretching of muscles, then the realization that she was pressed up to his hard chest. Jake knew when she was fully awake because her whole body froze. He was tempted to unwrap his arm from her, but he decided to have a little fun with the situation.

"I'd have to say Julia, this is the best morning I've had in a long time." Pulling her just a little firmer into his chest, he waited to see if she would freak out and pull away.

But Julia didn't do anything of the sort. In fact, she just seemed to cuddle in more. It took some will power not to pull her closer.

Clearing her throat, she kept her face away from his. "Morning. Sorry, I can be a bit of a cuddlier when I sleep. I thought since we weren't under the covers together it might not be an issue, but I guess I was wrong."

Since she hadn't moved away, he let his hand rub her back and take in the warmth of her body. She seemed to like that, she almost purred under his touch and that did nothing to help his current morning situation. Julia leaned into him, so he just kept rubbing her back, up and down, going a little lower each time, until he hit bare skin and the top of her underwear. He waited to see if she would pull away, but no, she just kept leaning into him. So he did a few more strokes and went a little further down, so his hand brushed over her bottom. Oh, it felt good, all that soft cotton over her tight ass. Oh God, he was in gentleman's hell. If this kept up he was going to embarrass himself big time.

Then the unthinkable happened. Pulling herself against him, there was no way she was going to miss how aroused he was. He heard her breath catch and his hand stopped moving. She held still for what seemed like forever and he was sure she was going to bolt.

He made ready to let her go, when cautiously, she leaned in and ran her lips along his collar bone and eased her pelvis against him in the sweetest kind of torture known to man.

He knew he should stop, but he felt his hand move lower and pull her tighter against him. As the two of them moaned, their lips met and it was like a detonation. He flipped onto his back and pulled her fully on top of him. His tongue swept into the hot recesses of her mouth and she sucked on it gently. Slipping his hand into the front of her night gown, he cupped her full breast in his palm. She gasped and pushed her breast further into his hand. Everything about her felt so amazing, so much skin, so little clothes and all he could think was, I want more.

Her hands slid down his chest, while her hips did a slow and painfully sweet grind against his erection. It was so good and the sexy sounds she made had him almost going out of his mind. Just as her fingers drifted along the waistband of his jeans he seemed to come to his senses. It took all he had to grab her hands and stop her progress. "Julia, we need to stop."

Slowly, she looked up and his heart hitched. Was that rejection he saw there? Did she honestly think he didn't want her, because the proof was more than prevalent in his pants. But she looked dejected and he had to make this right.

Running his hand along her cheek he stared deep in her eyes. "Julia, I'm not stopping this because I don't want you, because baby, I definitely want you. I could quite possibly pass out from all my blood being redirected south. But, after last night, I don't want you to think I'm taking advantage of you. You've got to know I wouldn't do anything to hurt you, I think, in this moment, we need to pull back a little. Trust me, if this had taken place at any other time, I don't know if I would be saying this. Because damn, I really want to, more than you can possibly know."

He lifted her off of his very hard, burgeoning cock and placed her beside him at a safe distance. She still hadn't said a word and he was starting to worry. He hoped she understood and he hadn't just screwed up the best thing to happen to him in a long time.

Looking at him, a slow, seductive smile spread across her face. If he hadn't just told her they should wait, he would have pulled her back on top of him and had his dirty way with her. She was breathtaking when she stared at him that way.

"You're right, I'm sorry. I shouldn't have made you uncomfortable. It's been a long time since I had someone in such an intimate situation, I guess I got carried away. I would say I'm sorry, but I think we both know it's been coming. If I'm being honest, I want it to happen again soon." She leaned in and kissed him softly. Then, she was up and heading to the bathroom, her hips swinging back and forth as she walked away.

Leaning forward so that he fell face first onto the mattress, Jake groaned in agony realizing he had been the first to pull away and now he was stuck with the most painful of all hard-ons with no way to relieve it. Cold shower time, and that's the best it was going to get for now.

Chapter 12

Once they had both cleaned up they had some breakfast. Jake left to pick up Hailey at his parent's place. He told Julia he would be back to pick her up tonight for their date.

As she sat at her desk working on the final edits to her book, she couldn't help but think about what had happened that morning. She wasn't sure what had come over her. Waking up in Jake's arms had felt so good. It had been so long since she'd been held. When he rubbed her back, each stroke had felt amazing, making her want to stretch like a cat with pleasure. Even as he went lower and she'd felt his hand on her bottom, all she had wanted was more. When she'd leaned closer and brushed against the bulge in his pants, that was all it took to push her into letting her desires get the best of her. She could tell how well-endowed he was and she was looking forward to their next encounter. Hopefully neither of them pulled back when it happened.

As the morning progressed, Julia got a quick text from Ian to say he wouldn't be home until a little later to pick up some more clothes. The last few weeks had gone by quickly and she felt like she'd hardly spent any time with him. He was so busy with school, swim tryouts and his friends she secretly wished they could go back to the last part of the summer when she had him all to herself. But that's what happened when kids got older – they moved on to the next phase. She knew someday he would move away, but in the meantime she just wanted to have some of his time.

Ian ran in the door mid-afternoon and gathered all he needed to take back to Wyatt's place. Walking quickly back to the front door, he stopped just long enough to kiss Julia on the cheek and say 'Love you'. She had gotten a text from Audrey saying the boys had plans tonight. In reality, it was just a bunch of their friends going over to have a video game playoff. She watched as Luke waved to her from the truck as he backed out to the road. Julia was alone again, but glancing at the time she realized she'd better start getting ready.

She jumped in the shower, making sure she spent some time primping, shaving and lady-scaping. Dressing in a black wraparound knee length skirt and a tight-fitting red blouse that showed off her curves, she felt pretty good. Sitting down at her makeup table, she added the finishing touches. She decided to wear her hair up, with tendrils down around her face to give it a soft look. Julia had never been one to use much makeup, but tonight she accented her eyes with shadow and painted her lips with a nice shade of red. Pulling on her low heels, she felt a strange pull in her stomach – she was starting to get nervous. Even though they had spent some time together – intimately today – she was still anxious about the date. He hadn't let her know anything about it, except to say it would be safe to wear a skirt, but to wear comfortable shoes.

She was just heading down to get her purse when the doorbell rang. Smoothing her clothes and fussing with her hair one final time, she took a deep breath and opened the door.

As it swung open her sights landed on a beautiful bouquet of flowers. It was a kaleidoscope of colors, all bright and vibrant. They were so pretty and she felt her heart give a tug. It had been many years since she had gotten flowers. Martin was never one buy them for her, so mostly she'd received them from others for special occasions.

In behind the lovely bouquet was Jake, looking drop-dead gorgeous. He was dressed in black pants and a black button-down shirt which showed off his muscular build and wide shoulders. He was clean shaven and his hair was neat. He looked good enough to eat! Smiling at her, his eyes scanned her from head to toe. He seemed to take in every detail and left her feeling a little exposed.

Staring into her eyes, he said, "If you tell me you'd like to just stay in tonight, I would be totally on board with that."

Julia laughed and told him to come in. She took the flowers and lifted them up to breath in their sweet scent. "Jake, these are so lovely! Thank you! Let me just go and put them in water and then we can head out."

Jake followed behind her as she made her way into the kitchen. She quickly located a vase and filled it with water. Arranging the bouquet in the vase, she set it in the middle of the island.

Julia was just turning around to thank Jake again, when he appeared right in front of her. The hunger was unmistakable as he whispered, "Let's just get this first one out of the way."

With that, his lips were on hers. She was swept up in the heat of his arms and the tenderness of his kiss. He tasted like mint and with each swirl of his tongue, she felt almost drugged. She didn't want this to end. His hard chest pressed against her and she could feel her nipples respond to the contact. He slowly pulled away and she heard a slight whimper come from her lips. Jake smiled and said, "Don't worry, there will be more, but right now we'd better get going or we won't be leaving this house at all." She only nodded, not trusting herself to speak as she knew her voice would betray how much that kiss had affected her.

The drive to the restaurant was about twenty minutes and the evening was cool but beautiful. They chatted about the kids and the fact that Danielle was also trying out for the swim team. Julia hopped she made it so she'd have someone to sit with in the crowd for swim meets.

They pulled into a quaint little building on the edge of the river. The sign read, Paradou Restaurant, and it had a wide veranda and double doors, with autumn wreaths on both. As they entered, they were met by a woman who made it obvious she liked what she saw where Jake was concerned.

Jake was oblivious to the woman and kept his focus on Julia the whole time. They were taken to their table in front of a large picture window that had a beautiful view of the water. He helped her into her seat as the hostess glanced continually at his butt. Wow, rude much? thought Julia. Once the lady had handed them their menus and reluctantly left, they reviewed the selections.

This seemed like an upscale place, minus the ogling hostess. The waiter arrived and introduced himself as Peter. He looked pretty young, but his manners were impeccable. He took their order and then came back to pour them each a glass of wine.

As they stared out over the water, the sun made the waves sparkle like diamonds. Jake leaned towards her and took her hand. He had been watching her the whole time and it felt as if he had something he needed to talk about. She took a sip of her wine and Jake smiled. "I thought after dinner we could go to the boardwalk. That OK with you?"

Julia nodded. "Oh, I'd like that. We've driven by a few times, but never stopped."

"I love this time of year. It's not too hot, but still nice enough to walk with a sweater." Jake picked up his wine glass and took a sip. Nodding his approval he asked, "Hey, I wanted to ask you if you finished your edits yet. You mentioned you hoped to have them done."

Julia told him she'd finished and would be sending it off in the morning. They talked about the progress Jake and the guys had made on the Firebird – he had run into a few issues, but nothing that caused too much delay. She liked listening to him talk about spending time with his dad and brother. They all got along so well and it was nice to see. When he spoke about the work they had done she could tell how much Jake loved working on cars. He was living his passion and not everyone got that opportunity.

Their dinners arrived. Julia had ordered the seafood linguine and Jake ordered the Porterhouse steak and baked potato. She smiled to herself at the very classically male meal in front of him. They started in and she could see him eyeing up her plate.

"Did you want a bite?" she asked as she speared one of the shrimp and spun a few strands of pasta onto the fork. Holding it up, she watched as his eyes tracked the fork as she brought it to his lips. He licked his bottom lip before opening his mouth and something about the gesture was very sexy. Wrapping his lips around the food on her fork, he took the bite and chewed, enjoying the flavor. Just watching him made her hungry, for something other than food.

She went back to her meal and when she glanced up, Jake had cut her off a dainty piece of steak and held if out to her. The steak looked really good, so she leaned in and slowly took the bite into her mouth. Pulling it off the fork slowly, she closed her eyes and moaned a little as the steak melted in her mouth. Opening her eyes, she glanced at Jake and the heat and need were plain to see on his face. He quickly cut her another piece and pushed the fork to her lips again. Smiling, she opened her mouth and took the offering. This time she moaned and licked her lips from the taste. She was sure Jake's eyes dilated and he looked ready to leap over the table.

They each went back to their own meals and once their plates were mostly empty, Peter came back to see if they would like any dessert. Jake leaned towards her and said, "I hear the mousse is fantastic."

It didn't disappoint. The raspberry was so good it was like a flavor riot in her mouth. Jake leaned over with a spoonful of chocolate for her and it was amazing too. After dessert they chatted over their tea and coffee. She was having a wonderful time. The meal, the sunset and especially the company made for an amazing dinner. Eventually, they decided to get the check so they could walk off the copious calories they had consumed. Peter came with the bill and cleared the teacups. Jake opened the bill folio and frowned. Julia was suddenly worried that maybe the dinner had been too expensive. Not knowing what Jake's financial situation was, she didn't want to embarrass him and ask if they should split the check. That would probably offend him. He pulled out his wallet and pulled out a gold credit card, so she figured he was fine, but what caused the frown? She glanced over and could see a hand written note on the back of the check.

Leaning over she could see Veronica, the hostess, had written her number on it, with a note that said, 'call me'. Peter came back and she quickly flipped the check over and waited for Jake to pay. Just as they were leaving the table, Julia grabbed it and slipped it in her pocket. She knew it was petty, but geez, couldn't this girl see they were on a date? As they walked up to the front, Veronica was at her station and she only had eyes for Jake. He, however, didn't give her the time of day.

Julia stopped and handed her the check with the number on it. "You can take this back, as he won't be needing it. Just be glad I don't report this to your boss. Very tacky move. Men like him don't resort to trashy; only classy will do." Julia spun on her heels and followed Jake out the door.

He looked at her as they made their way to his truck. Before opening her door, he said, "You feel better now?"

Watching his face she smiled. "If the tables were turned and some guy tried to give me his number while we were on a date, wouldn't you do the same? I let her off easy."

He moved in to pin her against the side of the truck. Whispering in her ear, he said, "Baby, if some guy had done that, he wouldn't be standing after I got through with him." His tongue came out and ran along the lobe of her ear, which sent all kinds of tingles straight down to her toes.

Jake stepped back and opened her door. She took a deep breath to steady herself then got in. This man was going to drive her crazy. Julia watched as he made his way around to the driver side. He had a great strut, like a man confident in his skin. The whole package was amazing and she felt even more drawn to him. Not just for the way he looked, but for everything about him.

They drove to the boardwalk and the sun had almost set, so Jake grabbed a sweater out of the back seat, and as they headed away from the truck he slipped it over her shoulders. Since they had left the restaurant the evening had cooled further and the breeze coming off the water would have chilled her skin. They stepped on the boardwalk and he grabbed her hand, lacing their fingers together. It felt so natural and sweet and she felt her heart melt.

The whole boardwalk was lit by old fashioned lampposts and it gave it a quaint, old town feel. They strolled along and Jake pointed out different things to her. He told her about the bridge she could see just down the way and how it had been dragged down river once during the spring thaw, and he pointed out an old boarded-up building that used to be an arcade back in the day.

Further down he showed her a spot where he and Luke had almost driven his dad's old El Camino into the river. They had managed to get it out and weren't planning on telling anyone, but by the time they got home someone had called his dad and ratted them out. The incident had earned him and Luke three weeks' worth of hard labor. Jake said his dad hadn't given them chores because of what they had done, but because they'd tried to lie about it.

Reaching a spot where the trees shadowed the boardwalk, they were suddenly secluded from sight. Jake decided to take full advantage of this fact. He walked her slowly backwards until she was pressed against a maple tree. With a mischievous look, he lowered his head and took her mouth in a slow, sensual kiss. She wrapped her arms around him, letting her hands explore his back, taking in the hard muscles and contours. He cupped her face in his hands as his pelvis pressed firmly against her. Moving his lips slowly, he kissed along her jaw and down the side of her neck. His kisses felt amazing and every moment they spent in the secluded spot made her not want to leave.

His breathing was heavy as he whispered, "God, you taste so good. If we don't leave now I think I might start acting on some of my really dirty thoughts. And even though I know all of the officers in this town, I don't think I'd be able to talk myself out of a public indecency charge."

Julia laughed and was glad she could take a breath. Her thoughts had been headed in the same direction as his, and this was definitely not the place for this to happen.

They both took a moment to gain their composure, then walked back to the truck. Just as they got there, Jake said, "Actually, my buddy Ted and his band are playing at The Rapids tonight. I thought maybe we could stop in and have a drink. They're actually really good. Do you want to go?"

Sliding her arms around his waist, she asked, "Is there dancing?"

"You bet, pretty lady. But if it's OK with you, I'd like to be the only name on your dance card." He stared deep into her eyes and she could see the heat lingering there.

She leaned up on her toes and gave him a slow, sweet kiss. "Trust me, I tossed my card. I'm all yours."

They walked the short distance to the bar. The Rapids looked like it was the place to be in town on a Saturday night. It was busy, and the sound of music poured out the doors as people came and went.

Once they were inside she could see it was a fairly big place, with lots a seating and a big stage over on the right side. As they made their way over to the front of the stage, she saw Jake wave to some guy where the band was setting up. A DJ was set in the corner and was providing music until the band was ready to start their set.

As soon as the guy spotted Jake, a huge smile spread across his face. As his eyes shifted to her they widened. He was tall, with dark hair and very dark eyes. Leaning over, he said something to his bandmates and headed in their direction. He weaved through a few tables and as he reached Jake he wrapped him in a big manly hug. Jake was smiling and Julia could tell they were really good friends.

Jake was the first to speak. "Hey, Ted! How you been? I heard you and Connie got back together, congrats, man."

Ted nodded. "Yeah, I'm glad we were able to work it out. Those six months were the longest of my life." Then he turned towards her and said to Jake, "Well don't keep me in suspense, Jake. Is this the beautiful Julia I've been hearing about all around town?"

Jake faced her. "Yes, this is Julia. Julia, this is Ted Delanie. We grew up together. And those guys over there are members of his band, Wicked Gear."

Before she could respond, Ted reached over and took her hand, then proceeded to kiss her knuckles. It was such an old-fashioned gesture she couldn't help the giggle that escaped her.

"It is a pleasure to meet you Julia. I've actually heard a lot about you. I was out at the shop today with Al. I can say he definitely didn't lie, you are gorgeous. Jake, please tell me you aren't planning on letting her slip away."

Jake had this look on his face like he was silently telling Ted to shut up. She thought it was kind of fun to watch him squirm a bit. Ted was still holding onto her hand and Jake gently reached over and pulled her hand into his. Ted glanced at their joined hands and said, "I always knew you were a smart man. Well, smart, and somewhat jealous. Anyway, come on over, I've got a table saved for you, one of the perks of having a brother who owns the bar. Best seats in the house."

They took their seats and a waitress came over and took their drink order. She seemed very nice and not overly interested in Jake, which made Julia happy. As they chatted about the bar, Jake mentioned that Terry, Ted's brother and the owner of the bar, were the same age as Grant and they had all hung around. He also gave Julia the low down on Ted and Connie.

Connie was a great lady and she had put up with a lot of shit from Ted over the years. She caught him kissing some girl one night after they played at a bar the next town over and she kicked him out. They have two kids and Ted was devastated. He had gotten pretty drunk that night after their set and he'd barely remembered kissing the girl. He had been sleeping in his brother's basement for six months until she finally agreed to give him another chance. He had been treating her like gold since then and she deserved it.

The band was warming up and the place filled up fast. It seemed like Wicked Gear had quite the following. Jake told her they played a lot of classic rock and Julia was excited to hear it. Once they were ready, they started off with Highway to Hell and every song they played was better than the last.

At one point Ted said he was going to slow things down for the new couples in the room and his eyes fell on her and Jake. The band started playing the Foreigner song Waiting for a Girl Like You. They made their way to the dance floor. She wrapped her arms around his neck and he took her waist. Moving to the rhythm they slowly danced to the music. They didn't speak at all, just swayed and enjoyed the feeling of their arms around each other. She ran her fingers through his hair along his collar and he wrapped his arms further around her, bringing her close. He leaned in and said in a husky voice, "You keep playing with my hair like that and I'm going to embarrass myself."

She stopped what she was doing and laughed at his worried face. She didn't want to say it, but she could actually feel his erection pressing low on her stomach. He didn't pull away, but she made sure not to rub against him again. Just as the song finished she heard Jake say under his breath, "Oh, shit."

He took her hand and quickly led them back to their table. Another slow song came on, but it seemed like the last thing he wanted to do was dance. She glanced around to see what might have set him off, but she couldn't see anyone. That was until she spotted a small woman making a beeline for their table. Something in the back of Julia's mind told her this was the person who had just changed Jake's demeanor.

She had long, dirty blond hair and blue eyes. As Julia glanced down, she saw the skin-tight jeans and pink T-shirt which was about two sizes too small. She had ample cleavage, which was clearly on display in the tight shirt. She would have been really pretty, except for the sour look on her face and the excessive use of makeup.

Julia watched as the woman walked up and stood right in front of Jake. His eyes slowly glanced over at her and before she could even say a word, he said, "Francine, this is not the time or place to discuss anything, so if that's why you're here, don't bother."

So this was Francine. She could see it now - around the cheekbones and chin she could see Dani and Hailey, but that's where the similarities ended. Francine stood with her hands on her hips, glaring down her nose at Jake. Julia disliked her instantly for the action. After all this woman had done to him, she had the nerve to look at him that way. Suddenly, Francine turned to her and sneered. Looking her over she said in a high pitched, whiny voice, "So, who's the skank?"

Before Julia had even registered what she'd said, Jake was out of his seat. He towered over his ex and a look of absolute hatred filled his eyes. Through clenched teeth, he said, "Don't you ever speak to her that way! Not Ever. Do you hear me? If you have an issue with me, that's fine. We can discuss it at an appropriate time. But do not ever talk to her like that again. You don't know her and you don't know anything about her. If you're here to stir up shit, just walk away."

Julia watched in silence as Francine seemed to be weighing her options. Jake continued to glare at her and Francine realized he was serious. She took a step back as she glanced over at Julia, her eyes truly assessing her for the first time. Just as Francine was about to walk away, a guy stumbled over to her and wrapped his arms around her waist. The guy, or should she say, kid, couldn't have been more than twenty-two years old. He seemed like a bit of a loser, with his hair all slicked back and a baseball hat on backwards. He focused on Francine then followed her stare to Jake's face. The kid pulled back, looking uncomfortable and was visibly quite drunk. He leaned into Francine, and, in a slurred tough guy voice, said, "Is this guy bothering you?"

Jake glared at the young guy. "More like she is bothering me. And just so we're on the same page, she's my ex-wife, so don't turn the tough guy act on around me, boy. Why don't the two of you just run along and let the grownups have a night out."

Jake was about to sit back down when Francine seemed to lose her mind. "You asshole! How dare you talk to my date like that!" She swung her arm out as if to hit Jake when a bouncer suddenly appeared by her side, stopping her progress. In a deep baritone voice, the big man said, "Franny, you've been warned before about your behaviour. I think it's time for you to leave."

Yelling ensued and Francine struggled against the bouncer. A second, larger man arrived wearing a shirt with the word 'Security' on it, and they eventually got her under control and took her outside. Her date had been standing out of the way during this whole scene, not wanting to be any part of the fiasco. He quickly stumbled off into the crowd.

Jake finally settled in his seat, staring up at the band, but he was clearly lost in thought. Julia laid her hand over his and he quickly linked them together. He pulled her closer, seeming to need some comfort from her. Leaning into him, they just sat and enjoyed the music. It took some time, but she felt his body relax slightly, although she could still feel the tension in him. Eventually, he whispered in her ear, "I think I'm ready to go."

She nodded and grabbed her purse. Since Francine had caused a scene, the evening had been strained. She thought perhaps it was best to go so it could be just the two of them.

Jake waved goodbye to Ted and they made their way outside. The cool, damp air felt good after the heat of the bar. They didn't say anything as they made their way back to the truck, each lost in their own thoughts. Julia felt disappointed and hoped they could get past this.

Chapter 13

Jake unlocked the truck and helped her inside. She watched him walk to the driver's side and could tell his mood had sobered. She wasn't sure what to do about it. He got in and started the truck. Heading out of town towards her house, she wasn't sure if she should let it go, or hit it straight on, so she decided it was best not to tiptoe around it.

"So...that was Francine? She seems... umm... I'm sure she has some redeeming qualities. Oh, I know, she has great kids. See? I knew I could come up with something."

Jake didn't look her way as he said, "How can you be so nice about this? She called you a skank!"

Julia waited to see if he would look at her, but he didn't. Sighing, she stared at him. "Well it's like this, Jake. I don't get too bent out of shape over that kind of stuff. Having been in the public eye as an author, I've learned that sometimes people can be rude. I've learned from the fan mail I get, that it's not all from happy fans, it's from angry fans, or people who don't agree with the way I've written my stories, or maybe they are looking for attention, even if it's negative. I've been called many things before, on paper and to my face. I won't lie and say it doesn't hurt, but I've learned to deal with it.

"Francine probably sees you're moving on with your life and even though she doesn't want you, it's hard for her to see you with someone else. Plus she must know you've probably told be things about the way she's treated the girls and she's feeling like I'm judging her. She can call me whatever she thinks will make her feel better about herself. I know who I am and nothing she says is going to make me feel bad. She's just not worth the time or energy it would take to worry over it."

Jake was quiet for a few minutes. When he spoke it was low and sad. "I just don't want her to push you away. I know she can be a lot to deal with. It just made me crazy hearing her call you that, because you are so far from anything like that. You're good and kind. You're generous and caring, and so much better than a lot of people I know. And you're starting to mean a lot to me. I can't have her hurting you – I just won't stand for it."

She moved a little closer and took one of his hands off the wheel where it had been gripping, hard. She rubbed her thumb over this knuckles. "Jake, she's not going to push me away. I really like you, too. And you mean a lot to Ian. You already know how I feel about your girls. Even if we don't end up together, I still want to know all of you and be part of your lives. You have wonderful kids, Jake, and that's all because of you. So, it would take a hell of a lot more than some crazy ex-wife to drive me away."

She could see his face still looking intense in the light from the dashboard. There seemed to be a lot of thoughts rolling through his mind, so she left him to think about what she'd said until they pulled into her driveway.

Turning to face him, she said, "I can see the wheels turning up there, Jake. I want to talk about what you're thinking, but if you just want to leave it for tonight I'll understand."

Julia focused on her hands and felt the gap between them growing. She was trying to think if there was something she'd said that would be pushing him away. Turning from him, she went to grab the handle to let herself out of the truck when Jake asked, "What are you doing?"

"I thought maybe you just wanted to end our date. You seem pretty wrapped up in your thoughts and if you need time to think about things, then I understand." She hesitated as she watched his face. Reaching out her hand to cup his cheek, she watched as his eyes closed and he held her hand to his face. The warmth of his skin seeped through her cold hand and she didn't want to leave. Jake surprised her as he pulled her towards him, wrapping his arms around her.

He breathed in and said in a whisper, "I'm sorry. I don't want to end our date like this. I was just lost in my head. I don't want to leave, because I really like being with you. You've been like a breath of fresh air since I first laid eyes on you. I feel better just being around you and it's been years since anyone has done that for me. I'm thankful every day that you picked this little hick town to be your new home. I know we haven't known each other very long, and you said even if we don't end up together we would still be friends.

But damn, I want to be more than friends, Julia. I want to be with you, in your life, every day. I won't push you, but I just wanted you to know how I feel. I think you know I don't go sleeping around. Hell, I haven't been with anyone in a long time, and at first that was for me. Then it was for the girls. They've seen so many men come and go out from Francine's life. I just couldn't do that."

He pulled her even closer and she wrapped her arms tight around him. He continued then, his breath caressing her cheek. "Then I met you and you changed everything. I've been out on other dates, but they never went anywhere because I just didn't feel anything at all for them. But tonight, with you, and every second I've spent with you to this point, I feel something. So I'm glad what happened tonight hasn't scared you off. I really want to give this a try."

With that, he kissed her softly. The kiss was so sweet and tender that tears appeared in her eyes and emotion overwhelmed her. He pulled away and stared at her. She knew he could see the tears and he kissed each of her lids and wiped away her tears before looking deep into her eyes. The porch light lit the side of his face and she could see the warmth and sincerity in his gaze. She liked what she saw and it loosened something inside her. Julia had been holding on to her grief for so long it had become like a blanket around her heart. Secretly, she had kept thinking if she didn't move on her memories of Martin and their life together would keep her sustained forever. But, she knew to live like that was wrong. For all her talk to Ian about moving on, it wasn't until this very moment she

really felt it. The tears were her way of letting go of the past –
allowing her a chance to rewrite love.

Moving closer to Jake, she kissed him again and he tangled his
fingers into her hair. Deepening the kiss she felt heat in her belly
and she needed him. Unfortunately, the confines of his truck were
going to make things pretty awkward. She wanted to have access to
him. To feel and touch him and have him do the same. She needed
this release, and she knew he did too.

Pulling away, she said in a breathless voice, "We need to go
inside."

∞ ∞ ∞

Jake looked into Julia's face and could see heat there. He quickly
nodded and hopped out of the truck. Before she could even locate
her purse and turn towards the door, he was opening it for her.
Pulling her into his arms, they practically ran the last few steps to
the house. Once inside he pulled her back into his arms, letting his
hands roam everywhere.

He could feel her pulling him towards the stairs, and he willingly
followed. When they reached the bottom of the stairs, he lifted her
up and she wrapped her legs around him. He heard her gasp as he
ascended, carrying her up the stairs. Knowing where those stairs
lead fueled his desires.

Once they hit the landing, they made the last few steps to her
room. Her hands were buried in his hair and she deepened the kiss.
His heartbeat ramped up and his total focus was on her and

everything she did. Just as they were about to enter her room he remembered this morning and how he had put a stop to their heated make-out session. It would take the house exploding around them to stop him at this point. He was consumed with his passion for her and if her response was any indication, she had no plans on stopping either. They made it to the bed and he laid her down, his arms still holding her tight.

Moonlight poured through the window and illuminated her body like a spotlight. Laying her down gently, he allowed his weight to press her into the mattress. He was just about to settle in when he heard her say, "Wait."

He pushed up and watched as she frantically tried to undo the buttons on his shirt. She seemed to be struggling, so he sat up and undid them while she dealt with her own clothes.

Just to break a bit of the tension, he laughed low and said, "Hey, pretty lady, it's not a race. We've got all night, so we can take it slow."

He held his breath as she peeled her skirt off. She lay before him in nothing but a black lace bra and a tiny pair of black lace panties. She was so beautiful that his mouth instantly went dry. Her creamy skin and rounded curves drew him, he wanted to feel and taste it all.

Just as he was thinking about how he would like to take his time, she reached down to the sides of her panties and pulled two ribbons and suddenly, her panties were no longer a barrier. They slid down between her legs and her sex was totally exposed to him. He could tell she was more than ready.

Growling, he reached down and popped the button on his jeans and unzipped his fly. "Change of plans, we'll go slow next time."

With that, she grabbed him and they kissed with a hunger he had never felt. He relieved himself of his shirt and could feel her silky skin rub against his chest. The friction seemed to push him over the edge. He needed her and the sooner, the better. Christ, it had been so long he feared he was probably going to come all over her stomach like a fifteen-year-old boy. He felt her slowly reaching down and taking him in her hand. Yep, he was definitely going to come. He had made sure to take matters in his own hand this morning at home, but, he had no idea he would be this excited.

Clearing his throat, he whispered, "Julia, it's been a really, really long time for me, and as much as I like you stroking me like that, if you continue I won't make it to the main event. Just give me a minute to catch my breath and I'll be good to go."

To his surprise she rolled him over on to his back. He was grateful she was willing to give him a minute to gain some control. He took a few deep breaths, willing himself to calm down. Before he knew what was happening she had taken his cock in her hand and swirled her tongue around it before taking him all in. He barely had time to process what she was doing, when the most incredible feeling rocked his body. She hadn't even hesitated, just took it deep and he groaned. Oh God, this was something that he'd only experienced a couple of times. Francine had tried it once then refused to even try again. He thought most women, except maybe porn stars, thought it was disgusting, so he'd never really considered it an option. It had happened after a date once, but the whole thing was awkward and he didn't even want to relive that moment.

He pushed his fingers into her hair and held on, watching her pleasure him like no one ever had. She took him in as deep as she could and started to fondle his sack, and he could feel the pressure building. He swallowed deeply and said in a lust-filled voice, "Baby, I've never had anyone make this feel so good. Mmmmm. But you gotta stop. I'm not gonna last. Oh, that feels so incredible. But I'm not going to be able to hold on much longer!"

She pulled off him, staring up at his face. "I'm glad you like it." Her hand slowly stroking up and down as she waited for him to answer.

Jake stared at her and she took his breath away. She looked so sexy touching him with firm fingers. In a shaky voice, he said, "I've only experienced this a couple of times, and wow that was amazing. But, seriously, I don't think I can go much longer."

A very dirty smirk appeared on Julia's face and she said in a husky voice, "Well, tell you what. How about we get this first one out of the way? That way we won't have to worry about any... pre-event mishaps." She took him deep again and Jake thought the top of his head was going to blow off.

He groaned, telling her to wait, but there was no stopping her. Her warm mouth was so tight and felt so good he couldn't help what happened next. Pulling her slightly deeper, his whole body tensed and his orgasm pulsed out of him before he could warn her. The sensation was incredible, like every bit of tension in his body flowed out of him.

Julia had taken all he had given her and slowly let his spent member lay against his stomach. Just when he was about to apologize for what had happened he could feel her slowly crawling up the bed towards his face. She paused to kiss his body along the way, running her tongue along his abs. She even took one of his nipples in her mouth and gently bit it. Jake didn't think he could recover from his initial orgasm so quickly, but the way she was kissing and touching him, he could feel himself stirring back to life.

Suddenly, she was staring down into his face. "Hope you didn't mind. I had a feeling you were close and thought maybe I could help you out. That way, when you're inside me we can make it last." She kissed him and he could taste himself on her lips. He wasn't sure what to think of that at first, but it seemed so intimate it only drew him closer to her.

Having his own plan in mind, he rolled her over. "I suggest you brace yourself, baby. I haven't had much practice with this whole oral pleasure thing, but I'm planning on returning the favor before we go any further."

Chapter 14

Julia panted as Jake's mouth traveled down her body. He went painfully slow, as he touched and tasted all of her sensitive areas. He pulled her nipple into his mouth and sucked gently. Her back bowed off the bed and her toes curled, it felt so good. Cupping her breast in his hand, he kneaded first one, then the other, running his thumb over the second nipple.

He continued kissing a path along her stomach. "You are so soft. Everywhere I touch is so soft. It's amazing."

Julia tried to smile, but he dipped his tongue into her belly button and it was slightly ticklish. Then he moved further down and a moan escaped her. Every brush of his lips made the walls of her sex pulse. He reached her pubic line and nuzzled his nose in the light dusting of hair she had. She could hear him breathe in deeply and groan loudly. In a whispered voice, she heard him say, "This is better than any dream I've had about you since we met. Damn, you're so sexy."

He pulled her thighs wide and the first swipe of his tongue almost sent her over the edge. Then he was all business, licking and kissing and she thought she would explode with sensation overload. She gripped his hair and pushed her pelvis into his mouth, desperate for more. For someone who hadn't had much practice he didn't disappoint as he pulled her hips up and his tongue dipped into the most intimate recesses of her body. She was overcome by need and said, "Please, Jake, please."

He stopped for a second and she wanted to scream in frustration. He quickly said, between heavy panting, "Hearing you call out my name could make me come again all on its own." Then he was back on her clit, sucking, and that was all she needed. She exploded and yelled out his name. Wave after pleasurable wave, she rode out the spiraling feeling that rolled through her body. She was sure she'd never felt anything so good. If that was how he did without practice she couldn't wait to see how he did when he was a pro.

As she lay there catching her breath, she felt Jake move off the bed. The next thing she heard was the crinkle of a wrapper. She still felt like she was floating. Jake moved back to the bed and suddenly he was hovering over her. The feel of the head of his cock nudging her core felt amazing. Slowly he pushed in, a bit at a time, until he was inside her. He watched her, holding her stare while he tried to communicate some emotion she wasn't quite ready for. He bent forward and took her lips tenderly. She cupped his face in her hands and kissed him deeper, tasting herself.

As she ran her tongue across his lower lip, he slowly pushed into her even further. They both breathed in as he penetrated deeper, forcing her passage to widen to accept him. She was so wet the glide was easy and she accepted all he had. Once buried inside her, Jake held still, holding her and she could feel his body tremble. She rubbed her hand along his back and could feel the muscles ripple under her touch. She wanted him to move; needed him to move.

Leaning up to his ear, she whispered, "Please, baby, I've got to feel you move. It's so good. Let me feel you."

With a growling response, Jake began to move and the two of them were elevated to another level of ecstasy. It felt as if every nerve ending in her body tingled with anticipation. He set up a steady rhythm, and her hips rose to meet his every thrust. She started to run her fingernails down his back and this seemed to push him further, feeding his need. It felt so good and Julia could feel their bodies grow slick from the exertion. It was the best kind of full body workout she'd ever had. Jake was almost frantic in his relentless pounding into her body and she loved every second. She pushed her head back into the pillow and gasped, "I'm coming!"

Black and white spots formed inside her eye lids as the orgasm ripped through her body. This was different than the first one, as it felt like her whole body exploded. She could feel the walls of her sex grip Jake's cock tightly and this pushed him into his own orgasm. He pumped furiously, then stopped and tensed. She could feel the heat as he filled the condom with his seed. He groaned and started to pump into her again, her sex still gripping him during the last of his climax. He lay on top of her, making sure to brace himself on his forearms, so as not to crush her.

They lay still for a while, letting the cool air in the room dry their skin. Julia gently ran her fingers along his back and she enjoyed the weight and the intimacy of the moment. Eventually she felt his lips on her shoulder and even though she had just had two mind-blowing orgasms, she could feel her body stir and come alive again.

She was enjoying his exploring lips, and then whispered, "How about we take this party into the shower? I'm feeling all sorts of dirty, and I think you're just the guy to find all those hard-to-reach places."

Jake pushed himself up so he could see her face. The sexy grin that spread across his face made her bite her lip. He swooped down and sucked her swollen lip into his mouth. He let it go and leaned down, saying, "Come on, dirty girl. Let's take that shower. We won't leave until I've scrubbed every single place, even those deep crevasses. It might take all night, but there won't be an inch left that I haven't thoroughly taken care of."

She felt him pull out and expected him to feel flaccid, but instead he was already starting to harden again. She was going to be one sore woman in the morning, but damn, it was going to be so worth it.

"I can't believe you can go again, already!"

Jake dipped down to hover his lips over hers. "I've been waiting a long time. If I'd known you would be the one I would be with after all this time, I would have known it was worth the wait."

Her heart fluttered as she watched the emotions in his eyes. He lowered his head, kissing her deeply, and she was lost in him again.

After their very busy night together, Julia woke up feeling slightly sore, but absolutely fantastic. Feeling the heat of Jake's body spooned behind her, she couldn't help pushing herself back against him. It had been some night. They had sex in the shower, then again in the kitchen when they went to find a snack. Also one more time, when Jake had woken her up in the middle of the night, because, as he'd said, "Damn it, woman, I can't get enough of you."

She smiled to herself and thought about everything that had happened. Jake was a very generous lover, always caressing, kissing her, touching her. He was always looking to make sure she was enjoying everything he was doing and he made the whole experience amazing. With the way he was, she could easily feel herself falling for him. He was the type of man she wanted in her life, kind, funny, hard-working, a great father, a good friend and an outrageously good lover. But before she got to ahead of herself, she needed to think about this. She needed to give it some time to see how things progressed.

A warm hand slowly made its way along her hip, curving its way down to where her clit was already tingling. Mmm, someone was awake, and oh my, did he ever know how to give a wakeup call. He pulled her tight against the rock-hard erection he was sporting, and his kisses lingered along her shoulder and neck. This was how a girl should greet the morning every day.

"Good morning, beautiful." His voice was gruff from sleep, but it was the sexiest sound she'd ever heard. "Are you really sore from last night? If you are I understand, but I would really love to be inside you again." His lips running back and forth along the back of her neck turned her to jelly.

Julia laughed and said, with a hint of lust in her voice, "Baby, you make it hurt so good. Don't make me wait."

Jake didn't even hesitate. Lifting her top leg up, he slid into her from behind. It felt so good, even with the slight twinges of muscle pain from all the lovemaking they'd done. A moan came from Jake as he buried himself as deep as he could go. Slowly pulling out and then back in again, he suddenly stopped. "Shit, I'm not wearing a condom. Damn it. I don't think I have any more."

He was about to pull out when Julia said, "I'm on the pill, Jake. I'm clean, I haven't been with anyone else since...."

She could feel him hesitate as he said, "I'm clean too. I was tested after everything happened with Francine. Are you sure you're OK with this?"

She laughed slightly, enjoying the feeling of being stretched wide. "Baby, if you pull out now, I might just tackle you. Do. Not. Stop."

He groaned his agreement and started to pump into her at a steady pace. He actually bit her softly on the shoulder at one point, which sent shivers down her body. He whispered in her ear, "Oh yeah, going bare feels so good." He paused only long enough to pull her body closer, and said, "Julia, I don't think I can go a single day from here on out without being inside you."

Panting loudly, Julia said, "We'll have to start finding quiet spots to rendezvous. You can come by the house for lunch, or if your office door locks, I can bring you lunch."

Pulling her earlobe into his mouth he bit it lightly and said, "Oh yeah? Now every time I look at my desk I'm going to be thinking about the possibility of having sex with you. I'll be walking around the garage with a hard on all the time."

She laughed and then yelled out as Jake shifted her body and hit her G spot just right. "Oh, don't stop, baby!"

It didn't take long for either one of them to reach their peak and tumble over into the abyss. Feeling Jake fill her with his warmth was incredible. They lay in bed, catching their breath, when Jake's stomach growled loudly. She smiled at him. "I satisfied one craving, now how about I go down and wrestle us up some grub to satisfy your other one?" She slowly pulled away from him and headed to the bathroom.

"You have the sexiest body I've ever seen. I could stare at you all day and still not get enough." Jake said, watching her.

Julia did a little wiggle and turned to look at him over her shoulder. "I'm glad you like what you see. Perhaps after breakfast, I'll let you study at all my parts up close and personal." She winked and then was out of Jake's sight.

Before she could fully close the door, Jake was in the doorway. "Damn woman, I need to take that look right now." Following her into the bathroom, he slowly closed the door. It was a long time before they came out again.

After some breakfast, that was actually closer to lunch, Jake headed out to pick up the girls and run some errands. Julia stopped by Audrey's to pick up Ian and then she was going to get groceries.

Standing at the front door, Julia knocked and waited. Audrey opened the door and a slow smile spread across her face. "If that's not the look of a satisfied woman who has enjoyed every minute of her evening, I don't know what is. And before you say anything, keep in mind he's my brother and the details can be saved for other women who haven't actually seen him in his birthday suit as a small child. But if the relaxed look on your face is any indication, it must have been fantastic."

Julia laughed and shook her head. "A lady never kisses and tells. Well, maybe a little. All I will say is… if I seem to be walking a little bowlegged, it's not because I was out trail riding all night. What's that saying? Save a horse, ride a cowboy? There you go; I did my part for horse kind everywhere."

Audrey held her hand up and saying, "Stop, stop, TMI! I'm just glad you had a good time. Come on in and have a cup of tea. I heard a rumor that a certain ex-wife almost put a damper on the party."

Julia followed her in and over tea, she filled Audrey in on all the details of her date and the incident with Francine, keeping all the naughty bits to herself. She loved having someone to talk to again. Paige had always been her confidant, but now with the miles between them, it just wasn't the same.

Audrey nibbled on a cookie as she sipped her tea. "Francine is like a thorn in Jake's side. I sometimes wish he'd never met her, but then we wouldn't have the girls. I love them so much, how can their mother be such a bitch?"

Julia shook her head. "I'm not sure. I know she wasn't very pleasant and I was only around her for a few minutes. I didn't say anything when she called me a skank, but then, I didn't need to. Jake freaked. But, she better hope I don't see her again because I have a few choice words for her if I do."

They finished their tea and Ian came down looking tired from staying up late two nights in a row. They said their goodbyes and stopped to pick up a few groceries. While they shopped, Ian informed her he'd been sent a text by the swim coach informing him that he'd made the team. Julia was so happy for him. She picked up stuff to make lasagna as a celebration dinner. As they were getting into the truck, Ian got a text from Dani saying that she'd also made the team.

They were just walking in the door when Julia received her first text from Jake since he'd left that morning. Waiting until she had everything unpacked and she could read it alone, she stepped into her office.

Hello gorgeous. I haven't stopped thinking about u for one second. U have me going out of my mind, woman!!! I need 2 see you again, like tomorrow. And if not tomorrow, then ASAP.

She smiled and quickly sent a text.

Hello handsome. You've been on my mind all day as well. I heard some good news today about Dani making the swim team. Ian did 2. We can be together at all the swim meets!

Pulling out all the ingredients for lasagna, she started to prepare while she waited for Jake to respond. Her phone pinged.

Hey, that is fantastic news. But there might be the odd Thursday I have 2 cover at the garage. But at least I'll be able 2 sit and ogle you the rest of the time.

She laughed out loud and texted back.

On the nights you miss I can bring Dani home or to Audrey's if that would help.

Jake texted right back.

That would be great. I actually have 2 work this Thursday. We can work out a plan this week.

Just texting with him made her suddenly want to see him. She was missing him already and it had only been a few hours. An idea formed.

Hey, have u started anything 4 dinner? If not, do u want to come over with the girls for lasagna? I really want 2 see u. We won't make it 2 late - school tomorrow. Just an idea.

She continued to get the pan ready and her phone pinged right away.

U had me at lasagna, baby. Be there in 20!!

She smiled to herself and pulled out an extra pan to make two. With both Ian and Jake eating, one would never be enough.

Chapter 15

Anthony stood staring at the buttons on the phone, a sense of anticipation coursing through him. He was so close to being out of this hellhole – just over a week to go and he would be a free man again. He could hardly wait to be able to sleep in his own bed, in his own house. No more shitty food, lights out rules or assholes trying to sell him drugs. All he wanted was a well-prepared sausage and spinach calzone, a fine vintage, and a big fat cigar. Oh, yeah, and a hot brunette he could pound his cock into to relieve some stress. Now that's what he really needed.

The line picked up and Gino's voice sounded better than it had the last time they spoke.

Hearing Gino shuffling, he knew he must be heading out to his garage. "Hey, Anthony, how you doin'?"

Anthony smiled and said, "I know I'll be better soon, once I'm out of this shit hole. You're still coming to get me right?"

"Absolutely, Anthony. And I have some good news, too. We found her." Anthony could tell Gino was smiling.

"You found her? Where the hell did she go?"

"It took some digging, but she's living in a place called Heritage Falls. It's way out on the southern Illinois border, about five hours from here."

She was only five hours from here? You'd think if she was running away from him she would have headed out to California or Texas, but she was still in the same state? Maybe he was wrong, maybe she just moved. But the abruptness of the move was puzzling. In his gut he didn't want to think the reason she had left was anything to do with him, but damn it, he couldn't take the chance on what information might be written in that book. He was going to have to figure out a way to get it.

Gino had been rambling on as Anthony pulled himself out of his thoughts. "Hey, Gino, when you come and get me we'll hash out our next steps to get the book back."

"For sure, Anthony. Just lay low and keep your nose clean for the next week and you're home free."

Anthony loved the sound of that. And hopefully once he had that book he would be free from worrying about that too.

The next few days were busy with work and Ian's schedule. It was Thursday and Julia was seated on the bleachers by the pool, waiting for the kids to finish their practice. She had stopped by Audrey's house and picked up Hailey so the two of them could spend some time together as they waited for the swim practice to be over. They were having a great time. Hailey was telling her all about the stuff that had happened at school that day with one of the boys in her class.

"So, then, he thought it would be really funny to make a farting sound when the substitute teacher sat down, only he didn't see the principal, Mr. Watson, at the door when he did it. He got in so much trouble! Mrs. Teagan, that's the teacher we had today, she was so embarrassed, too. I felt bad for her. Boys are so weird." Hailey was shaking her head. She was so mature for her age.

The whistle sounded and the team headed into the change rooms. Julia had told them they would go out for pizza after this. Jake said he would meet them there if he missed them at the end of practice. Julia and Hailey had made their way over to the one exit while they waited, and that's when Julia saw her. She could see Francine head into the building from the other parking lot. She seemed nervous and Julia could sense something was wrong when all the hairs on the back of her neck stood up.

Casually, Julia reached over and took Hailey's arm and pulled her closer. She reached up and brushed the young girls hair behind her ear and at the same time kept Hailey's back to her mother. She wasn't sure why Francine was here, but there was no way in hell she was letting the girls out of her sight.

Julia knew the moment Francine realized Hailey was with her. She seemed surprised, not expecting to see her here, and then she regained her composure. She marched right over to her and in an overly bright voice she said, "Well there you are, sweetheart! I've been looking everywhere for you. I was told you had come to Dani's swim practice, so I told your dad I would come and pick you two up and take you out for dinner."

Hailey looked puzzled, glancing at Julia. Then she stared at her mom and said, "Dad said that? We were already going out for pizza with Julia. Dad was going to meet us there."

Julia still had her hand resting on Hailey's arm and she hung on a little tighter as Francine answered her daughter. "He told me to tell you that the plans have changed and we can go out for dinner. He also said if you want, you can stay overnight at my place. Doesn't that sound like fun?"

No, that did not sound like fun to Julia, or even remotely possible. Something was definitely off here and there was no way in hell that was going to be happening on her watch.

Julia pulled Hailey back just slightly and stepped in front of her. "Actually, I haven't heard of this change in plans, so you won't mind if I text Jake and find out when he made these arrangements with you, would you?"

Francine's eyes grew large, but she recovered fast. "There's no need to check because that's what he said. I just got off the phone with him. So why don't you step aside so Hailey and I can wait for Dani."

Making a move to grab on to Hailey's arm, Francine lunged forward, but Julia blocked her. Just then Dani stepped out of the change room and walked over to where the women were facing off.

Dani looked mad and said, "Mom, what are you doing here? You know you can't just show up here and see us, right? The new rules say that..."

Francine cut her off so loudly and abruptly, everyone jumped when she yelled, "Yes, Dani, I know what the rules are, but your Dad said I could take you out for supper and you could stay overnight! So let's go get in the car. I'm really hungry."

Julia watched as Dani shook her head and said, "No, I can't do that."

Francine started to get really agitated then and Julia could tell something was really off with her. That's when she noticed the dilated pupils and shaky hands. Francine was high. Crap, this was just another layer of crazy Jake didn't need to deal with.

Julia turned to Dani and said, "Hey Dani, Hailey mentioned she needed to use the washroom. Can you take her?"

Dani glanced at her and seemed to understand. She held out her hand to Hailey and said in a calm voice. "Come on HaileyBug, I'll take you."

Francine called out to them as they walked away. "I'll be here when you're ready to go."

Once the girls were out of sight, Francine's mask came off. "Now you listen to me, you bitch. These are my girls and you can't stop me from being with them. I don't care what Jake or the courts say for that matter; no one can stop me from seeing them. Why don't you just run along so me and the girls can go for dinner?"

Julia watched as Francine stood there, her whole body sweaty and twitching. Julia pulled out her phone and said, "Well now, name calling isn't really my thing, so you listen to me. You're not leaving this building with those girls. For one, it's against the court order for

you to see them unsupervised, and two; you're higher than a kite –
don't try and deny it. Your pupils are dilated and you're sweaty and
shaking. You must be out of your mind if you think I'm going to sit
idly by while you endanger the lives of your kids."

Faster than Julia thought possible, Francine was right in her face.
"Don't preach to me about being a good mother, you piece of trash!
I'm the best mother on the planet. My girls love me! If it wasn't for
all of Jake's rules, I would have them all the time. They don't need
anyone else in their lives, especially not you and that little asshole
son of yours."

The gloves were off! Something in Julia just snapped. "Now you
listen to me, it's one thing to insult me, but talk about my son like
that again and I'll make you wish you'd never stepped foot in this
school tonight. Why don't you get back in your car and head off to
wherever the hell it is you came from. And in future, don't even
think about pulling this shit with me, do you understand? You will
not now, not ever, on my watch, take these girls anywhere,
especially when you're all doped up on whatever it is you've taken.
Before I pull out my phone and call the police and report a possible
abduction and the fact that you're driving under the influence of
drugs, consider where that will land you. Those girls deserve a
loving, caring mother who puts their needs first. Not some two-bit
slut who would put them in danger. Do I make myself clear? Good
night, Francine."

Julia stood her ground and watched as Francine glared at her.
The standoff lasted about a minute until, finally, Francine spun

around, wobbling, and marched the opposite way she came in. Julia never took her eyes off her until she was gone. Dropping her head down, she could feel the anger still crackling on the surface. She was furious. How could anybody even consider putting their kids in danger?

She felt hands on her shoulders, lightly squeezing and knew it was Jake. In a whispered voice, she heard him say, "I'm sorry you had to deal with her. I was already on my way here. Thank you for not letting her take the girls."

She moved around to stare at him. "I know the rules Jake, and I also know she is high on something. I would never have allowed her to take them."

Jake pulled her in and wrapped his arms around her. "You are an amazing woman, Julia. The girls and I are lucky to have you in our lives."

From behind Jake, Julia heard Ian say, "Oh my God!"

She and Jake both turned to stare at Ian. Julia was worried that perhaps seeing the two of them embracing might have upset him. She looked at his face and realized that, in fact, he wasn't looking at either one of them, but staring at the place Francine had just disappeared. Then, he turned towards the two of them.

He looked horrified, and started to back away shaking his head. "I'm sorry. I'm so sorry." Then he ran out into the hall heading deeper into the school.

Julia started to go after him, but Jake stopped her. "If this has something to do with Francine, which it just might, let me go. You took care of my kids tonight; let me take care of yours."

It killed her inside to think Ian was hurting, and she desperately wanted to go and find him, but she also knew if it did concern Jake or Francine or even the girls, Jake should handle it. She slowly nodded.

Jake rushed down the hallway to follow Ian. As she turned back, she saw the girls standing there, watching at her. Before she could say anything, Hailey ran to her and wrapped her arms around her waist. She gathered the girl in her arms and kissed the top of her head. She would never have been able to forgive herself if anything had happened to either of them. Dani walked towards her, much slower than Hailey, but once she reached Julia she put her arms around her and she heard Dani say, "Thank you for watching out for us Julia. You're what a mom should really be like."

Julia pulled both girls in tighter and held them. She didn't say anything, couldn't really, without betraying how she felt. But her emotions came through to the girls in the way she held them. How anyone could ever want to put their children in danger was something Julia would never understand.

Jake had gone to high school here, so he knew this place like the back of his hand. He stopped in the hall to listen for the sound of sneakers squeaking on the shiny floors. He heard one heading in the direction of the gym, so he started running at a good clip to catch up. He knew in his gut something had happened involving Francine. And more than anyone else, he knew what she was like.

He made a turn to the right just in time to see the doors to the gym start to close. Stopping just outside the door, he peered in. He could see Ian sitting on the bleachers, the light over the door shining on him. Ian was bent over with his head in his hands. Jake slowly opened the door and walked tentatively over to him. He didn't want Ian to take off again.

Not wanting to startle him, he quietly said, "Hey, bud." Ian glanced up at him and before Jake could say another word, there were tears in the young man's eyes.

"Jake, I'm so sorry. I didn't know who she was. I never would have spoken to her if I'd known. She never even let on she knew Dani or you or any of your family." Ian put his face back into his hands and Jake walked over and sat beside him on the bleachers.

Reaching out, he patted his shoulder, he said, "Just tell me what happened, Ian."

Ian looked over at him, his eyes wide with remorse and regret. "I was walking over to Wyatt's house on Monday after school. He was going to meet me there because he had to go with Luke to pick something up for the car. As I headed to his house, this lady pulled up beside me and asked if I need a ride. I thought it was strange and so I said, 'no'. I'm not stupid enough to get into a stranger's car. Then, she asked me if I went to the high school and I said, 'Yes'. She then mentioned a few teachers I actually knew and she seemed really nice. I still didn't get too close to the car, but she seemed nice enough to talk to."

Jake knew how charming and conniving Francine could be. He had fallen for it more times than he could count over the years.

Ian cleared his throat and continued. "She asked me if I was on any sports teams, because I looked athletic. I told her I had made the swim team and our first practice was on Thursday. She said she knew Coach Ruben and that he was a really nice guy. She asked me if I liked all the people on the team. I said I was lucky that a few people I had just met were on the team so it would be a lot of fun since I was new here. She asked if my mom and dad would be coming to watch me. I told her my dad had passed away, so it was just my mom. She seemed really sad for me and said how it was hard to lose a parent when you were so young.

"We chatted and I was thinking how nice she was. She asked if I had a girlfriend and I said I was working on it. She asked me what her name was and I told her it was Rachel. I only said her first name. She gave me a strange look when I said that and mentioned I probably had lots of options in the girl department, so I should make sure to play the field. I thought that was really strange, I mean what did it matter to her who I dated? Then she asked if I had lots of friends that were girls. I told her yes and then I mentioned how my friend Dani was on the swim team with me."

Jake took in a slow breath and could see where this was headed before Ian had even finished his story.

"We talked about parents coming to watch their kids and she said that sometimes, when she could, she went and watched her nephews play soccer. I told her that Dani's dad was going to be working the first night of the swim meet, but my mom would be there. It wasn't long after she checked her watch and said she needed to get going. Honestly, Jake, I didn't even think about that conversation until I walked out of the change room and saw her arguing with my mom. God, what if she had gotten the girls to go with her? I feel sick just thinking about what could have happened because I was so stupid and talked to a stranger. I was so careful not to tell her my name or where I live, but I mentioned my friends and put them in danger. I'm such an idiot!"

Ian's head dropped and his shoulders shook. Jake took him gently by the shoulders and turned him so they were facing each other. "Ian, she can be the most charming and kind person when she wants to be. I should know, I was married to her and witnessed it many, many times. So, I know she has the ability to make you feel special and I'm sure she was just a little bit flirty too, right?"

The young man didn't meet Jake's eyes, but nodded. Jake shook his head and said, "Yeah, that tends to be the way she handles things. She thinks by flirting she'll get her way with everyone, like they can't resist her. And until you get to know her and the type of woman she is, you think she's sweet and kind and nice. But instead, she used you Ian. She used you for the information she needed. You see, she's angry at me because she was irresponsible with the girls the last time she had them for the weekend. I told my lawyer and the judge changed our custody arrangements, so now all of her visits have to be supervised and she can only see them once a month for a couple of hours. I'm not sure what her plans were tonight, but I'll be contacting my lawyer and the police to make them aware of what happened. I hate to ask, but it would be helpful if you could share your story with them. Would you be OK with that? I mean, we'll have to talk to your mom first, but if you could do that for me I would really appreciate it."

Ian's head was nodding and he blurted, "For sure, Jake, whatever you need. I hate to tell my mom what I did because she's told me so many times not to talk to strangers, but I didn't feel in danger at all and I'm older now. I thought she just really enjoyed talking to me." Ian took a big breath, "My mom is going to be so mad."

Jake smiled and knew Ian was right, she would be mad, and disappointed, but also a bit protective too. "Yeah, she probably will be. But no one got hurt. I know my girls, especially Dani, and they would have never gotten in a car with her. They know all about the court ruling and Francine hasn't made the best impression on them over the years."

Ian nodded. "Dani talked to me about her mom, so I know how she feels about her."

Jake could only imagine what Dani had told Ian about her mother. The one question that kept running though his mind was how Francine knew who Ian was in the first place. It's not like she ran in the same circles as Julia, and she would have no reason to be around high school kids. Although some of her recent boyfriends looked as if they hadn't been out of high school long. All he knew for sure was she used Ian and he was going to have to do something about it.

Watching Ian now he could tell there was something else on his mind. "I know this might not be the best time to ask this, but, um, are you and my mom… serious about each other? I mean, I saw that hug and I've also seen the way you look at her. I know friends don't look at each other that way."

Well if that didn't knock Jake sideways! He thought he and Julia had been doing a pretty good job at hiding their affection for one another, but apparently not good enough.

It was Jake's turn to clear his throat and shift his eyes away. "Um, yeah, I guess you could say we really like each other, a lot, and we like spending time together. I enjoy being with her. I mean, she's funny and smart and very kind. She is really great with my girls, and I've enjoyed all the time I've been able to spend with you. Let's just say that I haven't ever met anyone like your mom and I would really like to have the opportunity to get to know her better. I hope that's all right with you?"

Finally Jake faced Ian and watched as a whole slew of emotions crossed his face. He could tell that his mother moving on was hard to adjust to. Her going on one date was way different then her actually moving on with her life and Jake could understand that.

Ian remained quiet for a few more seconds and finally said, "I knew, eventually, she would move on, but it's hard watching it happen. I mean, my mom is a great lady. She's smart and she's always been pretty, so of course men would be interested in her. Even some of my new friends have commented on how pretty she is. I guess what I'm trying to say is, if this was going to happen, I'm glad it's you. You're a great guy and I know you won't hurt her."

Jake smiled at Ian and gave his shoulder a squeeze. "I can assure you I would never hurt her, Ian. Your mom deserves to have a great life and I would never do anything to jeopardize it." Jake was glad their relationship was out in the open now. It was going to be hard to keep up the friend façade for any length of time.

Glancing towards the gym door, Jake said, "I think we best get out there and face the music. I'll try my best to have your back. But I've seen your mom's laser-eye stare, and to be honest, it kind of scares me."

Ian shook his head and said, "Wait until its directed right at you. It makes you feel like you're two inches tall." He let out a big sigh and stood up. The two made their way to the door. Just before they exited the gym Ian looked at Jake again. "I really am sorry, Jake. I'll make sure I watch out for both of them from now on. I really like your girls and I would never want anything bad to happen to them."

Jake put his arm around Ian and gave him a side hug. "Thanks Ian, I'd appreciate you keeping an eye out for them. Guys have to stick together and keep their families safe."

Ian nodded and they made their way back to the girls, who were still waiting near the pool viewing area. As they got closer he could see Julia still holding his girls, their arms wrapped around each other and quiet murmurs were coming from them. His heart swelled watching someone care for the two most important people in his world. They turned as they heard him approaching and Hailey was the first to break free and run to him.

She jumped into his arms and hugged him tight. Her voice was muffled as her face pushed into his shirt. "Don't worry, Dad. Julia wouldn't have let her take us. And we wouldn't have gone with her anyway." She gave him one final squeeze and let go. Dani was there and gave him a hug, too. She didn't say anything, but the look in her eyes said enough. Jake knew she never would have gone with Francine, that's why she had called him when she had supposedly taken Hailey to the bathroom.

Jake peered over and saw that Ian was braving his mother's stare and telling her what happened. Jake could tell by the straightening of her spine she was getting angry. When Ian was finished his story, Jake could see she was going to start in on her lecture, so he quickly made his way over and said, "Hey, I hate to interrupt, but it's getting late and I'm sure we're all hungry. Why don't we head over to the pizza place and get some food. This has been an emotional night for everyone and I think we could all use something to eat. What do you say?"

Julia turned to Jake and said, with a touch of the anger in her tone, "Fine. Let's go and eat. Just keep in mind you've only saved him for the time being. Ian and I will discuss this further when we get home. Don't think I don't see that the two of you are tag-teaming me, I wasn't born yesterday. Come on, girls."

He watched Julia as she gathered the girls and headed to the exit. With her back straight and hips swaying, even though she scared him just a little when she was mad like this, she was sexy as hell. All that sashay and attitude, who knew it could be such a turn on?

Turning to Ian, he spoke low, not wanting Julia to hear. "Sorry, bud. She's on to us. But at least I bought you a little time." Ian nodded and trudged along behind Jake, walking as if he was headed for his last meal. Jake felt bad for him, but he also knew there was nothing he could really say to change how Julia felt either. If the tables were turned he would be angry, too. But he also knew kids made mistakes; lord knew he had made plenty in his life time. He would try and calm her down over pizza. It was all he could do.

The girls had left in one car and the boys in the other. Julia was still fuming and didn't really want to see Ian at the moment. After all the years of telling him to stay safe and above all else, not to talk to strangers, then he goes and does this. It felt like she'd failed, like she'd wasted her breath. Why would he have done that? Gripping the steering wheel tighter she listened as the girls finally started to speak. The tension of the situation was starting to leave them. Yes, this is what they needed. Something that was ordinary so they could feel safe and not think about the fact their mother had just tried to wreck their lives.

Julia gripped the steering wheel again just thinking about how that woman had used her son. The most important person in the world to her and she'd used him to find out about her daughters. Francine was ruining any chance that she had to be part of their lives. Julia couldn't even comprehend never being in Ian's life. Not being there to experience every important event. She might be angry with him now, but she loved him with her whole heart. If she ever caught that woman speaking to him again, she wasn't sure what she would do, but it wouldn't be pretty.

Pulling into the parking lot, the girls piled out of the truck. Jake and Ian pulled in almost a minute later, so they waited just outside the restaurant door for them to catch up. She noticed Ian was walking much slower than he would have normally. She knew he was dreading the lecture that was to come. Julia didn't like to lecture. In fact, as a child she had hated when her own parents had done it, but as a parent sometimes it had to be done.

They were seated and she noticed Ian avoided her eyes as much as possible. The waitress came and took their order and brought them their drinks. Dani asked if they could go back and play the arcade games and Jake said sure. Ian didn't move. Dani turned and said, "Come on, Ian, you've got to see the game room, it's so cool."

Ian shook his head. "You go on ahead."

Dani looked puzzled, but made her way to the back with Hailey. Jake stared at Julia with a look that said, 'Come on, let him go'.

Rolling her eyes at Jake, she said, "Ian, go back and keep an eye on the girls, would you?" She watched as Ian bolted away from the table like his pants were on fire.

Looking back at Jake, she realized he was staring at her. It was unnerving. But then, a smile brightened his face. She wasn't sure what he was thinking. "You think you're real smooth, trying to keep him from getting in trouble? We both know what he did was wrong. I'm sure he is remorseful about it. I know he's older and probably thought it wasn't a big deal, but he put Dani in danger by telling Francine where she would be. How can you just forgive him for that?"

Jake reached over and took her hand. He rubbed his thumb over her palm and spoke quietly. "Julia, he's just a boy. Yes, it was wrong for him to speak to her. Yes, he should've known better as I'm sure you've told him a million times to be wary of strangers. As a parent, I'm totally disappointed he broke the cardinal rule. But as a guy, I know what she would have done. She would have made him feel special. She would have used her charms and flirted with him. She would have played on his self-esteem, making him feel good about himself, telling him how strong he must be, and how good looking he was. She would have totally had him eating out of her hand, and it would have been effortless for her because, men love that. Stroke his ego, build him up and get what she needed. Since she left me, I have heard the same story over and over from many guys. She plays with men to get what she wants. That's what she does, Julia. Ian just fell for the oldest trick in the book. Some women use this weakness and we're left at the end wondering what happened. We never learn the rules of the game until it's over. I'm just sorry Ian had to learn this particular lesson this way. But he'll be more perceptive next time."

Looking down at the palm Jake was stroking and feeling the warm sensation as it travelled up her arm, she felt sad for Jake. What must it have been like to be with someone like that? Hearing how jaded he was about the way women use men to get what they want, she hoped he didn't feel she was in anyway like that.

She was about to say just that when Jake spoke. "I can almost hear the wheels turning in there, Julia. I don't think you're like that. You couldn't be more different from her if you tried. That's why I like being with you. Not once during the whole time I've known you have you ever made me feel like you were just using me. Never once have you ever made me think you were saying what I wanted to hear because you wanted something from me. You are a kind, warm, loving person. You are the kind of woman men long for, and want to be a better person for. I look at you and see strength and integrity and someone my girls can admire."

Julia looked into Jake's eyes and could see how sincere he was as he laid out his emotions for her. She hoped he could see some of that reflected in her eyes as well. She felt the same way about him.

"Thank you, Jake. It means so much to know you would want them to look up to me. And my son gets a chance to spend time with a man who treats woman like they should be treasured and protected. I've been worried for a long time that without having a father, Ian wouldn't get to see what that should be like. You and your family are the kind of people that have let me rest easier at night. You're the kind of man women want in their lives, someone who is a partner and a protector and who values family. Not someone who takes and gives nothing in return."

The sounds of the restaurant slowly filtered in as they stared at one another. Julia never would have guessed that their first heart-to-heart about their lives and kids would take place in a pizza parlour. She smiled at him and squeezed the hand that had been stroking her palm.

Jake stared at her and a cocky smile appeared on his face. "So, what I'm hearing is, you like me. And you think I'm sexy and handsome and if you could you would ravage me right here, you know, if our kids weren't in the back."

Julia gave him a puzzled look. "No, I don't believe the words sexy ever came out of my mouth. Neither did handsome or anything about ravaging you."

He wagged his eyebrows at her and spoke in a whisper, "Baby, I can read between the lines."

Julia laughed out loud and Jake looked offended. "What? That's what I heard. And speaking of ravaging, when can we be alone again? Waking up in my cold and empty bed every morning is not my idea of a fun time. Do you know how hard it is to sleep when Jake Junior has you on his mind?"

Julia laughed harder this time. She wiped away a tear that had escaped and caught her breath. "Jake Junior? Is that what you call your... thing?"

Jake focused his stare on her with heat in his eyes. "Yes, that's what I call him. I called it Thor's Hammer once, but it didn't sound right. I always thought it was… bigger than that." A huge smile spread across his face as he waited to see what she would say.

Her mouth dropped open and she wasn't sure how to respond. She knew he was trying to get a rise out of her, so she decided to turn the tables on him. Leaning closer she whispered, "I agree, Thor's Hammer is much too small to describe the velvet steel between your legs." She sat back in the booth and watched Jake's eyes burn even hotter. Then she gave her lips one quick lick and watched as the nerve jumped on his cheek.

"I can see someone likes to play with fire. It's too bad we're not alone; I'd love to show you how much I've missed you the last few days. In fact if our kids weren't here I'd take you out to my truck right now and show you just how hard Jake Junior is. Is that something you would like?"

Julia could feel a full body flush come over her as she watched the hunger in his eyes. No man, not even Martin, had ever made her feel like this. He was so masculine and strong. When he looked at her like that, she felt powerful and wanted. She took a sip of her water and watched as Jake stared at her lips. Leaning forward again, she stared at his lips, letting the moment build. Biting down on her bottom lip she slowly looked up into his eyes. Jake's pupils had dilated and as he leaned in further to kiss her, she said, "Pizza's here."

She pulled back quickly as two waitresses brought over their pizzas and the kids suddenly appeared beside the table. Julia watched Jake as the kids took their seats and everyone started putting pizza on their plates. She grabbed a slice and was about to take a bite when she glanced back at Jake. He was looking at her and smiled.

He leaned a little closer and whispered, "This conversation isn't over, Mrs. Witmore. We will talk later." Then he took a bite of his pizza and turned to ask Dani how school went today.

Chapter 16

Later that night, after dinner and the girls were tucked in, Jake could hardly wait to call Julia. He locked up, turning off the lights, and headed for his room. Shutting off his bedside lamp, he undressed and crawled into his bed as he dialed the phone and waited for her to answer. Lying on to his back, he stared at the ceiling.

"Mr. Vincent, so nice of you to call. I assume you wish to finish our conversation?" He could hear her shuffling around.

"Why yes, Mrs. Witmore, I would love to continue our conversation from dinner. You never gave me an answer to the question I asked."

Julia's voice came over the line, quiet and seductive. "And what was the question again?"

Jake shifted his legs, wondering where she was. "The question was about whether or not you would have liked to go out to my truck so I could show you how much I've missed you. You know, so you could check out Jake Junior. He's really missing you right now."

He could hear the laugh in Julia's voice. "What are we doing here, Jake?

Licking his lips he spoke softly into the phone, "I thought maybe we could do something I've never done before."

A low chuckle came over the line as Julia asked, "Are you referring to phone sex? Because I've never done that either."

"Oh good, so it's your first time, too! Excellent." Jake's excitement about the prospect just ramped up one hundred percent. In a quiet, whispered tone, he said "I'm in my bed, with the lights out. Where are you?"

"I'm in my bed, with the lights on. I'm not sure I can do this, Jake."

He could hear the reluctance in her voice so rushed on, "Come on, let's just try it. If it gets too weird we'll stop. OK?"

"Umm, all right. God I can believe we're doing this. So, are you hoping I'm going tell you some kind of dirty bedtime story, Mr. Vincent? I've been told I tell great stories."

His mind spun with the thought of what they were about to do. "Oh yeah? How about you tell me a story about how you would have your way with me in my truck."

A low humming noise came across the line. "Let me see. Oh God, I can't believe we're doing this. OK, so I'm in the truck, lying back against the door as I watch you get in. You look really good filling out those Levi's, just perfect. You slide in closer to me and run your fingers up into my hair and kiss me really soft. I dip my tongue into your mouth and taste you. Mmm, you taste so good."

Jake started smiling and picturing her in that position in his truck. He could almost see her there. She continued, her voice soft and seductive, "I feel your hand slip under my shirt and brush against my skin until you cup my breast. Oh, your hands are so warm. Your thumb rubs over my nipple in a slow circle and it hardens."

He couldn't help but groan just thinking about her breasts. They were beautiful, so full with perfect, dark rose nipples. She must have known she was having an effect on him, so she continued. "I feel you lift my shirt and unhook my bra. The next thing I feel is your lips licking and sucking on my nipple. Oh my, it feels so good with your tongue swirling around the tip. I feel the pressure as you bite down, not hard, just enough to make it feel good." He could hear her breath speed up and that sound made his body flush all over.

Jake swallowed hard before saying, "Oh, so you like a little pressure, do you? I can't wait to try that in person. What do I do next? I want to hear you tell me all the dirty things I do to you."

He knows she must hear the strain in his voice. Her breathing is sending tingles all over his body. "Your lips travel down over my stomach and you dip your tongue into my belly button."

"Do you like that? Does it feel good?" Jake voice is gruff with need.

Jake closed his eyes as he waited to hear her answer. He could hear her hesitate like she was embarrassed, but then she continued. "Yes, it feels really good. I feel your breath over my skin as you travel further down. Your fingers slip along the waistband of my pants and undo the button on my jeans and pull them down, taking my underwear as you go."

Julia paused again, but she finally said, just above a whisper, "Now I'm totally bare to you. I can feel your breath on my sex, so warm it makes me tingle. I look at you as you stare at me."

She was breathing harder still and Jake's hand, of its own volition, travelled down his body to squeeze the length of his cock. Oh shit, that felt good. He whispered over the line, "What do you want me to do Julia? Do you want me to taste you? I know how fantastic you taste."

Her breathing sounded a bit ragged. Was she as turned on as he was? Was she touching herself? The thought of it made him crazy.

"Julia, what are you doing there in your bed all alone? Are you wearing anything?"

A small laugh sounded on the line and her voice sounded strained. "I'm in a very skimpy night gown, but I don't have any panties on. Are you naked?"

"Yes, I'm totally naked. And I'm stoking my cock while I listen to your crazy sexy voice tell me a story. Tell me, are you touching yourself? Damn, just thinking about you touching yourself while we talk is making me harder."

He groaned and he could hear Julia shift and a quiet gasp sounded. He knew she had just touched herself and it made him want to be with her even more. He was so turned on and then he heard her moan over the phone.

Jake's voice sounded rough as he said. "I can tell you're touching yourself, Julia. I've heard that moan before. Mmm, that sounds so hot. Continue the story, Julia."

She cleared her throat, and he could tell it took some effort for her to remember where they were at in the story. "You lift me off the seat and dip your tongue into my slick heat and lick me deep. So deep. Then you use your tongue to pleasure me, swirling it around my clit. Before I can come you stop and undo your pants. I watch as you pull them down and I see your hard cock. It's so hard and a drop of precum appears on the head. I lean forward and suck the head of your cock right into my mouth."

Jake was panting at this point. He could feel his orgasm right on the cusp. He moaned and said, "I can feel your tongue on me baby, and it feels so good."

Julia continued in a raspy whisper. "I slowly let you slip from my mouth and then you lean over and I can feel the head right at the entrance to my pussy. It feels hot and wet and all I can think about is you pushing deep inside me. Do you want that Jake? Do you want to feel your cock push into me, really deep? Feel my walls clench tight around you? I do. I want to feel your hard, hot cock pump inside me, pounding in and out. Oh yeah, can you feel it? All you have to do is push, Jake."

Seven Hells, she was so incredibly amazing. His grip on his cock was hard and his strokes were getting shorter as he drew nearer to his release. "I am totally pushing it in, baby. Hot and deep. Yyyyeeessss."

Just before he lost it, he heard her say, "Yes, Jake, just like that! Take me hard."

Shoving off the covers, he went over the edge and could hear her on the other end as she, too, lost her control. Straining as he stroked, he spiraled out of control. Once he could focus, he realized he'd been laying there just breathing into the phone.

It was quiet on the other end. Oh God, had she hung up? "Julia, are you still there?"

"I'm here." He could tell by her tone that she was feeling embarrassed.

Wanting to make sure she knew how amazing it was, he said, "Wow, baby. That was crazy hot. I wish we were together though, because I would love to do that in real life."

Julia chuckled low. "I can't believe that we just did that! I've written a lot of scenes in my time, but I've never talked that dirty out loud before."

Smiling, Jake said, "Julia, you really do know how to tell a great story. But, it's no substitute for the real thing. I need to touch and taste you in the flesh."

He could hear her shift as she said, "I want that, too. We'll figure something out. Hey, how about this weekend we do something with the kids during the day, then see if we can get some time alone?"

He started to clean up as he said, "Yeah, sounds perfect. The Fall Fair is going on this weekend. Hailey loves seeing the animals and I'm sure Dani and Rachel were already planning on going, so that means Ian and Wyatt were too. If you're good I might even win you a stuffed animal."

"A stuffed animal? Well, how could a girl refuse an invite like that? And what else might we see at this fair? Will there be rides and stuff?"

Jake walked into his bathroom to finish getting ready for bed. "Absolutely. Why do you think the kids want to go? There is also a tractor pull, 4H ribbon presentations, horse shows and the smashup derby."

"That sounds very exciting indeed. Might they have candy apples?"

With a seductive tone he said, "Would you like a candy apple, milady? Because I would love to watch you eat one. All that juice and sticky candy. Mmm, yeah, I can totally get you one."

"Only you can make eating a candy apple sound dirty. But yes, I would love a candy apple. I haven't had one in… I can't even remember."

Jake crawled back into bed. "Then have one you shall. Well, beautiful, it's getting late and I have to get up early tomorrow. Thank you again for the most amazing phone call I've ever had in my life. I'll call you tomorrow and we can discuss our plans for the weekend."

Hearing Julia shuffling around, he knew she was snuggling under her covers. "OK, we'll talk tomorrow. Good night, my knight."

They hung up and Jake laid there thinking about her. She was the most incredible woman he had ever known. He knew he'd told himself he wouldn't rush it, but he wanted her so bad. How amazing would it be to have her in his life, in his bed, in his world every day?

Waking up with her beside him and falling asleep with her in his arms every night. Talking about their day, making plans for the future. Just having someone to talk to about his girls, and all the craziness that went along with bring up teenagers would be great. Being there when Ian needed a man to talk to. How long would he have to wait to have her want him as much as he wanted her? He decided he'd just have to show her every chance he got, show her they were meant to be together. They had something special, he could feel it. Now all he had to do was make her feel it too.

Chapter 17

Julia couldn't help but smile as they pulled into the parking lot. The sounds and smells of the fair surrounded her and they hadn't even gotten out of the truck. She could hear the music coming from the midway, along with the squeals and screams of excited people as they spun and twirled. The oily smell of French fries and the sweet smell of funnel cakes filled the air. Memories of fairs from long ago came to her. Those memories were special, but today was about making new memories with Jake and both their kids.

She watched Jake as he got out of her SUV. Hailey was climbing out of the back seat, as was the rest for the crew they had brought. Ian, Wyatt, Dani and Rachel were all talking excitedly and it warmed Julia's heart to see them together. As she climbed out, she heard Wyatt's name being called from behind her. Turning, she saw a young girl and boy walking towards them. The girl was short, with long blond hair and a cute smile. She remembered meeting her once at Audrey's house. She also knew this was the girl Wyatt liked. Looking at him now she could see the telltale twinkle in his eye.

The guy with her had to be her brother, as he had the same face and eyes. He walked over to the group and as he passed Dani he did the most subtle of moves. He brushed his hand against hers and Julia watched as Dani kept her eyes away from him, but the shyest of smiles appeared on her face. Ahh, so this was him. Hailey had entrusted her with top secret information about the boy Dani liked. She had made her pinky swear she wouldn't tell Jake. She never broke a pinky swear, and she wouldn't start now.

She walked over to the group and put her hand on Dani's shoulder. Being as nonchalant as possible, she said, "Who are your friends?"

Dani's eyes grew wide as Ian turned to her and said, "Mom, this is Alyssa, and that's her brother Owen. Would you mind if we went ahead and bought our ride tickets?"

Julia opened her purse and handed him some money. "Sure, you go ahead."

Ian smiled at her and started walking with the group. Thinking she wasn't watching, he walked beside Rachel and bumped her shoulder. She looked at him and smiled. Ian thought she didn't know they were dating, but she totally knew. The lovesick look he got in his eyes every time he saw her had given him away.

Jake came up behind her, and, as if reading her mind, said, "Man, that boy has it bad for her." Then whispering into her ear, he said, "I know how he feels. I've got a bad case of that myself."

She turned to look at him and smiled. "Well, aren't you just a smooth talker?"

Before she could move, Jake leaned in and kissed her. It was very sweet and soft, the kind of kiss you could find yourself drowning in. He pulled away when loud whistling and calls of 'way to go Jake, she's a hottie', came from the direction of the kids.

"OK, if that's not a mood killer, then I don't know what is." Jake spoke low so that only she could hear.

They were about to head towards the entrance when saw Hailey watching them. Julia wasn't sure what to say or do. Jake cleared his throat as if he was about to speak when Hailey smiled. "You don't have to say anything, Dad. I know that you like her. I've known it for a while now; I've seen the way you stare at each other. Don't worry, I'm not upset. I think Julia's great, and you deserve someone like her. And you're a great guy, and she deserves to have someone as special as you in her life, too. So, let's not make this weird where you talk about life changing and how much you'll still love me even if you have someone new in your life. I know you love me and Dani, even when we drive you crazy. We've been waiting for a long time for you to find someone. Besides, Ian, Dani and I already talked about this and we're happy for you."

With that, Hailey turned and started running towards where Dani and Ian were waiting for her. Julia couldn't believe what she'd heard. Looking on, she watched as Dani put her arm around Hailey and Ian ruffled her hair as they were swallowed up by the crowd.

Glancing over at Jake she could see he was shocked too. Turning to look at her, he said, "Wow, she's like an old woman inside a ten-year-old body. How did she get so wise? Sometimes she amazes me."

Julia laughed. "I know. She's like Yoda sometimes. She has her own special force or something."

Jake stared at her with wide eyes. "Did you just use a Star Wars reference? It is official; you are the woman of my dreams!"

Shaking her head again, she started walking towards the entrance. "Come on Han, let's go see if we can find the Millennium Falcon; and yes, I know what that is." She could hear Jake gasp behind her. Not bothering to check over her shoulder she added. "If I'd known all I had to do to impress you was talk about Star Wars, I would've shown you my movie memorabilia all ready."

Jake was beside her in an instant. "You have Star Wars memorabilia? Oh baby, you were already a ten on the hotness scale, but now you're a fifteen – no, a twenty." Suddenly, he picked her up and spun her around before his lips came down on hers again. This kiss was a little hungrier than the last one, and she was now wishing they could go back to her truck for a little while.

From just up ahead she heard a familiar voice, "My, my, my, little brother, you keep kissing her like that in public, and Mama's going come over here and throw a pail of cold water on you."

They stopped kissing and looked over at Audrey, Luke, Jennifer and Grant, who were all smiling at them. Great, looks like most of the family had seen them kissing now. Just as she was going to say something, Lillian yelled out, "Jacob Michael Vincent, did I just see you kissing that girl like that in public? Don't be going and corrupting that sweet girl, Mister. If you want to kiss her you better wait until later and do it in private."

They watched as Jake's parents started making their way over. Fantastic, now the whole family had seen them kissing. Lillian came over and gave them both a hug. Al gave her a squeeze and a kiss on the cheek. Then they all made their way into the fair.

Concentrating hard, Jake tossed one more ring and the sound of it spinning around the bottle was music to his ears. He looked over to see Julia clapping her hands. If that didn't make him feel like a he-man, nothing would.

"What prize would you like, darlin'?" The carnie asked, as he watched Julia with just a little too much appreciation.

Julia looked the animals over and said, "Oh, I want the purple and blue dragon. He's adorable."

The carnie handed it over and smiled a little longer than necessary at her until he saw Jake giving him the eye. He quickly wiped off the smile and said, "Have a nice night, you two." Then he moved onto the next customer.

Julia held up the dragon so Jake could see it. "He is so cute. Do you know why I picked him?"

Shaking his head, Jake looked at her puzzled.

"Because I already have a knight, it only makes sense I have a dragon. Besides, he has the most beautiful eyes. He reminds me of you."

Jake's heart melted. He was having the best time. Earlier, he and Julia had taken a ride on the Ferris wheel, and he paid the guy twenty dollars to stop their chair at the top for a few minutes so he could get in a really good kiss. As it turned out, Julia was scared of heights, so she had clung to him like a second skin, allowing him to get even closer than he thought he would.

Next they went on the Scrambler and the ride went so fast she had been mashed up tight against him, with her face pressed into his chest. They found Hailey with the group and she wanted them to go and see the animals. Jake watched as Julia and Hailey giggled and cooed over all the baby animals, as they fed the little lambs and piglets and held bunnies and chirping little chicks. It was incredible watching them together, enjoying the simplest of things. He took their picture as each of them held up a fluffy bunny. To be honest, he had taken at least four dozen photos of Julia and the girls today and he was glad; now, Jake would be able to see her beautiful face anytime he wanted.

They were heading over to the amphitheater to listen to some music when Julia stopped suddenly, staring into the crowd. She seemed puzzled and Jake wondered what was going on.

Taking her hand and pushing her hair behind her ear he said, "Hey, you, what's wrong?"

She stared up at him and shook her head. "Nothing, I just thought I saw someone I knew from Chicago, but I must have been seeing things."

"This fair does bring people from as far away as Chicago."

She frowned. "No, I don't think he would come all the way here, it's not really his scene. I must have been mistaken."

They finally found a few seats so they could watch the show. Jake wandered over to the concession stand to get them something to drink. While he was standing in line, his father walked over.

"There's my boy! How's it going today? It looks to me like you're walking on cloud nine. To be honest, I don't think I've ever seen you this happy." His dad was beaming at him.

Jake smiled back. "It sure feels like cloud nine. And you're right; I don't think I've ever been this happy."

His dad reached over and squeezed his shoulder. "She is a great woman Jake, don't let her get away."

Jake laughed. "It is my intention to hold on as tight as I can."

Giving Jake's arm a gentle squeeze, Al headed off. It meant a lot to Jake that his dad thought so much of Julia. He already knew his mother was over the moon about his relationship with her. And now the kids had voiced their approval. He was thrilled everyone was glad to see them together. Now, all he had to do was convince Julia they were ready to be more. But he was getting a bit ahead of himself. He would just enjoy his time with her, let her ease into it and then tell her he wanted to be with her, in a more permanent way.

He got their sodas and made his way back to where Julia and Hailey were sitting, enjoying the show. He waved to several people as he went. Growing up in a small town meant everyone knew you and your business. When it came to his garage business it made him happy that people knew who he was. Word of mouth was his best advertising, but so were all the many community events. He sponsored floats and soccer teams, or, in the case of the fair, one of the cars in the derby.

It was Grant's turn to drive this year, but Jake secretly wished he could drive instead. He wanted to impress Julia with his driving skills. Maybe he should see if his brother would cut him some slack. Spotting the man in question, he made a quick beeline over to talk to him.

Grant smiled at him as he walked over and before Jake could even say anything his brother said, "You want to drive today, don't you?"

Jake gave him a puzzled look. "How could you possibly know I was going to ask that?"

Grant shrugged. "I just knew. You had that determined look on your face. I should say no, as it is my turn, but if I had a new lady to impress I'd want to drive too. Plus, Jenn hates when I drive. She says it freaks her out. So, you drive and I'll be your pit crew. And yes, you will owe me one."

Jake grabbed his brother and gave him a huge bear hug. "Thanks, man! And I do owe you. I'm going to tell Julia right now."

Before Jake could move away, Grant said, "The derby is in just over an hour so go and kiss your girl then get over there and do your pre-check. I'll be there shortly."

Racing back to Julia, Jake whispered in her ear, so as not to disturb the act that was on stage. "Hey, I'm going to drive in the derby for Grant. It starts in just over an hour, so I need to go and get ready. You all right with that?"

Julia stared at him and whispered back, "Is it dangerous?"

Jake was shaking his head then said, "No, it's just really about smashing into one another and whichever car is still running in the end is the winner. I've done this many times before. Come over soon so you can so you can get a good seat." He gave her and Hailey a quick kiss and was off.

He was excited he was going to be part of it. He'd always loved being the driver, smashing into cars and hearing the familiar crunch of metal. Plus, knowing Julia would be watching and cheering him on, it was going to be a blast.

Julia and Hailey made their way over to the grandstand so they could get a front row seat. This was Julia's first smashup derby. They met up with Ian and the others and told them Jake was driving, so everyone followed. As Julia glanced around, Jake's cheering section was getting pretty large.

She watched as the cars were lined up and drivers were doing their last minute inspections. As she waited, her mind drifted back to earlier when she thought she'd seen Anthony. It was bizarre to see someone out of context. It had certainly looked like him. The hair, profile and build were exactly as she remembered. But really, what would he be doing at a country fair in Heritage Falls? She just couldn't shake the feeling like a memory from her past had crept in.

Just then, the announcer came over the speaker stating the race would start in five minutes. She turned to see Dani and Hailey talking and pointing down to where their dad was about to get in his car. He was driving an orange Dodge Charger. They had it done up nice, but it wasn't fancy like the ones she saw on the walls of the garage. This one was strictly a derby car. Jake looked up at them and waved. They all waved back and Ian yelled out, "Good luck!"

Suddenly, a horn sounded and the cars were off. They had been split into two groups. As Julia watched, cars sideswiped and smashed head long into each other. Some cars were going in reverse, so as not to damage their front ends. Others seemed like they were tag teaming and ganging up on others. The sounds of crunching metal mixed with the cheers from the stands and the smell of exhaust. Jake's car sped up in reverse and he took out an old Chevette, totally crushing the front quarter panel. Next, he started driving forward, hitting the back end of a Lincoln Town Car that had definitely seen better days.

All of a sudden, a yellow Mustang came out of nowhere and hit Jake on the back bumper. Beside Ian she heard Wyatt say, "Aww, crap, that's Dylan's car. He is such an asshole." Wyatt seemed to realize he was in the presence of adults and he glanced at Julia saying, "Sorry."

Julia smiled and said, "You don't need to apologize, I completely agree. He is an asshole."

Wyatt smiled back at her before looking down at the field.

Ian was watching her. His eyes were sad and it was then she knew he must have heard about what had happened at the bar. She'd been careful not to mention it, but it was a small town and he was sure to hear it from someone else. She put her hand on his arm. "Don't worry about it, babe. I'm fine. I can take care of myself you know. You would have been proud to see how I dropped him like a bag of stones. So don't be sad, sweet pea. Your mom can handle herself."

Ian tried to smile, but said, "I just wish it had never happened."

She put her hand on his shoulder and squeezed. "Me too, babe."

They looked back at the field in time to see Jake chasing down Dylan's car. There was a blue Pontiac Firefly that cut in front of Dylan, making him swerve. Jake was then able to T-bone the Mustang. They watched as Jake backed up, and accelerated forward hitting it a second time, closer to the front end this time. Smoke started billowing out from under the hood of Dylan's car and flags went up. The announcer called a timeout while Dylan got out of his car. As he was walking off the field, he flipped Jake the finger and the crowd booed at the poor sportsmanship. Julia smiled and knew this particular smash had been done just for her. She glanced over and Ian was smiling too.

The derby continued and finally they were down to the last three cars. A grey Crown Victoria, an old Chevy wagon painted in rainbow colors, and Jake were all that remained. The wagon was already limping on a soft tire and the whole back end of the Crown Vic was crushed. Just as Julia was thinking it was over, the wagon started heading right for Jake and he wasn't backing down. At the last second, the wagon turned to the right and Jake hit it on the front quarter panel. Smoke puffed from the hood and the flag went up. The driver left the vehicle and it was down to two.

Jake seemed to be circling the last car, waiting for it to make a move. The Crown Vic made a valiant effort to catch Jake, but it swerved at the last second, hitting the side of a broken down car. It was quiet for a moment until a small fire started under the hood. As the crowd cheered, workers rushed out and got the driver, while fire extinguishers were used to put out the fire.

Jake was handed a flag and he drove around the field waving it, showing he was the victor. Julia was thrilled for him and the kids were ecstatic. They made their way down to the field and waited for Jake to come over. Grant and some guys were down on the field. Jake walked over to them as they all cheered and handed him a beer. He clinked his can with all of theirs and took a swig. Spotting her, he smiled and made his way over. His girls were calling to him and he stopped and gave each of them a hug and kiss. Ian and Wyatt were next getting fist bumps and handshakes. Lillian and Al were there to say congratulations as well. Guys were calling out his name and he was waving, but his eyes never left hers.

Finally, he was standing in front of her. He looked handsome, with his fancy racing overalls, his hair all messy, sexy with adrenaline still pumping through him. He was a sight to behold.

Julia smiled at him and said, "Congratulations, handsome. That sure was some show you put on. I've never seen anything like it."

Jake's voice was low as he said, "Did you notice I took out the asshole? That was just for you, baby."

Julia leaned in and said, "That was my favorite part. Thank you."

Jake moved in slowly and kissed her. There was a hunger in his kiss and Julia was wishing they were already at her place.

Pulling away, Jake stared into her eyes, and in a low whisper, said, "I can't wait to have you alone tonight. Let me go and get cleaned up and I'll meet you out front."

He headed off, eyes still lingering on her, while she and the group made their way back out to the fair. Lillian and Al said they were ready to head home and Hailey was going to leave with them since she was staying overnight. Dani was going to be staying at Rachel's house, so they were going to hang out for a while; Audrey and Luke would make sure they got home. Ian and Wyatt were going over with the girls to watch the horse show. Ian kissed her goodbye and told her he would see her tomorrow. Hailey gave her a quick hug, and then she was off with her grandparents.

As she waited alone for Jake, she thought she saw Anthony again. It was only a quick glimpse, but she could have sworn it was him. She wandered over to see if she could get another look, but whoever it was had disappeared. It was so weird. She must be seeing his doppelganger.

Just as she was turning around to head back to the front of the grandstand, someone grabbed her and pulled her into a side entrance. Whoever had grabbed her put their hand over her mouth, so she took the opportunity to bite down, hard. From behind her she heard a male yell, "Son of a bitch!"

He let go and she spun around. There stood Dylan, waving his hand around, distinct teeth marks pressed into his skin. She backed away and Dylan's eyes flashed. Grabbing onto her shoulders and keeping his crotch turned away from her, he pushed her up against the wall. Julia could feel his breath as his chest heaved, the smell of hard liquor like a cloud around him.

Sneering at her with a mean glint in his eye, he watched her close. "We're finally alone at last. You're definitely a feisty one, Julia. How about we go out to the parking lot and I show you my new Dodge Ram? The back seat is so wide I could fit two others in there with us. Trust me, I've done it."

He dipped his head forward as if to kiss her and Julia closed her eyes as she pushed with all her might. Unfortunately, he barely even budged. Just as she was about to scream, the pressure was removed from her shoulders. She opened her eyes just in time to see Jake punch Dylan so hard Julia was sure he was seeing stars. Jake was pulling his fist back before she could comprehend the move and he hit him hard again. He was winding up for a third as she yelled out, "Stop!"

Jake's eyes were filled with rage and she had to yell out again before he seemed to hear her. He didn't look at her, but he held off swinging his arm for another punch.

Jake glared at Dylan and gave his body a shake. "What the fuck is wrong with you, Dylan?! She doesn't want you! Why can't you seem to get that through your thick skull?"

Dropping his hold, Jake backed away and Julia could see it took all of his will power to do so. She looked back at Dylan and watched as he ran his hand over his face, as if trying to feel if anything was out of place. Holding the wall, he staggered up and stood on unsteady feet.

"What the hell, Jake? You know, you used to be cool. Now you're just an asshole. It's no wonder Franny left you. You're such a control freak, especially when it comes to your girls. She's their mother, and she deserves to see them, too. I'm glad I helped her get the information she needed, even if she didn't get to have the girls for the night! How can you treat her so bad?"

Jake stepped forward the same time as Julia, but she was the one to speak. "Help her how, Dylan? What did you tell her?"

Dylan wiped his nose on his sleeve, blood smearing on the fabric as he stared at her. She could see his face puffing out over one cheek. "I pointed out your kid to her. I figured she might be able to get some information from him since he wouldn't know who she was. She told me that if she knew when Dani's swim practice was, she could go and pick her up and take her for dinner. She said Jake here hasn't been allowing her to see her girls. That's not cool."

Surprising her, Jake laughed, not in humor, but in anger. "Dylan, it's not me stopping her, it's the law. She has screwed up so many times where the girls are concerned. She left them alone in a house with her recent boyfriend overnight. They didn't even know him. And thanks to you, she tried to come and pick up Dani while she was stoned. Stoned, Dylan! I don't give a flying fuck if she kills herself, but letting her go anywhere near the girls when she's like that, that's what's uncool, Dylan. If she had called me I would have told her when the swim practices were and she could come and watched as long as I was there. But instead you had her use Ian to get the information. I don't know what bullshit story she fed you, but apparently you fell for it."

Dylan was staring at Jake with a questioning look as his eye starting to swell shut. He hung his head as he said, "Shit. She told me it was you keeping her from the girls. I told her the last time I saw her to lay off the drugs, guess she didn't listen." Glancing up at Jake he shook his head. "I'm sorry, Jake, if I put the girls in danger. I had no idea Franny would do that. Shit!"

Jake just continued to glare at Dylan. Julia took the opportunity to have her say. "Dylan, I'm going to say this once, and only once, I'm not interested in you. I don't want to date you, I don't want to get to know you, and I definitely don't want you to proposition me for sex. You and I will never be a thing. If you come near me again, I will get a restraining order, and that's a promise. I've never shown any interest in you. If that hurts your pride, I really don't give a shit."

She could see the corner of Jake's lips quirk up in a slight grin. She spun towards the exit and heard Jake behind her as he said to Dylan, "Come near her again and she won't need to get a restraining order. I'll make sure to put you in a full body cast, asshole."

She walked out into the light and it felt good to take in a full breath. Her shoulders were tense and all she wanted was to get as far away from here as possible. Jake walked up behind her and wrapped his arms around her waist. That was what she needed. Taking another deep breath she could smell his scent and it calmed her.

Jake's voice was low as he asked, "Are you all right?"

She nodded. Then, feeling like she needed to lighten the mood she said, "Tell me, Mr. Vincent, how does it feel to be the Heritage Falls smashup derby winner?" She extended her hand as if she held a microphone.

Jake leaned over her shoulder like he was speaking into the mike. "Well it was a bit touch and go there for a while, but once I saw the smoke and fire I knew I had it in the bag. I owe all my inspiration to a pretty little lady who was cheering me on from the stands." He kissed her cheek and her heart was filled to bursting.

Whispering into her ear, Jake said, "I see the family has abandoned us, so let's make a run for it before we see anyone else we know. Oh, and one more thing…"

Julia watched as Jake walked in front of her and put his hand into his jacket pocket. Slowly, he pulled out not one, but two candy apples. "For you, milady. As promised."

She smiled wide and took the apples. "You remembered?"

Jake looked at her, puzzled. "Of course I remembered. I really want to watch you eat one. But let's wait until later; I don't want to have to pull off to the side of the road on the way home to ravage you."

As they made their way to the car, she was glad they weren't going to talk about what had happened with Dylan. It had been such a wonderful day before the incident she didn't want to taint it any further. All she wanted now was to go home and spend some time with Jake. Hopefully the evening would be just as great as the day.

Chapter 18

Damn it, she almost saw him, twice! He really hadn't expected to see her there. That had been his first stop and he was hoping to get some information, but not in this hokey little town. If he'd mentioned her name it would have been around town quicker than a bullet that someone was looking for her. You could get away with asking around in a big city because people didn't care. In a little town like this though, everyone knew everyone, and that was something he needed to avoid. Small communities made him itchy, so many busy bodies and no one minding their own damn business.

He and Gino had checked into a local motel and were trying to figure out what angle to use so as to not raise any suspicions. Even though he almost got caught today, it had given him a chance to see who she was hanging out with and what she was up to. He had a chance to see Ian from afar, too. He was filled with guilt for a few minutes while watching him. Losing his dad had to be tough, and Anthony would probably always feel bad for his part in that, but if Martin hasn't been so careless, he wouldn't have had to do it.

Now all he had to do was get the notebook and they could hightail it out of here. Anthony wondered again if she had taken the stuff and put it in the bank or if it was at the house. God, he hoped

she hadn't read it. He really didn't want to have to take her out, too –
Ian deserved to have at least one parent alive.

Glancing over at Gino, he said, "Tonight we scout the house and
see if we can find it there. Hopefully she is out at her new
boyfriend's place so we can have a good look around. We need to
keep our eyes open for bank documents just in case she put it in
another safety deposit box. Hopefully we can get in and out of this
town without alerting her or the authorities."

Gino studied him and said seriously, "And if she see us, then
what?"

Scratching his head, Anthony said, "I make up an elaborate lie
and hope she believes it. If we do see her then we'll learn if she
knows anything."

Nodding, Gino added, "You could always ask her for it. Then
you'll know for sure."

Anthony shook his head. "No, then we run the risk of her reading
it before she gives it to us. We can't take that chance."

"If that's what you want. We'll go tonight and see what we find. I
have her address and checked out the map to see what was around
there. It's out in the country, so hopefully her neighbors are far
away, and aren't the nosey kind."

Anthony propped himself up against the headboard of his bed
and watched the television for a while. All he wanted to do was get
that notebook and get the hell back to the city where he belonged.

Hours after they left the fair, Jake and Julia lay sprawled over her bed, not a stitch of clothing to be seen. Jake was staring up at the ceiling, feeling like he had just completed a marathon, but one he would be willing to run many more times. He couldn't get enough of this woman. Focusing on Julia, he found her lying on her stomach, eyes closed, her breathing just leveling out. Letting his eyes drink her in, he admired her shapely legs, and the sexy globes of her rear, up the smooth skin of her back, all the way to the sexy tumbled hair he had just had his hands buried in a little while ago. They had both already had an orgasm, but he felt his cock stirred to life again just thinking about her.

She was so generous as a lover and willing to try anything he asked. He had never had that before. Francine had been a cold fish in bed, especially once they were married. He was so glad to be with someone who understood that relationships were give and take.

Slowly moving towards her, Jake hovered over her body, starting to slowly kiss and lick down her back. Running his lips in soft circles at the base of her neck he could hear a low murmur of pleasure come from her. He knew she loved to be touched and kissed, and he loved pleasing her. As his lips skimmed along the edge of one shoulder blade, he moved slowly to the other. His tongue slid down her spine, tasting her skin and loving every inch. Eventually he was angled over her luscious ass and he cupped both cheeks and kneaded them in his hands. Surprising her, he bit one gently and Julia moaned. Oh, so she likes it a little rough! He was just fine with that. He bit the other cheek and watched her squirm. He let go and allowed his fingers to play along the valley, hearing her breathing speed up. Slowly he ran his fingers lower and lower until he could dip his fingers inside her already wet passage. Leaning down so he could watch as his fingers pleasure her, Julia pushed back on his fingers to urge them deeper. Well, if she wanted more, who was he to deny this beautiful woman?

Pulling her hips up and strategically placing his cock at her opening, he buried himself in her. Julia gasped and grabbed the sheets to help her gain some leverage so she could push back. She thrust herself up and back on her hands and knees, glancing over her shoulder at him. He wasn't sure why, but seeing her heavy-lidded stare was so sexy. She smiled and he thought his heart would explode. Leaning over, he kissed her as he drove in deep. Julia threw back her head and groaned out her pleasure. She felt so good and Jake reached under to rub her clit. As he added another layer of sensation, she moaned out his name. He loved hearing her say his name while he gave her pleasure. Feeling the tingle in his spine, he knew he was getting ready to explode. Shifting to an angle he had learned would push her into an orgasm, he started relentlessly stroking in and out of her.

Just as she slipped over the edge, his cellphone sounded on the bedside table. There was no way to stop this freight train, nor would he want to, so he let it go to voicemail. His orgasm felt like it was coming from his toes. The spirals of pleasured pain kept rolling through him. He would never have enough of her. He lay pressed against her back, making sure he didn't crush her.

They were both panting as Jake said, "I love… that. I really loved that." Shit, he almost said 'I love you'. Geez, he told himself he wouldn't rush it, and here he was almost blurting out those three little words that could possibly scare her away. Did he really love her? He lay there thinking about her and he knew he did – he knew deep in his heart that he had for a while, but he couldn't tell her yet. It was way too soon, and she still needed time to sort out what her own feelings were.

He heard the smile in her voice as she said, "I loved that, too. You are a machine, Mr. Vincent. A hot ass sex machine. Wow, you really know how to tire a girl out. Babe, did I hear your phone go off? Maybe you should check it in case it's the girls."

Jake kissed her shoulder and slowly eased himself out of her. The cool air on his cock made him want to push right back into all that wet warmth. But, he knew she was right. Crawling over to the bedside table, he grabbed his phone. Flipping over to lie on his back, he checked the last number. He didn't recognize it, but it was a local number. He checked his voicemail just in case it was something important. He could feel Julia crawl over and gently start pressing slow kisses along his chest. "Careful now. Isn't kissing how the last round started? Just keep in mind if you start something, we'll be finishing it."

He could hear her laughing as his voicemail connected. "Hey, Jake, it's Dwayne calling from the hospital. We brought Francine here this evening. We picked her up earlier for driving under the influence of narcotics and alcohol. Once we got her out of the car we realized she was bruised up pretty bad and she had cuts on her wrists. She was yelling saying she was going to drive off Falcon Canyon road. She said someone hurt her but she's refusing to tell us who. I know this is probably the last thing you need, but she was asking for you. Actually, she was screaming for you, so I told the nurses I would call and see if you would come up here and talk to her.

"She's under arrest, but we brought her to the hospital to get her checked over and bandage her cuts. We also wanted to have her under surveillance to keep her from harming herself. Once her bail is set she's going to need someone to take care of her. You might want to call her parents and see if they'll come and get her. If I'm being honest, Jake, Francine needs some serious rehab as this isn't the first time we've been down this road with her. There's no one to post bail for her, so I'm sure she'll ask you. Call me at this number or if you could come down to the hospital it would be much appreciated."

Jake deleted the call and stared up at the ceiling. Son of a bitch, why did that woman have to continue to be such a pain in his ass? If it was just him, he'd let her rot there, but as mad as the girls were at her, they wouldn't want that to happen. Francine really did need to go to a place where she could dry out, if she ever wanted to have a chance to have a relationship with the girls. Damn it, why did this have to happen now?

Letting out a big breath he could sense Julia knew something was wrong. She'd stopped kissing him and had started rubbing his chest, trying to comfort him. He took a minute to gather his thoughts, and then sat up so he could talk to her. She had a look of concern on her face, but she didn't push him to tell her what was going on.

"That was my friend Dwayne. He's a cop with the Heritage Falls Police Department. Francine got picked up for driving under the influence of drugs and alcohol. They put her in the hospital under surveillance because she had cuts on her wrists and was threatening to hurt herself. She also has bruises on her that look like she was beat up, but she won't say who did it. She's been asking for me, well, screaming actually. He called me because there's no one else to call. She's got no one to bail her out, so I'm going to need to call her parents. He also said he thinks she needs go to into rehab. This isn't the first time she's been picked up on a DUI."

Taking his hands and rubbing them over his face, he was pissed that he needed to be the one to handle this. "Had I known when I met her how taxing this relationship would be I never would have married her. But as exhausting as she is, and the fact that I loathe her most days, I don't like the thought of someone beating her up. The girls would hate to see her like that. Damn it, she needs to clean up her act or she will never have a relationship with them. Why can't she just grow up and take responsibility for her life? I blame myself sometimes because I made things too easy for her when we were together – I covered for her so many times until I just couldn't anymore. Her family tried to help her, but she ruined all her relationships with them and they've all turned their backs on her because no one trusts her any more. She just makes me so tired."

He fell back on to the bed, staring up at the ceiling. He remembered just forty minutes ago he had been staring at this same ceiling thinking his life was amazing with this special woman beside him. Now, he had to go and deal with his ex who couldn't get her shit together to save her life.

What was Julia going to think if he left right now to go and handle things for Francine? She had every right to be pissed at him. Hell, he'd be pissed if she needed to do the same. But at least he knew he didn't need to worry about that. Her husband was long gone and there was no baggage to deal with from him. His shoulders sagged as he continued to avoid her stare. "I'm sorry Julia, but I need to go down there and take care of this."

She was silent and this forced him to finally glance over at her. Sadness was in her eyes and it gutted him to see it. She nodded and said, "Yes, of course you need to. It sounds like Francine is going to need a lot of help. It's important for rehab patients, especially those with suicidal tendencies, to have a good support group, so she's going to need the girls and you more than ever now."

She nodded her head as if she were confirming something in her mind. Before Jake could take ahold of her hand she pulled away. She mumbled something about needing to get cleaned up. Julia went directly into the bathroom. Fuck! If that wasn't a sign she was upset, he didn't know what was. He sat there focusing on the door, and waited to see if she would come out. The sound of water running was all he could hear, and he knew she wouldn't.

Getting up, he grabbed his pants off the floor. He found his shirt halfway in the hallway, where Julia had pulled it off. They had frantically peeled their clothes off the moment they hit the landing. It felt like a cavern had opened up between them since that point and now he needed to go and deal with Francine.

Walking back to the bathroom door, he leaned his head against it. "Babe, I won't be too long. I'm just going to go and deal with this and I'll be right back."

There was a long silence and Jake didn't think she was going to answer. Just as he was about to say it again, she said, "Jake, it's getting late and you don't know how long you'll be. You should just go home after."

It felt like all the wind had been knocked out of him. He could hear the tremor in her voice as if she was on the verge of tears and it made him feel like shit that he was making her cry. "You know what? Maybe I'll just call Dwayne and tell him I can't come. I'll give him the number and he can call her parents." Even saying it he knew it was too late to tell her this option. He'd chosen to go and handle it in person – this wasn't going to fix anything.

Now he heard frustration in her voice as she said, "Just go, Jake. You need to take care of it, so just go." Then in a faint voice he was sure she thought he wouldn't hear she said, "She's obviously going to need you."

Damn it, why was Francine always ruining his life? God, he'd done so much for her in the years they were together and he'd been paying for it ever since. Clearing his throat as he could feel himself getting emotional as he said, "Babe, don't do this. You know how I feel about you. Don't be mad, ok?"

Julia sounded closer to the door as she said, "Jake, Francine needs some help and all she has is you and the girls here to count on. I'm not mad. Please, just go and take care of her." Then he heard her move away from the door and the sound of the shower turning on.

Fighting the urge to barge in there and demand they talk wasn't going to make this situation any better. He just needed to go and get this over with. Running his hands through his hair, he swore and grabbed his phone off the bed. He would be coming back here after since he needed to use her SUV as they had left his truck at his house. He couldn't leave her without a vehicle, not that it mattered because even if he had his own vehicle here, he was going to come back. He needed to make his feelings known to Julia.

He made his way downstairs and grabbed the keys off the side table. Slipping on his shoes, he switched off the alarm and unlocked the door. He didn't actually know how to reset it and he would need to get back in when he came back, so he left it turned off. Pulling the door shut behind him he was sure to lock it and then headed to the truck. This was the last thing he wanted to do and now Julia was upset or pissed off. He hoped she'd be willing to talk about this when he got back. She had to know he was in love with her. The only reason he was going to deal with Francine was because of the girls. She was their mother and as much as he despised her, he needed to get this sorted out and get her some help.

Pulling away from the house he headed to the hospital, but all her could think about was Julia.

Julia stood under the spray of the shower and let the water bead off her back. Her hands covered her face as tears streamed from her eyes. She was trying to keep her sobs quiet, but she hoped he was already gone so he wouldn't hear. It had been so long since she had felt this kind of heartbreak. Oh God, it hurt so bad. When she'd lost Martin, that pain was a different kind of deep ache, the kind that had no way to be healed except with the passage of time. But this pain felt like it was slicing though her like a knife, because as much as he didn't want to hurt her, he had. She tried to be understanding of his situation, but she felt like he was making a choice, one where she would be on the losing end.

What if she lost him? If Francine needed help with rehab and depression she could see Jake feeling responsible for her. He would want to work on getting her better so she could have a relationship with the girls. And how could she blame him for that? But it just hurt because he said he didn't want to be part of Francine's life, but apparently if she needed him he would help her.

Maybe it wasn't fair for her to be upset, but damn it, they had just started to get to know each other and now that might all come to an end. Julia also felt guilty because somewhere in her heart she felt maybe Francine was just going to try and use him like she had done before. Hadn't he been the one to say she was a user? And where was this so-called boyfriend? Was he the reason she was all bruised up? Julia didn't like the thought of anyone being in that kind of situation and she felt sorry for Francine if that was the case. Maybe Julia was wrong and Francine did truly need Jake. She felt like she had just started to see a future and now it was being pulled away.

Her anger flared up when she thought about him saying, 'I'll call Dwayne back.' She was angry because either Francine needed him or she didn't and it felt like he was just saying it to placate her. She had wanted to yell out, 'Too late!' but she didn't want him to come in and talk to her. He'd already made up his mind to go. He didn't need to do her any favors.

The final straw for her was when he actually thought he was going to come back tonight. Her head and heart were feeling too much turmoil to want to rehash this later. She needed some time and distance to sort out what she felt. Julia knew what she'd been feeling for Jake and she had been headed for the deep end of the love pool for sure, but, now she needed to get some perspective on their relationship.

The more she thought about the whole situation, the more she got lost in her head and emotions. She was willing to deal with Francine when it came to the girls and what was best for them. But Julia would be damned if she would sit around and act like it was fine if that woman was going to wedge herself into their relationship. Julia was a level-headed person, but even she wasn't willing to play this kind of game with her heart. And she couldn't help but feel like this situation with Francine was part of some game. She feared Jake would get there and she would use his emotions against him. He said he knew she was a user, but Francine was a seasoned professional who knew how to play the game. Julia prayed she was wrong about that.

Suddenly, the pain in her heart was too much and she knelt down on the floor of the shower and cried harder. As unreasonable as it might be, she felt betrayed. She had finally felt ready to move on, that this was a relationship that could last, one they could build on. Now it felt like it was dissolving before her eyes and washing down the drain with her tears.

After sitting there for ten more minutes the water went cold and she turned it off. Drying herself off, she walked back into the bedroom. The sight of the rumpled bed had her shaking her head. She couldn't sleep in here with the bed like that and she had no energy to strip and remake it. Plus, the smell of sex still hung thick in the air and she couldn't bear to be reminded of something she may have just lost.

Grabbing a nightgown, she headed towards the guest room. It had a comfy double bed with a pretty blue and grey comforter on it. She wrapped her hair in a towel and crawled under the covers. She was cried out and drained; her body sagging from the physical exertion from the times she and Jake had made love. She didn't want to think about that, even though she could feel how sore her muscles were. She felt emotionally rung out. Julia needed to sleep and forget about the situation.

Chapter 19

Jake pulled into the visitor parking lot at the hospital and stared at the front doors. Why was he here? Why had she been asking for him and not her new boyfriend? She couldn't honestly think he gave a shit about what happened to her after everything she had put him through? Sighing, he pulled the door handle and made his way to the front entrance.

The Heritage Falls Hospital wasn't a very large facility, but it took a few minutes to locate Francine's room. The three-level building was just a series of hallways running out like spokes on a bicycle, with the main nurses' station centralized in the middle on the second and third floor. Jake had always hated hospitals; the pungent ammonia smell mixed with sickness and dying carnations, the pale green and blue walls and the blinding glare of the florescent lighting. No wonder people hated hospitals. Maybe if they made them more inviting people wouldn't mind visiting.

As he rounded the corner, he saw Dwayne slouched over outside of the room. Jake laughed to himself. Time had not been good to Dwayne. He'd lost most of his hair and had filled out with a fair size pot belly. They had gone to school together, but Dwayne looked like he was at least ten years older than Jake. It must have been all those free pastries and not enough physical activity.

He walked up to Dwayne and nodded. Jake didn't even really know how to start this conversation so he waited for Dwayne to tell him what he needed to know.

"Hey, Jake, thanks for coming down. She was pretty belligerent when we picked her up. She refused to cooperate with the nurses when we first got here until Patty threatened to put her in a strait jacket and gag. It didn't shut her up, but she definitely toned down the language after that. She was better still after we agreed to call you. I still haven't been able to find out why she has the bruises, but I have a few other officers out asking questions so we can get to the bottom of this. You can go on in when you're ready to talk to her. Then, we can call her parents and see what they want to do."

Jake didn't bother voicing his opinion; he just wanted this over with. Dwayne opened the door to her room. He could see Francine sitting up on the bed beside the door, staring up at the ceiling. As expected, as soon as she saw him, she started crying and saying how the police had it all wrong – she was the victim and she wasn't drunk. Even from his position by the door, with over ten feet of distance between them, he could smell the booze fumes rolling off of her. She sat up straighter and reached out her hand to him.

Keeping his temper in check he studied her. She looked like she hadn't slept in days. Her hair was dirty and her skin had a dull paleness to it that he had never seen. Bloodshot eyes stared back at him from a face he hardly recognized. When they'd seen her at the bar and again at the school she didn't look like herself, but at least she seemed healthier, and definitely cleaner. Watching her now, all he felt was pity. He glanced down at her hand and without reaching out he said, "Why did you want to see me Francine? You can't possibly think I'm going to bail you out. You should have called Mike or Marc or whatever his name is."

She looked at him, tears streaming down her face and said in a heavy, slurred voice, "He's out of the picture. He said he didn't like me going out all the time, so I gave him the boot. Told him I was going back to my husband because he knew how to treat a lady."

Jake stared at her as all the hatred and anger he felt earlier came back. "You told him what?! I can barely stand the sight of you, let alone be with you. Why the hell would you think I would be willing to do that? I agree with him, you do go out and party too much, and I don't need the girls to see that shit."

Her eyes became wild as she screamed, "They're my girls, too! You wouldn't have them without me. You owe me for giving you those sweet baby girls. All you do now is take them away. What kind of father are you anyway, hanging out with that snobby bitch and her son? She's not the one for you, Jake. The girls need their rightful mother!"

Jake stepped forward and she leaned back as the fury was plain on his face. "I told you before never to call her anything, didn't I? She is a wonderful woman and if you wouldn't have gotten yourself arrested, I would be with her right now. Instead, I have to come down here and deal with your shit. And what kind of father am I? I'm the kind that cares about his kids. The kind that goes out of his way to make sure to set a good example for them and take care of them the way they need to be taken care of. Julia has taken better care of them in the short time she's been in their lives then you have in the last nine years. Don't pull this crap, Francine. If you'd been capable of being responsible and not jump in bed with every Tom, Gary and Dylan, then perhaps things would be different, but here we are. As far as the drinking and drugs go, you need help Francine, but it's not going to be me that helps you. You have parents for that."

Francine focused on him and tried to put on a sweet face, all the while she was sweating and her hands trembled. "Come on, Jake, you know you still love me. You've always loved me. Remember what it was like when we were in high school? We had such great times. We could have that again. Just get me out of here and we can start over, just you, me and the girls."

Jake couldn't help it. He laughed without humor. "You've got to be joking. High school was a long fucking time ago, Francine, and I don't think we remember it the same way. I spent most of my time trying to keep you out of trouble. So no, we will never go back to that time, and as for loving you... I can't even remember loving you. I'm going to call your parents and they can decide what rehab center to send you to. I'm done Francine. Don't call for me again, because I won't come. You need help. The kind of help you can only get in a place that deals with your issues. Maybe once you clean up and get control of your life, you can see the girls. Until then, I don't want to hear from you."

As he moved towards the door, Jake heard Francine call out, "Jake, wait, I need some money! I owe this guy a lot of dough for giving me some stuff. I needed a fix and I promised him I'd pay him. He found me tonight and when I told him that I didn't have his money he hit me and told me if I didn't have the money for him by tomorrow I'd be sorry."

Jake saw red as he turned back to her. She was staring at him, her last hope. But the truth was becoming clearer by the minute. She didn't want him back, she wanted him to pay her debts and save her from some asshole drug dealer. She was in trouble and he was the only person she felt would help save her. Damn it.

Letting out a huge sigh, Jake said, "Ah, the truth comes out. Well, Franny, that's not my problem. Guess you shouldn't have given up on your boyfriend so quickly. Maybe if you'd called him he'd come and help you out."

He grabbed the handle. She yelled from behind him, "He kicked me out and told me never to come back! I did call him and he said he wouldn't come!"

Shaking his head he called out over his shoulder, "That makes him the smart one then, doesn't it?" As the door closed behind him he could hear her screaming profanities at him.

Pulling out a slip of paper from his shirt pocket he jotted down the number for Francine's parents. Dwayne stood as he handed it over. "Here's the number for her parents. I'm not staying while you call. You should have told me you called her boyfriend. I have no legal connections to her, with the exception of the girls. Her parents can find a rehab center for her."

He was just about to leave when he glanced at Dwayne. "She got those bruises from a drug dealer that she owes a lot of money to. That's why she wanted to see me, to once again pull her sorry ass out of the fire. I suggest you get the name from her, he doesn't sound like the kind of guy you want to leave out in the general public. I won't come back to see her, so if she asks, tell her she can go to hell for all I care."

Dwayne looked at Jake with understanding in his eyes. "Sorry about this, Jake. Marc said he couldn't handle her either. Said she'd drained him dry, so he couldn't have posted bail even if he wanted to. Thanks for the number. I'll call them and see what they want to do. What should I say if they ask me to contact you?"

"Tell them if they ever want to see their grandkids again, they better get off their asses and handle this themselves. She's their child. I've done my time babysitting her and I'm done."

Letting out a breath, Jake walked down the hall, away from a screaming Francine. He heard one of the nurses say it was going to be a long night and Jake couldn't help but agree with her. Making it down to the first floor he pushed the door open to the cool night air. The stuffy, oppressive feel of the hospital was swept away with the slight breeze coming from the north.

She had only called him because the other guy wouldn't come and she was in trouble. Typical Francine move. She was never going to hurt herself; she was trying to get sympathy to get what she wanted. She played the game and Jake fell for it, again. And to top it off he'd hurt Julia. Shit. Julia must have known what would happen.

She probably knew what Francine was trying and do, and he didn't even think before he came running. No, he just jumped into Julia's truck and rushed down here. Now he was standing here feeling like a first class asshole.

His heart squeezed again at the thought of hurting Julia. She was such a wonderful person. Why should she just sit around waiting for him to handle all the crazy shit his ex-wife got into? God, he hoped she would understand. He needed to fix this, and fast.

Jogging over to the SUV he got in. He was heading back there even if she wouldn't talk to him. If it took him sleeping out on the porch until she spoke to him, he'd do it. He raced back as fast as he could. He never should have left, he knew that now, and he would never do it again. Please say she didn't hate him. She was meant to be in his life. She was the only one he wanted and he would do whatever it took to win her back.

Anthony peeked in the front porch window while Gino scoped out around back. They had gotten lucky, as there was no sign of a vehicle in the driveway. She must be staying overnight at her boyfriend's house. It had been strange to see her with that other guy. The new guy had been so different from Martin. He was quite large, with broad shoulders, and if Anthony was honest, a little intimidating. Martin had been tall, but muscular he was not. He had been average, to say the least, land Anthony had always wondered what Julia had seen in him. She'd always been a beautiful woman, with a sexy body and a sharp mind. It was her sharp mind that had kept him from trying to claim her himself. Woman like that were too inquisitive and he never would have been able to keep his lifestyle a secret from her. No, he would stick with his variety of goomars. They all had their specialties and that kept it interesting for him.

They had pulled their car around to the other side of the barn so if someone did drive in, they could just hide out until it was safe to leave. Anthony walked up and checked the front door. It was locked, but that had never stopped him before. He wondered if she had a security system. Living out in the sticks, he hoped she felt safe enough not to need one. Not that it would matter because he had tools to take care of that. Taking his lock pick out of his pocket he had the door open within ten seconds. He pushed it open and could see the alarm on the wall but it wasn't armed – someone had failed to turn it on, and for that Anthony was grateful as it saved him some time. He made his way in and shut the door. He pulled a flashlight out of his pocket and started to explore the place.

The house was really nice inside. She must have bought new furniture as he didn't recognize anything he saw. Glancing around the front room he didn't see anything that would provide any information on where the notebook might be. He made his way to the kitchen and flipped through a pile of bills sitting on the counter. Nothing of interest there either. He knew he needed to find her office. That's where she would keep her important stuff. Hopefully, she had a safe in there and had kept all the stuff from the safety deposit box. Moving down the hall, he finally found the office and made his way over to the paintings on the wall. Checking each one, he found the safe behind the third.

Anthony had always prided himself on being an excellent thief, which included having the best tools for the job. Pulling out a special case, he withdrew a rare earth magnet wrapped in a sock. It was very powerful and could hurt you if you didn't handle it properly. It could open just about any safe in no time. He attached the magnet to the upper part of the door and within three seconds he turned the knob and it opened. This was why anytime he bought a safe is was commercial grade, not the cheap ones.

Opening it up, he found a few folders and a bunch of USB keys and CDs. This must be all her book stuff. On the top shelf she had an envelope with about three hundred dollars and some contracts. Then, he finally found something. There was a document from the First National Bank in downtown Heritage Falls. On it he saw she had moved her accounts and had also signed for a safety deposit box. OK, so now he knew which bank. Taking note that is was box number 235, he searched for a key inside the safe. Nothing. Not a single key inside. Actually, that was smart of her to put it in a different place, but damn, it was a pain in the ass for him.

Putting everything back into the safe mostly the way he'd found it, he locked it back up and pushed the picture back in place. He started to search her office desk to see if he could find the key, but no luck. She must have another hiding place for things like that. He had a sinking feeling he wasn't going to be able to get what he needed without talking to her. Honestly, it was the last thing he wanted, but there just seemed no other way now.

He was just turning back to the hallway when he heard the front door open. It was probably just Gino. Heading towards the hall the light came on in the kitchen. Damn it, that wasn't Gino! Tiptoeing to the edge of the doorway he peered around to see Julia's boyfriend. Fuck, he looked even bigger up close. Ducking down, Anthony crouched low to the floor and hoped this guy wasn't going to be a problem. He heard the fridge open and then the jingle of keys and something that sounded like a glass being put on the counter. Apparently, the big guy was thirsty.

Anthony was getting impatient. He tipped to the right to see if he could locate the boyfriend, but ended up knocking over a bag that had been sitting by the door. Shit! He scrambled back, hoping the boyfriend would brush it off. But soon he heard footsteps coming down the hall. Scanning the area close to him, he saw a huge piece of rock on display on the shelf beside his head. Grabbing it tight in his hands, he waited. He didn't want to shoot the guy if he didn't have to. That would be way to much clean up to do, so he would just knock him out. The steps got closer and Anthony lifted the rock over his head. When the big guy came into focus, he bent down picking up the bag that had fallen. That's when Anthony hit him as hard as he could on the back of the head. The guy groaned and slumped to the hardwood floor. Ouch, that was going to leave a mark.

He heard the front door open and Gino whispered, "Anthony, you OK?"

Anthony responded and came out to see Gino making his way down the hall. The two of them picked up the boyfriend and struggled to get him into a chair. They proceeded to tie him up with some butcher's twine they found in one of the kitchen drawers. Then they blindfolded him, so if he did wake up he wouldn't be able to identify them.

As they finished up with the boyfriend, Anthony saw Gino stare at something on the counter. Anthony looked and it took him a few seconds to process what he was seeing. It was Julia's purse. If that was here, than that likely meant she'd been in the house the whole time. Letting his head fall forward, he knew she'd probably just heard the whole thing. God damn it! Gino stared at him and nodded. They knew they had to go and find her before she had a chance to slip out of the house, if she hadn't already. Luckily he had some leverage. If she didn't cooperate, he'd shoot her new man.

An unfamiliar noise woke Julia. She lay there trying to figure out what the sound was. Maybe Jake had decided to come back. Well, he could sleep on the couch for all she cared. There was no way she wanted to discuss Francine now. She heard footsteps go into the living room and then it was quiet. Then they went into the kitchen. Maybe he was thirsty. She listened and thought she heard him go into her office. That was strange. Why would he go in there? All her important papers and stuff were locked away, but still that seemed a bit private and she didn't think they were quite at that stage where he would have the right to look through her private stuff. No, he wasn't the type to do that, anyways.

Maybe he was just making sure the house was locked up. That had to be it. And really, why did she care? It wasn't like they would be sleeping together tonight anyway, so he could do whatever he wanted. She had told him not to come back.

She lay there waiting and then she heard the front door open. That was strange – did he just leave? No, she could hear him now in the kitchen again and the sound of keys being put on the counter. How did he get from her office at the back of the house to the front door without her hearing him? It was an old house and the floors would squeak in certain places.

The fridge opened and she could hear the sound of something being poured. She had made a pitcher of iced tea earlier that day because she knew it was his favorite. Now, she wished she hadn't bothered. She apparently was way more concerned about him then he was about her since he couldn't wait to run off to his ex-wife. No, she wasn't going to think about it. It would just make her angry and upset again.

There was a thumping noise that came from her office and she wondered how Jake had gotten back there from the kitchen so fast. It was then she heard someone making their way from the kitchen. It almost sounded like... were there two people downstairs? Listening to the movements, she suddenly felt something was very wrong. Sitting up slowly in the guest bed, she listened.

There was a groan and a heavy fall and something told her that had been Jake. Oh my God, oh my God! She held her hand over her mouth to keep from calling out. Was he all right? The implications settled into her when she realized someone else was in her house. But why hadn't they come up to find her? Julia's mind raced and then it hit her, the truck! Jake had to take her truck to the hospital as she had picked him up today. Whoever it was probably thought no one was home. She sat there for a second trying to wrap her mind around what to do next when she heard the front door open again. Oh God, now there was someone else in her house! She slipped the covers down and was just about to climb out of the bed when she heard a whispered voice say, "Anthony, you OK?"

Anthony? As in Anthony Farachelli? Then she heard a different voice say, 'yeah'. Oh my God. That was Anthony's voice. But why was he here, sneaking around her house? This made no sense at all. If he wanted something, why didn't he just call her? They had been good friends up until he disappeared. Why would he break in?

She could hear them dragging something across the floor, presumably Jake, and she prayed to God that he was all right. She struggled to decide what to do. If she could make it into Ian's room she could sneak out on the second floor porch and climb down the trestle. Damn her phone was in her room. There was no way she was going to go back to her room as she would have to go past the top of the stairs and that was too risky. Think, Julia, think! Then, she remembered Ian had a walkie talkie that he and Wyatt used. It was a good set that could travel over fifty miles. She could grab it and see if she could call out to Wyatt or try a different channel to see if she could reach someone.

Julia could hear the men rummaging around in the drawers and she quickly got out of the bed and tiptoed to the door. She was careful not to step on any spots that would squeak. Glancing out into the hall and seeing no one, she quickly made it to Ian's room. He hadn't cleaned his room in a few days and there was stuff on the floor. She was careful not to step on anything that would give her away. She could see the walkie talkie in the charger and gave a silent thank you that it wasn't on the floor somewhere. Grabbing it, she walked over to the sliding door that opened to the porch. Sliding it open as quietly as possible she opened it just enough to get through, then closed it behind her. She made her way over to the side of the house on the opposite side from the kitchen. As Julia peeked over, she could see the trestle. It had been a lot of years since she had climbed down the side of a house, but Jake's life was at stake and she didn't think too hard about it – she just started climbing down.

Moving as fast as possible, she was part way down when it felt like the trestle was starting to detach from the side of the house. Thinking it might be less noisy to jump she looked down, but couldn't see anything. No, she would just have to take it slow. She took two more steps down and could feel it come loose. With blind faith she jumped and hit the ground. It was sloped on this side of the house so she hit at an angle and pain radiated through her ankle. She stifled a scream. Damn it, that really hurt! Getting up as best she could, she limped to the front of the house. There was no other vehicle in the driveway, so how did Anthony get here?

Contemplating for a second she almost started to head to Alfred and Lillian's house. But with the way her ankle was feeling it would take her forever to get there. She decided the best place to hide was the barn. From there she would call Wyatt on the walkie talkie. Careful to stay in the shadows, she limped over. She took the long way around so as not to be seen from the house. There was a door on the paddock side, so she climbed through the fence and made her way into the barn.

Julia had only been in here a couple of times since they moved in. Her and Ian had scoped it out and had been talking about maybe getting a couple of goats, but nothing had come of it yet. She felt her way along the wall and stopped when she felt a bale of hay. Sitting down, she switched on the walkie talkie. It was loud and she quickly turned down the volume. She had used one a few times before so she knew how it worked. Pressing the button on the side, she whispered as loud as she could, "Wyatt, Ian, do you read me?" There was nothing but static. She tried again, "Wyatt or Ian or anyone do you hear me, please?" Nothing happened. Crap. Fine, she would try a different channel. Fiddling with the dial she listened to see if she could hear anyone. This seemed to be taking forever until she heard a faint voice on one of the channels. Pressing down, she said in a low voice, "Hello, is anyone there, can you hear me?"

There was silence until a young boy's voice came over the speaker. "Yes, I can hear you."

Relief filled Julia. She spoke again. "Oh, thank God! Who are you?"

The voice came again. "I'm not supposed to talk to strangers."

Julia smiled and said, "You're right, you shouldn't talk to strangers, but I'm in trouble and I need your help. My name is Julia Witmore, what's yours?

There was more silence and then he spoke again, "David."

Julia listened to the noise outside the barn to see if Anthony had come out of the house. When there was nothing she said, "David, can you go and get your mom or dad?"

There was static and then David said, "But I'll get in trouble for playing with the walkie talkie. I don't want to get in trouble."

Julia leaned her head back on the barn wall and decided there was no time to be reasonable and she would promise him the moon if he did what she said. "David, sweetheart, I know you don't want to get in trouble. But if you do me this huge favor, I will get you anything you want."

She could hear the excitement in David's voice, "Really, anything I want?"

Inside she felt horrible because she should scold him and say how bad people would promise him things and then hurt him, but she couldn't think about that now. "Yes, David. Anything you like!"

David spoke so quickly she could hardly make it out. "I want to ride in a derby car. We saw them at the fair today and I really wanted to ride in one."

Smiling Julia said, "David today is your lucky day. I can make that happen. So run and get your mom or dad. I need you to be my hero. Can you do that?"

David said in a small voice, "I would be a hero?"

Julia was straining to hear any sound outside. "Yes, David, you would. Hurry, please."

Then there was silence on the other end. God, she hoped he was running. Her heart was in her throat as she focused again on the sounds outside the barn. Then there was a man's voice on the walkie talkie, "Hello?"

Julia was relieved, but kept her voice to a whisper. "Hello, my name is Julia. I live out on Portage Road, 2250, in the old Bulger place. There are men in my house and I need you to call the police."

The man on the other end said in an angry voice, "Is this some kind of joke?"

Julia covered over the speaker so it wouldn't be so loud "No, sir, this is no joke. My name is Julia Witmore and my boyfriend, Jake Vincent, has been hurt. Two men are in my house. One of the men is named Anthony Farachelli. I've snuck out of the house and I'm hiding in the barn. Please call the police."

The man on the other end said, "Wait, did you say Jake Vincent? Julia, it's me, Ted Delanie."

Yes! Thank God for small towns. She remembered Ted from the date Jake had taken her on.

Ted then said, "I'm dialing the police as we speak. Hang in there Julia, help is on the way."

Julia let out a sigh of relief again until she heard movement outside. Turning the volume down she whispered, "I think they found me, Ted! Tell them to hurry." Then she buried the walkie talkie in behind the hay bale and moved deeper into the barn.

She moved into the shadows as she heard footsteps beside the door she had come through. Pushing herself in behind some other hay bales, she hoped they didn't hear her. The door opened and she saw a flash of light. Oh no! Julia made herself as small as possible, hoping if they didn't see her they would leave.

The beam of the flashlight moved back and forth over the area and she held her breath. The light eventually disappeared and the barn door closed. She waited as she heard footsteps retreating. Should she run now or go back and get the walkie talkie to check in with Ted. It was dark and it would be a struggle to run, especially with her ankle aching like it was. But if she waited they might come back and find her. Yeah, her best chance would be to get out to the road and try and keep to the trees if possible. Now was her chance. She could make it out and hopefully someone would come by.

Pulling herself out from behind the hay bales, she made her way to the door. She thought about getting the walkie talkie, but she decided she didn't want to get caught with it. They would know she'd called for help and that might make the situation worse. Opening the door slowly she stuck her head out to see if she could see anything. That's when someone grabbed her.

Arms came around her body and crushed her in a bear hug. Hot breath in her ear said, "Hello Julia, long time, no see." Then he put a hand over her mouth and she knew she was in trouble.

Chapter 20

Jake's head throbbed as he tried to lift it. He struggled to open his eyes and realized he was blindfolded. Moving his hands, he could feel that they were bound behind his back and he was tied to a chair.

He faintly made out sounds around him, but it almost sounded like he was underwater. Trying to take stock of his body he felt sore on his left side, but didn't know why. His head felt like someone had hit him with a baseball bat.

Where was he? He struggled to remember what he was doing before waking up. He had the faint taste of sugar on his tongue. Why? When had he had something sweet? He took in a breath and could smell something floral and berries. Julia. That was Julia's smell. Her hair always smelled so good. He was at Julia's house. Yes, he'd come back. He went to the hospital to see Francine and then came back. Damn Francine. She was always turning everything in his life upside down.

He remembered he'd come back in the house and had been thirsty. Yeah, he was thirsty and he'd gone to the fridge and saw iced tea. Julia had made it just for him. He didn't know why he thought that, but he knew it. Yes, iced tea, and it was really good. Then there was a sound in the office. He had walked down the hall and there was a bag lying on its side in the doorway. He'd bent down to pick it up. That's when he'd felt a sharp pain in his head. Someone had hit him. Did Julia hit him with a baseball bat? Was she scared or was she mad at him? She didn't give the impression she was the violent type. Wow, that girl could hit! With a swing like that she should be playing for the Cubs.

Jake tried to laugh, but that just sent shooting pain through his head. No, there was no way she would have done that. No, something was very wrong. There was no way in hell Julia would have done this to him. For obvious reasons, she wouldn't have been able to lift him into the chair if he was out cold. Things just weren't adding up. He heard a faint sound. Was that Julia's voice? She sounded muffled. Sitting still, Jake decided he would pretend to still be knocked out. He might learn more about the situation if someone thought he was unconscious. He laid his head back down against his chest and waited for whoever had done this to him to come in the house.

It took a few minutes, but soon he heard Julia struggling to speak. It sounded like someone was covering her mouth. His blood started to boil at the thought of anyone touching her. He would kill whoever it was. She was his and no one was to lay a finger on what was his. He knew that was a very caveman point of view, by he didn't care. A door opened and heavy foot falls came towards the kitchen, and he held as still as he could. The sounds of someone struggling to hold onto her made him, once again, want to rip someone's head off, but he didn't move.

He could hear the sound of a chair being scraped across the floor and an out-of-breath voice say, "Grab the twine." Shuffling feet and Julia's muffled voice was all he could hear. They were tying her up and his anger had him almost shaking.

They must have removed whatever it was they had covering her mouth, because finally he heard her speak. "What the hell is this all about, Anthony? Jesus Christ, you come to my house in the middle of the night and break in. I haven't seen you in over a year-and-a-half and now I see you like this. It was you I saw you at the fair today, wasn't it? What could you possibly want from me that you couldn't just ask me for? We were friends, for Christ sake. Why would you do this?"

Jake heard a man's voice on the other side of the kitchen rummaging through the drawers, dropping things all over the floor.

"I'd rather not say Julia, but I need the key to your safety deposit box. I believe there's something in there that belongs to me."

Waiting for Julia to ask her next question, Jake was just as curious as she was. "My safety deposit box? There really isn't a lot in there, just some coins, folios and notebooks that Martin put in there."

Anthony's voice was suddenly closer to her as he said in a deadly whisper, "You didn't look through that stuff did you?"

Julia, as if sensing Anthony's anger said, "No. When we moved, I just put everything in a cardboard box and when I got to the new bank, I put the whole thing inside. I didn't want to deal with anymore of Martin's stuff."

He could hear the man let out a breath. Then, he said, "Just tell me where the key is and I'll be out of your hair."

There was a long pause from Julia. Suddenly, Anthony yelled, "If you want your boyfriend to live, I suggest you tell me where the damn key is, Julia!" There was a clicking sound, like that of a revolver spinning to a new chamber.

Holy shit, this guy was going to shoot him! Ok don't panic. Just think, Jake, think! They would get out of this.

Julia said in a small voice, "If I tell you where it is, how do I know you won't kill us both anyway?"

Anthony's laugh was sinister. "Damn, Julia, I always knew you were too smart for your own good. Guess we each have something at stake here. For you, it's the life of the meathead here, and for me, it's the possibility of going back to prison. Yes, that's where I've been, Julia – that's why I disappeared. So, if you don't mind, I would love to just get that key and walk away. Where is it?"

Jake was trying hard to act unaffected, but this guy was going to shoot them. He was trying to figure a way out of this when Julia said, "Anthony, I don't care what's in the box. That's your business and it obviously has something to do with Martin. Why didn't you just say, 'Hey Julia, Martin was holding onto something for me, so can you let me into the box so I can retrieve it?' I might have thought it was weird, but then you would have had whatever it is you need, and we wouldn't be here trying to negotiate for our lives."

From the other side of the room another voice spoke. "I told you that you should have just asked her, Anthony. Now we're here in another stupid, shitty situation."

Anthony yelled again. "Shut up, Gino!" Then, he spoke to Julia. "I'm not kidding around Julia, tell me where it is!"

Jake could hear the tickling of the clock that hung over the stove. Time stretched and Jake was busy trying to get his hands free of the twine on his wrist. He barely moved and he hoped no one was focused on him.

When Julia spoke, it was quiet. "The key won't do you any good, Anthony. You aren't the owner of the box and I have to sign for it. Unfortunately, you still need me."

Jake could hear Anthony move closer to him as he said, "But I don't need him."

Julia was silent for a moment, then she said in a strained voice, "If you kill him, you might as was well kill me too, because there's no way in hell I'll tell you where the key is."

Jake heard Anthony move towards her and the sound of a loud thump and a gasp filled the room. Jake couldn't stop himself when he yelled out, "Keep your fucking hands off her!"

Panting, he waited for a blow to come his way. Instead, the blindfold was ripped off so roughly his head throbbed. The light was blinding and he squinted against the piercing pain.

Focusing on Julia, he could see her lip was bleeding and a dark purple welt was forming on her cheek. He saw red and turned his head towards the man standing in front of her. "You touch her again and I will kill you!"

Anthony glared at him. "And how do you plan on doing that? You're holding no cards here, asshole. So, why don't you just stay quiet while Julia and I work this out? And if you can't stay quiet, try talking some sense into her."

Jake glared at him, but stayed silent. Looking around he saw a young guy standing on the other side of the kitchen. This must be Gino. Hmm, Anthony and Gino. It was like he was stuck in an episode of the Sopranos. He glanced back at Julia. She wasn't looking at him, but he could see the wheels turning in there. What had happened while he was knocked out?

Anthony began to pace, sarcasm ringing in his tone. "I sure hope we figured this out before Ian comes home. I would hate for him to be involved."

Jake watched as Julia's head snapped up. Hatred rolled off her. "Don't you dare threaten my son, Anthony! Don't even think of going near him. How could you even consider hurting him? That's Martin's child."

Anthony spun to glare at her and said, "I don't care about Martin, Julia! He's the reason we're all in this fucking mess to begin with. I should have killed him long before I put a contract out on him. He has cost me so much, and he's still screwing me from beyond the fucking grave."

Julia's eyes went big and she whispered, "You had Martin killed?"

Jake could see the devastation in her eyes. It was like she was losing him all over again. He could feel the shock and pain coming off her in waves.

Anthony frowned at her and Jake caught just a glimmer of remorse in his eyes. "Damn it, Julia, I didn't want to, but he was getting sloppy. He got greedy and lost two hundred thousand dollars of my money. I can't support someone who can't abide by the rules. I had no choice but to put a contract on him, he couldn't pay it back. I have people to answer to. And now we're here, having both been screwed over by your dear, sweet, dead husband. But, hey, it all turned out for you before I showed up, right? This big strapping man in your bed. I'm sure he's better than Martin ever was."

Julia hadn't said a word, silently staring at the floor. Tears welled in her eyes, but she didn't let them fall. His heart ached for her and all he wanted to do was scoop her up in his arms.

Anthony resumed pacing and everyone was silent. Gino was watching Anthony's back, while Anthony was staring at the floor. Neither one of them saw the headlights of the car that had pulled on to the side of the road. Jake could just see them through the trees. Then the lights went out and he couldn't see anything at all. Jake quickly moved his eyes away from the window. He didn't want to give anything away. Could someone be coming here? How could they know? Jake hoped whoever was coming here realized what they were facing.

As silence filled the room, Jake turned to Gino. "Hey, why don't you get her a glass of water? She looks like she could use a drink. I could do with a drink too, and maybe an aspirin. My head is throbbing."

"What does it look like we're running here, Goddamn room service?" Gino looked pissed about being treated like the hired help, but he waited to see if Anthony would refuse. Anthony nodded. While Gino was getting water out of the tap, Jake thought he could see shadows making their way to the house. He hoped Gino didn't take the time to stare out the window and see what Jake was seeing. He knew it would all be over if the two mob guys figured out that someone was on to them. If whoever was out there could get in undetected, then there was still hope. Damn, he hated not being able to protect her. He needed to keep trying to get loose, or he needed to stall to give whoever it was outside a chance.

As Gino finished getting the water, Jake managed to get his one hand free of his restraints. He kept them together behind his back so it still appeared like he was tied up. They had tied him around the waist to the chair, but the chair was light and he knew that with his hands and feet free he could at least defend Julia. Anthony was still holding the gun, but seemed lost in his thoughts. Jake could sense that he didn't want to kill Julia, but if push came to shove, he would.

Gino took a glass over to Julia first and helped her take a drink, since her hands were tied. Both men had their attention on her, so they didn't see the shadow of a head that popped up just outside the window. Jake couldn't see a face, but if it meant they were almost out of this mess, then he didn't care who it was.

Gino had found some Tylenol beside the sink. Bringing a glass of water over to Jake, Gino waited for Jake to open his mouth, slipping the pills on his tongue. Gino held the glass to Jake's lips and watched as Jake took a long drink. Just as Gino pulled the glass away, he said, "There, now your headache should go away just in time for Anthony to blow your head off. You're welcome."

Jake just glared at him. He hoped he would get a chance to pound the shit out of this guy; he'd thoroughly enjoy it.

He could see Anthony's patience wearing thin, so he watched Julia. She was still not looking at him. He needed some way to convey that help was here. Or did she know that? Had she been able to make contact with someone? She had been outside when he came to, so it was possible she'd told someone that these guys were in her house.

Everything happened fast then. Anthony looked at Julia and said, "Time's up, sweetheart. I'm tired of waiting and you don't seem to be taking this seriously. So, I think I'm going to take your new beau out of the picture, then you can concentrate on what you want to have happen next."

Anthony held the revolver to the side of Jake's head, the metal pressing hard into his temple. Just before the mobster pulled the trigger, Julia screamed and Gino yelled, "Holy shit, the fucking cops are here." Anthony pulled the gun away from Jake's head and that was when he knew he had to make a move.

Grabbing the gun, Jake stood up as best he could. With their hands over their heads, they struggled against one another. Jake pushed Anthony into the kitchen island and felt the man arch back, still trying to get control of his gun. The two shoved and Jake swung his arms so the gun flew out of both their hands, sliding under the kitchen table. They both scrambled for it and Jake fell, totally smashing the chair he'd been tied to. Crawling across the floor to the table, he could see that Anthony had already reached the gun.

Anthony swung around, pointing the gun right at Jake, when a loud voice yelled from the doorway, "FBI, put your guns down!!"

It wasn't until then that Jake glanced over and could see that Gino had his gun out and it was pointed at him, too. Jesus, if Anthony didn't get him, then Gino would have!

The house was suddenly filled with FBI agents and cops. They grabbed Anthony and had him in cuffs before Jake could take in the whole situation. Gino had dropped his gun as soon as the FBI agents walked towards him. As the two were escorted out, an official looking gentleman walked towards Jake and helped him off the floor.

Holding up his FBI badge, he said, "Hello, my name is Agent Robert Horton. The FBI has been tracking Mr. Farachelli's activities for quite some time. Your lady here is a smart one. It was because of her call for help using the walkie talkie that you're both alive."

Jake watched as an agent checked Julia's lip and cheek. Turning back to the FBI agent, Jake said, "She is one very special lady, for sure."

Jake walked over and stood beside Julia until the agent was done checking her injuries – then, she was in his arms. She held him so tight he thought she might squeeze the breath out of him, and he didn't mind a bit. She pulled back eventually, not letting go, just easing back so she could see his face. "I thought I was going to lose you. I never would have forgiven myself." She clung to him.

Jake ran his hands up and down her back saying, "It's my fault! If I hadn't gone to the hospital I would have been here. And I didn't turn the security system on when I left because I didn't know the code; it's my fault they even got in here."

Agent Horton cleared his throat and said, "Actually, he would have been able to get around that. He knows all the tricks."

Jake shook his head, "I took the truck and they thought no one was home. They might not have come in if I was here."

The agent glanced at him again, "Maybe, but it's possible he would have come in and checked the place out. But, we'll never know for certain. Anyway, I'm going to need to take your statements."

Julia looked at Agent Horton. "If it's OK with you, I'd like to put some proper clothes on." Jake touched her arm and felt how chilled her skin was in only her nightgown. Jake peered down at her and said, "I'll go and grab you some, then you can change in the bathroom down here if you want."

She seemed so fragile as she nodded. This had been a very long night and they had both been through so much. He quickly went and grabbed a pair of pants, a shirt and sweater that were piled on a chair in the bedroom. As he came down, he saw an ambulance had pulled in and an EMT was checking Julia over. He gave her an ice pack and had put some ointment on her lip.

Jake handed her the clothes and she went off to the bathroom down the hall. The EMT asked Jake to sit so he could assess his head injury. Jake hadn't even realized the back of his head had been bleeding. They took a look but the cut wasn't too bad. They were more concerned with the headache that Jake had. He didn't show any other signs of head trauma, so they gave him an ice pack after they checked all of his vitals. They mentioned he should go to the hospital, but there was no way he was leaving Julia again tonight.

Before Agent Horton took their statements, he told them how they ended up here. "We've been watching Anthony for quite some time. He's been involved in a lot of criminal activity before and during his time in prison. Gino is his right hand and has been doing all his dirty work on the outside, along with a few other guys. Money laundering, extortion, burglaries and drug running are just a few of the things he has going on, not to mention murder. Unfortunately for him, he has pissed off a few people with the risks he's been taking. Even from prison he was taking chances and didn't seem to care. So an informant came forward and gave us some Intel to take him down.

We had no idea why he decided to come to Heritage Falls until we put two and two together from something the informant said. Martin Witmore was Anthony's legal counsel before he got in too deep. When we did a search on Martin we realized he had been killed in a car accident so we decided to investigate his next of kin. That's what led us to you. Your background check uncovered your move to Heritage Falls and that could be the only reason why Anthony would come here. At first, we thought perhaps the two of you were involved, but as he had no contact with you in well over a year we decided that didn't fit. We went back to the informant and that's when he mentioned Martin had been one of Anthony's friends and maybe he thought you knew something.

One of the deputies in Heritage Falls happens to be a relative to one of our agents and he contacted him when we got into town. When you asked your neighbor to contact the police, the deputy got ahold of us. It's a good thing you mentioned Anthony's name or we never would have made the connection. We had a tail on them, but they slipped past our men. We called in a few more agents to come and check out your place just in case. After a quick scan of the area, we found their vehicle behind the barn and knew we were running out of time."

Julia looked up at Agent Horton. "Anthony mentioned Martin had a journal or a notebook he thought had information against him. I think it's in the safety deposit box at my bank. I didn't really flip through the contents of the box when I moved here, I just put it in the box. He wanted the key, but I told him he wouldn't have been able to use it without me. Not sure what his plan was, but since he almost shot Jake, attacked me and threatened Ian, I hope he rots in a cell for the rest of his life."

Agent Horton nodded and proceeded to take both of their statements. Jake overheard the agent say something to Julia about witness protection and he would explain more tomorrow. Jake didn't want to think about that, he had just found her; he couldn't bear the thought of losing her because of something like this. They finished up and made arrangements to meet him at the bank to get the notebook from the safety deposit box.

They were just wrapping things up when Jake thought he heard his mother's voice. Glancing towards the front door, he watched as Lillian came barreling through, followed by his father. She hugged Jake hard and looked him over. Alfred came over and hugged him, too. He didn't need to see his father's face to know he was going through a whole slew of emotions. Hailey was still asleep and one of the neighbors was at the house. They had seen the lights over at Julia's and heard on the police scanner that the FBI was here.

Then his parents descended on Julia and she wasn't given a choice about accepting the hugs. They both fussed over her and it totally warmed Jake's heart to see how much they cared for her. They were safe now and everyone needed to get some rest. Lillian and Alfred left to go back home. All the agents had left except for two that were going to be outside the house to keep watch through the night.

∞ ∞ ∞

Jake picked up the pieces of the chair he'd broken and made a note to replace it. He tried not to focus on what could have happened. Every time his mind started to stray to why he had left and what might have happened if he hadn't come back, he would move on to another chore.

Julia stepped into the kitchen and stared at him. "Are you coming to bed?"

Jake looked at her sadly and said, "I don't know if I deserve to share your bed." He stared down at the piece of wood in his hand.

Walking over to him, Julia wrapped her arms around him. "Jake, what happened tonight could have played out in so many different ways. Who knows what could have happened? He might have come back on a night when just Ian and I were at home. He could have come when I was by myself. You heard Agent Horton; he knows all the tricks to get around security systems. He would have eventually needed to get to me as he never would have found the key. You can think as much as you want about what happened, but it doesn't mean I blame you in any way. He is a criminal, and would have done anything to get away with his crimes."

Jake rubbed his face in her hair and held her close. They stood like that for a few minutes until finally, Julia mumbled against his shirt, "The sun will be up soon. Let's get some rest before we go and meet Agent Horton at the bank."

He nodded and they shut off all the lights, locked the doors and switched on the alarm system, which seemed pointless after what the agent had said.

They walked into the bedroom, the bed still all disheveled from their earlier lovemaking. Julia crawled into the bed and pulled up the covers and set her alarm. Jake climbed in beside her and pulled her towards him so they were spooned together tightly. His head throbbed, reminding him he was probably not going to fall asleep.

As they lay there he decided not to waste another moment. Leaning in close to her ear he said, "Before one more minute goes by, Julia, I need to tell you that I'm in love you. I need you to know that. With everything that happened tonight, I feel like I almost missed my opportunity to tell you. When I think about the possibility that I might never have told you, well, it's too much to think about now."

He waited for her to answer and for a second he thought maybe he'd pushed too hard. But she tilted her face so he could see her. "I love you, too. I think I've known for a while, but the thought of losing you tonight made me see that I don't want to live without you."

They kissed each other tenderly, and held each other close. They talked softly to one another about mundane things, anything but what had happened tonight. They drifted off a couple of times, but with everything that had happened neither of them fell completely asleep. They both watched as the sun behind the curtain lightened the room. He breathed her in as much as possible and enjoyed the knowledge that they were together.

Chapter 21

They both got out of bed, still exhausted after their night of trauma and not much sleep. Mechanically, they both dressed and got ready to meet Agent Horton at the bank. Jake's sister-in-law, Jennifer, was the general manager at the bank so they had contacted her once they were ready. She told them that Agent Horton had already been in touch and she would meet them there. Julia went into her bedroom and took down the figurine that Martin had given her. Flipping it over, she pulled out the key. She stared at it for a moment, thinking they could have lost their lives over this little key. Shaking her head, she put the figurine back on the shelf. There was no time to dwell on that now – they needed to go.

They got in the truck and drove to the bank. Neither one of them spoke, both lost in their thoughts of all that happened. Julia felt like she was walking in a fog. The whole event seemed unreal and dream like. Would Anthony really have killed them last night? The way he had pointed that gun at Jake in the last moments, yes, she was sure he would have killed them if the FBI hadn't shown up. She'd known him for over sixteen years and never had she ever suspected anything about his life or his connections to a crime ring. He was a businessman, an upstanding citizen. It was as if he led a double life.

Thinking of that made her realized Martin must have been leading a double life, too. Never once had she noticed anything about the things he was doing. How could she not have noticed? He had been working a lot, especially before he died, but he was trying to make partner, so of course he worked hard. He had seemed stressed, but he said it was from trying so hard to get ahead so he could make a better life for them. She never would have thought in her wildest dreams that he had turned to a life of crime to make that happen.

It had been such a hard blow when Anthony told her he had put out a contract on Martin. How could he have done that? The two of them had been friends almost their whole lives. How could he so easily have thrown away a life time of friendship? It was baffling for her to even think about why anyone would do that. All this time she had thought Martin's death had been an accident, but, really, Anthony had put a price on his head. She dreaded telling Ian about everything, but especially dreaded that. If he was younger, she might not tell him. But, he was older now and he deserved the right to know the truth – the truth that Anthony had his father murdered.

She didn't know how to break the news to him about having to go into witness protection. They had just gotten settled and he'd made some great friends here. It was as if their life from the city had followed them, just to ruin the wonderful new life they had both just started. She couldn't even let herself think about losing Jake. It just seemed overwhelming and it was too much to think about. There had to be another way.

As they pulled up in front of the bank, Julia could see Jennifer at the door speaking to a few agents. Jake got out and came around to open her door. Just as she stepped out, he wrapped his arms around her. Pulling her in tight he asked, "You OK to do this? We don't have to stay. They probably already have a warrant to open it, or can get one."

He examined her face. There were so many emotions there, but the main one was concern. He didn't want her to hurt anymore. She smiled sadly up at him and said, "I can do this. I want to cooperate with them and I need to be here. Thank you for coming, by the way."

Jake gave her a questioning look. "Where else would I be? You didn't think I would declare my love for you and then not come and support you, did you?"

Julia grinned. "I guess not. It wouldn't be the knightly thing to do."

Jake kissed her sweetly and whispered, "Well, I'm nothing if not knightly, malady."

She laughed softly and they made their way to the door of the bank. Agent Horton greeted them, and then Jennifer swooped in and hugged them both tight. They returned her hug and then everyone went into the bank.

It was eerily quiet as they made their way inside. Jake stayed back as Agent Horton, Jennifer and Julia made their way to the safety deposit box area. Jennifer opened the vault and waited as they went in to open the box. Walking in, Julia found Box 235 and unlocked the little drawer. The day she'd been here to put her stuff in this box, she never would have imagined she would be back here under these circumstances.

She pulled out the tray and handed it to Agent Horton. "My husband had special coins he was saving for our son. I hope you don't need to take those. They aren't stolen property. They were a collection Martin was putting together for Ian since he was born."

Agent Horton nodded. "Let me just take a look through the items. I can leave your things and you can lock it up. I know those will be special to him since his dad saved them." Then, clearing his throat, he said, "I wanted to tell you your husband wasn't as deeply involved as Mr. Farachelli might have made it seem. We knew he'd been gambling with mob money, but that was as far as his involvement went. But unfortunately, the mob frowns on those who can't pay their debts. Anthony was on the hook for your husband's gambling. He handled it the only way he knew would appease the bosses. I only wish we would have known about that part sooner. Perhaps we could have saved him."

Julia's eyes were filled with tears as she nodded. She didn't speak as she watched him take the cardboard box out of the tray. He opened the box and took out everything Julia had put in not so long ago. He inspected the coins and placed them back in Julia's box. He opened the first folio and read what was inside and placed that back in her box as well. The last item he picked up was a black, embossed notebook. Agent Horton flipped it open and a single sheet slid out. He read the page, and then stared at Julia. Slowly, he handed her the page and continued to flip through the notebook.

With trembling hands, she started to read the handwritten note. She recognized the handwriting.

My Julia,

If you're reading this, then something has happened to me. I need you to understand that everything I've done I did because I love you and Ian with all my heart and soul. I wanted you both to have the best of everything life has to offer, but I fear that in my pursuit to give you those things I got lost in the game.
I got involved in something that I never should have. But, to right this wrong, I want to make sure that those who need to be brought to justice will be. It is important that if something does happen to me, the authorities know what they're up against.
I need you to do one final thing for me. Do Not Read This Book. It has information that you should never know. If you were to read it they would probably kill you. Please take it directly to the FBI.
I never meant to hurt you. I'm so sorry. You've always been my everything, Julia. You are a strong person and I hope that serves you well once I'm gone. It's hard for me to write this, but find someone who will take good care of you and our boy. It breaks my heart to think I won't get to watch him grow up, but with you by his side I know he'll be a great man. I hope you find someone who can help him to be that great man. And please, chose someone who won't make stupid choices for greed and money like I did.
Please tell Ian that I love him so much, and that I'm so proud of him. Tell him I wanted only the best for him, but I made a mistake, and

I'm sorry. I want him to be better than me, better than I should have been. Tell him he needs to take care of you, and to be happy, because that's what I wanted for him.

I love you, Julia, with all that I am. I want you to live, my beautiful wife, and make a life that will make you happy, because you deserve the very best.

Forever and always yours,

Martin, XO

She stood there with tears streaming down her face. Her heart ached for the husband that was taken from her life. He knew something was going to happen. How could he have lived with all of this? How could she be unaware of what was happening? She would never forgive herself for not seeing what was right in front of her eyes.

Wiping her face and folding the letter, she glanced over to see Agent Horton still reviewing the book. He looked over to her then and said, "I need to discuss with you how the witness protection program works."

Taking in a huge breath she said, "I can't do this right now. I need a day to figure this out. I need to find some strength to speak to my son and tell him everything. I understand this is for our protection, but we just moved here and he was doing so well. I need to figure out how to break this to him. I wish there was another way."

He nodded and said, "I can give you a day to discuss it with him, but we will need to talk. Unless by some miracle Anthony is wiped off the planet, I don't see how you'll be safe."

They made their way out of the vault. Jake walked over and put his arms around her. She could tell he had questions about why her face was blotchy with tears, but she couldn't talk right now. Her heart was crushed knowing somehow she would have to leave him behind. It wasn't fair to have her heart be torn in two again. She didn't know how she was going to handle this. But if it meant keeping Ian safe, she would need to find away, even if it meant she would be leaving her heart in Heritage Falls.

As they all headed towards the door, Agent Horton's cell phone rang. Feeling numb, Julia didn't even notice as he spoke to someone on the phone. She was wrapped up in her grief and sadness until Agent Horton yelled into the phone. "What the hell do you mean they're dead?!"

Everyone stopped to watch him. It felt like forever, but it was probably just a minute or two. He started to nod and then his questions started. "How many officers are hurt? Are emergency personnel on their way? Fine. Let me wrap up and I'll come straight there. Call Branagan and see if he can get some more agents to help out with the mess."

Julia watched as Agent Horton ended the call, staring at the floor, frustration pouring off him. Then he said, "About thirty minutes ago, there was an ambush on the transport team that was taking Mr. Farachelli and Mr. Valcavi to our facility on the outskirts of Chicago.

A few of our men were hurt; thankfully, none critically. Anthony and Gino were the targets of the ambush and unfortunately, they were both shot. Neither of them survived. It looks like someone might have had a contract on them, or it could be that the big boss was just tired of Anthony's antics. I'm sorry to say Julia, but there will be no justice by the courts for your husband's death. However, this does mean we won't need you to testify and we no longer need to have that discussion I just mentioned."

Julia was stunned. Anthony was dead. A contract was placed in his head and now he was dead. She nodded to the agent, but in her head she felt justice had been done, on some level. He wouldn't have to serve time, but he would no longer get to ruin anyone else's life. His life had been taken away, just like Martin's. In a way, this seemed more fitting.

Jake turned her towards him and studied at her face. "Julia, are you OK?" He pulled her in and hugged her tight. She gripped onto the front of his shirt and let him comfort her. Even though she was glad she wouldn't need to leave Jake, she felt numb. Her mind was still reeling from the letter she'd just read. She needed some time to deal with this and the only person that would feel the same way was Ian. The need to go to him was overpowering.

Letting out a big breath, she held Jake for another few moments, then pulled away. Jake squeezed her arms and tried to draw her in again, but she didn't allow it. Composing herself, she nodded solemnly and everyone exited the bank. She could tell Jake wanted more from her, but she didn't have it in her to give.

Jennifer locked the door and the agents said their goodbyes. Agent Horton turned to her and said, "Mrs. Witmore, I'll keep you posted if we need anything further."

They watched as the agents drove away and once they were out of sight, she stood, overwhelmed by everything that had happened. It was over. She could hardly believe it, but her heart was heavy. Turning to Jake she admired at his profile. He was a good man, the kind of man that Martin would have wanted to help raise their son. He was a great father to his own daughters and was more than she could hope for. But, she just needed some time to talk to Ian and process everything. This new information was going to be hard on him. She needed to do this now.

Turning away from Jake, she asked Jennifer, "Do you think you could drop Jake off at home? I need to go and pick up Ian."

Jake spun towards her and spoke abruptly, "What? No! I can just come with you to Audrey's house. I need to get the girls and I wanted to talk to you."

She focused on her feet and said in a quiet voice, "Jake, I need to be alone before I pick up Ian. I have a lot to tell him, including something that was in the box for me, and I wouldn't mind a few minutes to gather my thoughts."

He looked sad and confused. She wasn't trying to hurt him, but she needed to deal with this her own way. Nodding slowly, he turned away and she made her way over to her truck. Getting in the driver's seat, she took a few minutes to close her eyes. She didn't want to cry again before she saw Ian. She needed to be strong for him. How would he deal with this knowledge about Martin's death? Pulling the letter from her pocket, she stared at it. Thinking someone had accidentally been killed was one thing, but knowing they were taken from you on purpose was quite another.

Starting the truck and pulling away, she glanced in the rearview mirror. There, still standing outside the bank watching her drive away was Jake and her heart broke. She hated herself for pushing him away, but she just needed this time. One lone tear slid down her cheek and she knew it had nothing to do with Martin and everything to do with the man she was driving away from. She hoped he understood. Time is what she needed and hopefully he would understand.

Julia pulled up in front of Audrey's house and she couldn't bring herself to go in. She quickly texted Ian and asked him to come out so she could take him home. Peering around nervously, she hoped it would be quick because she knew Jake would be here right on her heels if she didn't make it fast. She couldn't bear to see him watch her pull away again.

Ian was out the door in less than thirty seconds, so he must have been waiting for her. Watching him run to the truck, she thought about what Martin had said in the letter. How proud he was of their son. She was proud too, so proud that sometimes it overflowed from her heart. He pulled open the door and practically jumped into the truck. Before she could say a word he had her in a bear hug. She could feel his body shake as he held on to her tightly, silently crying. Holding him just as tight, she ran her fingers into his hair. God, she loved this boy and she would give anything to keep from hurting him. But he had to know the truth.

They held each other like for a few minutes. He stared into her eyes and she could see the fear and pain in his stare. His cheeks were wet as he said. "They told me some of what happened just this morning. I was thinking about what I would do if I had lost you too, Mom. I can't lose you, I just can't! Promise me you'll never leave me."

Julia couldn't speak for a few moments as the lump in her throat made it impossible. Finally she said, "Oh, babe, I'm here! I'm not going anywhere." She held his face and rubbed away the worst of the tears, then kissed his forehead.

"Ian, there are some things I need to tell you, but not here. Let's go home." She watched as he seemed to realize that this was serious.

Looking afraid, he said, "Are you OK, Mom? You didn't get hurt did you? They said you were fine." He focused on the bruise on her face and the cut on her lip. She could see the moment his anger surfaced.

She lifted his chin and said, "I'm fine, babe. The bruised cheek and split lip will heal. It isn't about me, but there are still things you should know."

Ian nodded, still seeming unsure if she was fine. She was, at least everything but her heart.

Once they made it home, she and Ian sat on the couch and she told him everything that had happened. He seemed torn between anger and shock. She pulled out the letter and let him read it. The string of emotions that crossed his face was hard to watch. She knew when he read the part about himself and that's when the tears started. He yelled and ranted as his anger over took him. He had a right to his rage and she let him get it all out. After that, he hugged her, saying he would always take care of her, always. Holding one another, they both cried thinking of the man that had been taken from them, and the son he would never see grow up.

Julia told Ian that Anthony was killed that morning, along with his partner. Ian was mad at first, saying that there would be no justice for his father. Julia explained that at least he wouldn't be able to take anyone else's life and his death meant that they wouldn't have to go into witness protection. Ian seemed relieved that they didn't have to move again because he loved living here. She said perhaps this morning's event had been Martin watching over them, knowing how happy they were in Heritage Falls.

They sat together for a while and Julia enjoyed just being close to him, since he usually pulled away from her affection now. Eventually they heated up some leftovers and turned on a cheesy movie. They really didn't watch it, but instead they talking about Martin and the things that they loved about him. It was hard at times, but it was a way to relive the best moments they had while he'd been alive.

It was late when they went to bed. Julia was exhausted since she hadn't really slept in forty-eight hours. Just as Ian was headed for his room, he came in and sat on the end of her bed. "I've been thinking about what Dad wrote. You know the part about you being with someone else?" She glanced at him and nodded.

He picked a piece of lint off his pajama pants. "I think he would really like Jake. He's a good man, Mom. He is the kind of guy I want to be like. He's funny, smart, and people really like him. He treats you really good, too. That's the kind of person to look up to." Sadness seemed to overwhelm over him and he continued, "But I still want to be like Dad, the best parts of him. He was a great man too, even if he made a mistake."

Julia walked around and sat on the foot of her bed and held him. She spoke softly, "He was a good man, babe, the best. You are like him in a lot of ways. But don't worry about being someone else. You just be the best that you can be. And as for Jake, I really like him too. I just need a little time to grieve again. That letter really sent me for a loop. But when I'm ready, and if he still wants to be with me, he'll be the first one to know."

Chapter 22

"Bloody hell! It's been a week since I've spoken to her, for Christ's sake! How long do I have to wait?" Jake ranted in his parent's kitchen while his mom, dad, sister and brother all stared at him like he had lost his mind.

Audrey cleared her throat and said, "Actually, it's only been five-and-a-half days. She needs time, Jake."

Jake glared at her. "Close enough to a week. And what was with the switch up last night for swim practice? I left work early so I could see her and instead it was you. When had that little schedule change happened?"

Audrey huffed out her impatience. "What is the big deal? We made arrangements that I would go and get Dani as Julia was heading out of town early the morning before. Ian was staying at my place anyway so it just made sense. She made sure that everything was taken care of."

Throwing his hands in the air, he said, "And that's another thing! She leaves town and doesn't even tell people?"

Audrey stared at him, smiling. "She told me, Mom, and Jennifer, and even Dad knew she was going. I'm sure if you ask Luke he knew too. Grant, did you know?"

Grant glared at her. "I'm not getting involved in this."

Jake turned his stare on his brother. "You knew? And you didn't tell me? What the hell, Grant?"

Grant gave his sister a 'thanks a lot' look, and then he turned back to Jake. "Jen told me, but just the day before and told me I had to keep it to myself, or else."

Jake glared at him. "Or else, what?"

Looking angry Grant said, "Well excuse me if I happen to like having sex with my wife, and the 'or else' was no nookie for me. Sorry, Mom."

Lillian just shrugged and said nothing.

Jake looked at his father and Alfred lifted his hands. "I'm not getting into this either. But I will say she said she needed time. Geez, she just found out the damn mob had her husband killed. If she needs time then I say give it to her."

Turning to his mother he watched as she shook her head. "Jake, I love you, but you can be so impatient sometimes. No one knows what's going through her mind right now, so time is what she needs."

Peering around the room and feeling disgusted with the whole group, Jake headed for the door. Turning back, he said, "Well, if you'll all excuse me, I'm going to go where people will be reasonable. If I can't be with her, then I'm going to be with the next best person I can think of. Audrey, text Wyatt and tell him to get the PlayStation set up because I'm coming over for a Call of Duty beat down."

If he couldn't be with Julia then he'd go and spend some time with Ian. He was growing more attached to that kid every day. Plus, he might just find out some information about her, and that would make his day. He felt like it had been a month since they'd spoken, even though according to Audrey it had only been five-and-a-half days. He just missed her so much, and with everything that had happened they needed to talk. He still hadn't really had time to apologize properly for screwing up and going to the hospital to see Francine. He wanted time to do that, and time to just hold her in his arms and breathe her in.

When she'd pushed him away at the bank and told Jen to drive him home, he didn't think he'd ever felt so rejected in his whole life. He knew she just needed to prepare to talk to Ian, but what was the thing she got from the safety deposit box. Why had it changed everything? Whatever it was had put sadness in her eyes that he had never seen, and all he had wanted to do was wrap her in his arms and take way the pain.

Jumping into his truck he headed over to Audrey's house. Maybe he should have just stayed and worked in the shop for a bit, but, he knew that wouldn't get her off his mind. Not that going and hanging out with her son would help get her off his mind either, but at least he could be with someone she loved.

He stopped and picked up chips, soda, beer and other junk food. Dani was at Rachel's house and Hailey had been invited to a sleepover birthday party. That meant he was free for the night, so he might as well make an evening of it.

Pulling into the driveway, he grabbed all of his supplies and headed up to the house. Before he got there, the door was opened wide and Luke was standing there, offering his hands to take something. Jake gratefully handed over the beer and bag of snacks. They wandered in and he could see the boys had the den all set up for game night. Yeah, this is what he needed. A guy's night to clear his head. Drink beer, play video games and talk about cars. This would be good for him. Although, if he was honest, he'd take a romantic night with Julia over a guy's night anytime.

They all got snacks and soda, beer for the men, and the tournament began. It was great just hanging out. He and Luke loved to take on the young guys and talk smack. They were always competitive and did their best to take the boys down. However, the younger generation had the hand-eye coordination that the older generation lacked. They were laughing and having a great time. He had heard Ian's phone chime a few times. When there was a break in the action, Ian glanced at it and did a quick text then put it away.

Jake smirked and said, "You got a hot date or something?"

Ian gave him a shrug and said, "No. That was my mom. She just got home and wanted to let me know. Guess she didn't stay in Seattle as long as she thought."

Jake just stared at Ian as he took in this new information. He was desperate to ask him more about what she'd been doing there. Just knowing she was back at home alone was killing him. She was so close; he could be there in ten minutes. He quickly looked away trying not to let Ian see how much he wanted to ask him how she was, and if he knew when she would call him again. Dear Lord, he felt like a damn teenager wanting information on his first crush. No, that wasn't fair to Ian to be pulled into this. He would just wait.

Getting up and clearing the soda cans and empty chip bags, he headed to the kitchen. He'd ended up drinking a soda as the beers just weren't going down too well. Dumping the cans into the recycling bin, he saw Ian come into the kitchen.

Jake watched Ian as he leaned on the island staring at his feet. "Do you still want to be with my Mom?"

The tone of Ian's voice was sad and Jake wasn't sure where he was going with the question. "Yes Ian, I really do want to be with her. She told me she needed some time, so that's what I'm giving her. I have to tell you though; it's killing me to not see her. And it hurt that she didn't tell me she was going away."

Ian nodded. "I wasn't going to say anything, but that day at the bank, my dad left a letter for her in the safety deposit box. It made her sad to think that he knew something bad was going to happen. I think it made her feel guilty too that she was moving on. She didn't say that to me, but I heard her talking to one of her friends on the phone. I also happened to hear her say she missed you." Ian finally looked up and smirked at Jake.

Jake couldn't believe it. She said that? If that was so, why hadn't she called or texted him? He so desperately wanted to see her that his heart ached. Would she be mad if he went out to see her? Everyone said give her space, but damn it, he needed her.

Studying Jake, Ian said matter-of-factly, "My mom has a tradition when she signs a contract for one of her books, like she did today. She opens her favorite bottle of wine and lights candles. Then she plays these old sappy love songs and sings and dances. It's her thing and she's done it for all of her books. I've been her partner for the dances and she sometimes lets me have a sip of her wine, which is really gross by the way. But since I'm here, it might be nice for her to have someone else to share her special night with."

Running his hand though his hair, Jake stared at Ian. Would she like it if he just showed up? He would love to be with her on her special night, but he didn't want to upset her if she still needed time.

Ian smiled while shaking his head. "My mom thinks she needs space, but I think she needs to spend time with a really great guy. Trust me, I wouldn't send you there if I thought she would kick you out. We'll finish our tournament of Call of Duty another time. Besides, Rachel and Dani are going to be coming over soon. So go, man. She really does like you a lot."

Jake didn't know what to say, but hell if he was going to stand around here staring at her son when he could be holding her in his arms. Grabbing his keys off the counter and giving Ian a fist bump on the way by, he headed for the door. Luke was just coming out of the den when he spotted Jake. "Hey, where you going? We got a tournament to finish here!"

Opening the front door, he looked over at his brother-in-law, "I'm going to see Julia, and don't try and stop me."

Luke lifted an eyebrow. "Why would I try and stop you? I can't believe you waited this long. Go, man, and don't take no for an answer. You've been like a bear with a sore ass all week."

Jake just smiled as he headed for his truck. If she needed time, she was going to have to deal with him being right beside her.

It had been a long couple of days, but Julia was thrilled. The publishing company had invited her to come out to their head office in Seattle. There had been meeting after meeting and at the end of it all she signed the deal. She and her agent Tanya had gone out to dinner the night before and had a lovely time. Tanya had been Julia's agent and friend for about seven years and they got along really well. It was nice to talk to someone who knew her work and understood her passion, but she was glad to be home.

The whole time she'd been away, Jake hadn't been far from her mind. She'd told Tanya over dinner about the whole situation with Martin and Anthony. Tanya was sad to hear the real truth about Martin's death. Julia told her about Jake and how they had started into a relationship over the last month or so. Tanya was a great listener and Julia shared a lot of how she was feeling since reading the letter from Martin. She explained her guilt and how the grief had felt fresh just reading the letter he'd left.

At the end of the story, Tanya nodded and said, "Julia, I know it must feel like you've lost him all over again, but it has been over two-and-a-half years. No amount of time at this point is going to help you move on – you were already moving on. Jake sounds like a really great guy. If I were you I wouldn't make him wait another day. You sound like you need each other. Keep moving forward."

Julia had been thinking about that conversation all day and she knew Tanya was right. When she texted Ian to let him know she was home safe and sound, he had told her Jake was hanging out with them. She was disappointed, as she'd hoped to call him and see if they could talk tonight. However, she didn't want to break up the boy's night. She decided to wait until tomorrow.

There were a lot of things she needed to tell him. First, she wanted to say how sorry she was that he'd been pulled into the situation with Anthony. She still couldn't believe everything that had happened. It all seemed right out of a movie. The image of both Anthony and Gino pointing their guns at Jake would be forever branded in her mind. What would she have done if she had lost him? She shuttered at the thought and pushed it out of her mind.

Second, she needed to explain why she had pushed him away after she'd read Martin's letter. She had felt so raw she couldn't cope with the feelings that had come from reading those words. She could have handled it better, though, and she wished she would have.

She also needed to apologize for not reaching out to him sooner. He had been through so much with Francine that he didn't need her to make him feel bad. Julia should have been more understanding about that. She knew he didn't have feelings for his ex-wife anymore, so she didn't know why she'd been so upset. Perhaps she just didn't want Francine to make a fool out of him again. Women like her were users and she just hoped Jake had figured that out for good.

Hopefully, she had a chance to tell him all of that tomorrow. She prayed it wasn't too late to say all she needed to say. She had fallen for him hard and she didn't know what she would do if he decided she wasn't worth his time. There wasn't anything about him that she didn't like and she hoped they could get on the right track again.

When she had first gotten home, she changed into her favorite yoga pants, the ones with the hole in the knee, and a too-small, tank-style pajama top. The outfit was hideous, but so comfortable. Keeping up with tradition, even though this was the first time she had done it alone, she poured her wine and lit her candles. Pulling up her love song mix on her phone, she hummed along.

Julia couldn't remember why this had become her thing, but it always made the deal final. It was like giving herself a way to symbolize all the sweat, tears and hard work that went into every book she wrote. The last couple of books, Ian had been around and she had made him sit and listen to her music and even dance a song with her. He'd never been overjoyed to do it, but he knew it was important to her. She'd just have to dance by herself tonight. That was OK; she could sing as off-key as she wanted and no one could complain.

She was just reaching over to top up her wine glass when there was a knock on the front door. Her eyes went wide as she glanced at how she was dressed and panicked. Who the hell could it be?! Damn it, there wouldn't be enough time to change and get the door. The knocking came again and she resigned herself to just tell whoever it was that she wasn't up for company and send them away.

Tiptoeing over to the door she looked through the peep hole. Oh my God! It was Jake. Why had she chosen to wear her rattiest clothes tonight? Oh that's right; she wasn't supposed to have any company. Quickly running her fingers through her hair to try and fix the worst of the mess, she slowly opened the door.

To say Jake looked good at that moment was an understatement. He was hotter than a GQ model standing there on her porch. His low rise blue jeans and tight-fitting white t-shirt had her mouthwatering. His hair was messy-sexy, like he had been running his fingers through it, and the few days' growth of beard were just icing on the sexy cake. She tried to keep her face neutral as she feasted her eyes on all his yumminess, but she was sure he could see how much she wanted him.

"Hey, Jake." That's all she said as she watched emotion play over his face. He looked sad and worried, like he wasn't sure what she would say. Then, as if he couldn't help himself his eyes travelled the length of her body and finally returned to her face. She could see the heat in his eyes; he wanted her just as much as she wanted him.

Clearing his throat, he leaned on the door frame and said, "Hope I'm not bothering you. I just wanted to come over and say congratulations on the book deal. Ian told me that's where you'd gone."

He apparently wanted to make it clear he had to find out from Ian where she had gone. She'd known he would be upset she hadn't told him directly.

Stepping back, she needed to give herself some breathing room. She could smell him, all clean soap and maleness. She struggled to concentrate on the conversation as she said, "Thank you. It went really well. I signed on to do the trilogy. I'm pretty excited." This felt awkward. She didn't want to be standing here making small talk.

Jake smiled. "You said you were hoping for that. I'm glad you got what you wanted."

She watched as he briefly let his eyes linger on her lips. Her heart sped up and she could feel her body flush. Nodding her head, she said, "Yeah, it will be a lot of work, but I can hardly wait."

He moved forward just a fraction and she could feel his body heat. It made her want to curl up against his chest and take in a deep breath. God, she had missed him over the last several days.

Jake moved a little closer still, his voice low. "I'm sorry, I couldn't wait any longer to see you." He had pain and longing in those beautiful green pools. Her heart ached knowing she had put that look there.

She lifted her hand and put it on his cheek. He leaned into it and closed his eyes.

"I didn't mean to hurt you Jake, and I'm sorry if I did. I just needed a little time." She wanted so badly to pull him close, but she'd been the one to push him away and she needed to know if he still wanted her.

Without opening his eyes he said, "Please tell me you've had enough time, Julia. I don't think I can take being without you one more day."

She waited until he opened his eyes and she smiled at him. "Then I won't make you wait."

Within seconds Jake had his hands in her hair and his lips on hers. He tasted like salt and sugar and she couldn't help it when she licked across his bottom lip. He groaned and pulled her tighter against him. Somehow, he'd managed to step inside and close the door without Julia even noticing what was happening. Leaning her back against the front door he took his fill of her mouth. His hands explored her everywhere, caressing and pleasuring. She ran her hands up the back of his shirt and teased him with her nails. He gasped at the sensation and kissed her again, deeply. She wanted all of him now, and she was sure they wouldn't make it upstairs.

Stumbling thought the house, they managed to make it to the living room. Their clothes left a path directly to where they lay on the couch together. Crawling on top of him, she needed more and she wasn't waiting for an invitation. Before he realized what she was doing, she tipped his cock against her very wet entrance, and slid down his length. They both moaned out their pleasure at the same time. As her body stretched and expanded to accept him, he pulled her down and kissed her. Staring into his eyes she was thrilled to see her passion echoed. She loved this man.

Running his hands slowly up and down her back and over her buttocks, he gripped onto her and pushed faster and harder. It felt amazing as she sat back and he rubbed his thumb over her sensitive nub. The sensation was building and she didn't know how much longer she was going to last.

Pounding into her now Jake said, almost breathlessly, "Come now, baby, I want to feel you soar."

That was all it took. She felt spiral after spiral as her release tore through her and she could feel Jake's warm seed inside her. Leaning down over top of Jake, she enjoyed the feelings of his hands on her back, stroking tenderly. As they lay together, still joined, the air felt cool. He pulled the throw blanket off the back of the couch and spread it over the two of them. Neither of them wanted to move.

Eventually Jake whispered, "I think we better go and get cleaned up, before we make a big mess on your couch."

Julia smiled – she had been thinking the same thing. Slowly lifting herself off of him, she instantly felt empty. She loved having her body wrapped around him, with him buried inside her. Grabbing his T-shirt off the floor, she pulled it on and headed for the small bathroom by the kitchen.

Once she was finished, Jake ducked in there while she got him a drink. He stepped out of the bathroom and his smile could have melted the panties off her, had she been wearing any. "Mmm, you look good wearing my shirt. And just knowing there is nothing covering you under there is making me think very dirty thoughts."

She laughed and handed him his drink. "Cool down there, cowboy. I was hoping we could talk. I think we both have things we want to say, and I know I'll feel better once I apologize."

Jake stopped mid-swallow and stared at her. "Why do you need to apologize? I'm the one who should apologize. This whole mess with Anthony would never even have happened if I'd never left that night. I don't care what Agent Horton said, if the truck had been here and I hadn't left the alarm system off, he wouldn't have come in. He would have waited for a better time."

Julia shook her head. "We will never know what he would have done, but I need to apologize for the whole mess. I got upset about Francine and that was just so petty on my part. I know you don't love her; I was just upset that you chose to go to her after everything she has done to you. I understand she's the mother of your children, but I knew she was going to try and use her ways to get to you. I didn't want you to go because I just knew she was going to play you."

Jake nodded and glanced away. From that look she could tell that he'd been played and that just made all the events of that evening all the more frustrating. Looking back at Julia he said, "First, she said she wanted me to bail her out because she wanted us to be a family again. I told her no way in hell would I ever take her back. She said the girls needed her because she was their mother, but, when push came to shove the real reason she called for me was her boyfriend wanted nothing to do with her, and she owed some guy money for drugs. So yeah, she played me." Letting out a huff he said, "I heard from her dad on Tuesday. They've moved her to a rehab center in Florida. I'm just glad they did something with her. She needs help but she's not my responsibility anymore."

Julia was relieved to hear him say that. Just knowing Francine wouldn't be lurching around every corner of this town made her feel better.

She was quiet for a moment then she said, "I'm sorry about pushing you away Jake. I... Agent Horton found a letter that was addressed to me from Martin in the safety deposit box. I was so stunned when I read it. He knew someone would try and take him out. He told me not to read the notebook and to turn it into the authorities. He said he was sorry for everything and that he loved me so much. Martin spoke about Ian and you could tell he knew he wasn't going to be around to see his son grow up. And, he told me to move on with my life. Find a great man who would take care of me and help Ian grow into someone who would make us proud.

"It was so hard. I felt gutted reading it, I felt like I had lost him all over again. It had been hard enough when Anthony had told me, but to see that letter, knowing Martin knew he was probably going to die, it just overwhelmed me. I pushed you away and I don't know if I could have changed how I felt in those first couple of days. But I was missing you and I was worried you would think it was something else. I took a few extra days because I got the call about the publishing meeting and that was a whirlwind. Truthfully though, I couldn't bring myself to know if you were going to push me away."

Jake came over and wrapped his arms around her. He was only wearing his pants, as she had his shirt, and she rubbed her cheek over the tight skin on his chest. She gripped him harder and loved the way she fit perfectly into his body.

"Julia, I could never push you away. It has taken me years to find the perfect woman, and I finally found her. You are perfect for me, I love everything about you. I don't think I have ever met a more beautiful, thoughtful, more caring person in my life. Just being in the same room with you lifts me up. And don't even get me started about how amazingly sexy you are. I want to be with you all the time, not just when we get a chance to sneak in time. I want to wake up with you and fall asleep with you and have Sunday morning breakfast with both our kids and be together to live through all the ups and downs that happen in life. Being away from you for even those handful of days has been enough to show me that I don't want to live without you. I'm not saying we have to rush into it, but I want you to know I won't ever push you away."

She focused into those amazing green eyes she loved, and smiled. She could totally see a future with him. They would make a great couple and knowing someone was there to help raise Ian and she could help him raise Dani and Hailey sounded like a dream come true.

She leaned in slowly and kissed him softly. He was exactly the man Martin would want for her, and she would never let him go.

Pulling back, she said, "So… looks like we talked. What do you want to do now?"

A sexy grin spread across his face. "Oh, baby, you know I'm good for another round, or five. Let's you and me go upstairs and play 'Never Have I Ever', the dirty version. If you haven't ever, you get to try it out on the other person. Mmm, I am thinking up all sorts of things I haven't ever, so we could be here for days."

Running his lips from her earlobe to her collarbone she felt her body shiver. Hmm, this could be an interesting night indeed.

Epilogue

(One year later)

Jake stood and stared out over the turquoise waters of the Caribbean. The sun was just about to come up and he still couldn't believe he was here. Having never really travelled beyond the borders of Illinois before, this was the first time he'd ever seen an ocean. He'd seen plenty of pictures, but it was even more breathtaking in person. Hearing the waves crash onto the shore, he remembered leaving the window open last night, while he and Julia had made love for the first time as husband and wife.

She'd been so beautiful walking down the beach, the wind blowing her white sundress as she smiled at him. Yesterday had been perfect. All their friends and family had come to watch them take their vows. It wasn't a traditional ceremony, as they had wanted to incorporate their kids and it had been more special than any he had ever seen. The girls wore pretty floral sundresses and had been Julia's bridesmaids. Audrey had been her matron of honor and had taken the role very seriously. Grant had been his best man and Luke and Ian had also stood with him. Everyone had been barefoot in the sand and it had been way more fun than any other wedding he had ever been to.

Taking those vows with Julia had been a dream come true. She was everything he could ever want in a wife. She was loving and kind, smart and funny, and she loved his girls like they were her own. Saying 'I do' was the easiest thing in the world as he'd gazed into her eyes. Life had definitely turned around for him and he owed it all to Julia.

Thinking of her, he said, "Hurry, babe, I don't want you to miss it."

Just then she came thought the doors, bringing a coffee for each of them. They had a coffee maker in their room and had decided to enjoy their first morning as a wedded couple watching the sunrise. He took the cup she offered him and gingerly took the first sip. Wincing only a little he said, "Well it's no Starbucks, but it'll do. Thank you for making it for me."

She took a sip and grimaced. "I'm not exactly sure what brand of coffee was in that packet, but I can only work with the tools I'm given." She held out her cup and they clinked them together. "Here's to many, many years of morning coffee together."

He leaned in and kissed her. They pulled apart just in time to see the sunrise. Its light seemed to grow out of the water, almost as if it was pulling itself back together after it has dissolved. Pink, gold and orange burst across the surface, highlighting the clouds that were sitting just along the horizon. It was spectacular. They both watched as seagulls hovered and dipped into the water and he realized this was the most relaxed he'd felt since he had asked Julia to marry him.

She peered up at him as if hearing his thoughts. "Yesterday was amazing, wasn't it? Everyone had such a good time. I'm glad we decided to do a destination wedding, the kids are loving it. I heard Audrey is taking the girls to get beads in their hair today. I can't wait to see it. Oh, and Ian and Wyatt are going to try snorkeling today with the guys that run the resort water activities. I'm so glad they're enjoying themselves."

Taking another sip of his coffee, he just stared at Julia. It was like he was living a dream. She snuggled deeper into his arms. He kissed the top of her head then moved her in front of him, so her back fit snug against his chest. Wrapping his one arm around her, he held her while still holding his coffee. Slowly, he began to move his body so he was leaning into her from behind. She felt so good and he was starting to enjoy the fact that the balcony had a solid wall around it for privacy. Setting his coffee down, he put his hands around and slipped them into her robe. He leaned over and started kissing her neck and gave her earlobe a lick. Oh yeah, he was really starting to like this sunrise watching. Leaning his body forward he could just hear her moan over the crashing of the waves. He lifted the back of her robe up and over so he could see the globes of her bottom. It would be so easy to slip into her while they watched the sky and water turn from pink to blue.

Parting his robe below the waist he was just about to enter into her moist heat when he felt Julia tense. He glanced up just in time to see some of his family waving from down below. Apparently some of them had enjoyed the party so much yesterday they were just finishing up now. His brother yelled up, "Get a room!"

Biting back a curse, he waved back as he yelled out, "We are in our room, and we're trying to christen every part of it." This was met with hoots and cheers. Deciding perhaps it would be best to go inside where there were no prying eyes, they went back into their room.

"Christ, another minute and they would have caught me making love to you on the balcony!" Jake cringed at the thought.

He looked over at Julia in time to see her start laughing hysterically. "Another minute and I don't think I would have cared if we got caught. How about later tonight, we go back out there when it's dark and we reenact that again. Only this time, we make it happen."

Hot damn, he loved this woman. Pulling her into his arms, he kissed her deeply. She was the fulfillment of all his dreams and fantasies. "Baby, I don't think I can wait until tonight to have you again. There's a part of me that requires attention right now. Do you think we could do something about that?"

Walking him backwards towards the bed, she pushed his robe off of his shoulders so he stood before her in all his naked glory. Kissing him along his collar bone she said, "Hmm, let me see what I can do to fix that." Then she stared up into his eyes and said in all seriousness, "But after, can we go and get some real coffee for breakfast? I don't think I can handle one more sip out of that cup."

Jake laughed as he gazed into her eyes. "Absolutely, malady, anything for you."

THE END

ABOUT THE AUTHOR

Lana Pickering lives in beautiful Northumberland County, Ontario, Canada, with her husband, son and crazy dog Mater.

By day she diligently crunches numbers and provides support for many. But in her free time, she writes and fulfills her passion as a story teller. A lover of love, Lana reads and writes all she can, whether new budding teenage love or hot, passionate adult love, it inspires her.

This work is Lana's first attempt at publishing. She wrote this story for her very first Nanowrimo writing project in 2016. Lana's next romance novel is underway and she is also working on a young adult fantasy novel. You can follow Lana on Facebook and Twitter.

Links:

https://www.facebook.com/LanaJPickering/

Twitter:

@LanaJP